THORNS OF HOPE AND BETRAYAL

A MAGE'S INFLUENCE SERIES

Seeds of Glory and Ruin

Vines of Promise and Deceit

Thorns of Hope and Betrayal

Forests of Grandeur and Malice

And set in the same world:

A MAGE'S APPRENTICE SERIES

Winds of Courage

Storms of Allegiance

Tempests of Truth

THORNS OF HOPE AND BETRAYAL

A MAGE'S INFLUENCE BOOK 3

MELANIE CELLIER

LUMINANT PUBLICATIONS

THORNS OF HOPE AND BETRAYAL

A Mage's Influence Book 3
First edition published in 2022 (v1.3)
by Luminant Publications

ISBN 978-1-922636-35-5

Luminant Publications
PO Box 305
Greenacres, South Australia 5086

melanie@melaniecellier.com
http://www.melaniecellier.com

Cover Design by Karri Klawiter
Editing by Mary Novak
Proofreading by Deborah Grace White
Map Illustration by Rebecca E Paavo

For my fun and creative niece, Zoe—
I hope you enjoy these books one day

HIDDEN CITY
NOMAD LANDS
Kingdom of CALISTA
VIRIDIAN RIVER
CELADON RIVER
CALINARA
LAKE ATERRA
CADENCE'S HOUSE
HUNTING LODGE
Kingdom of TARTORA
CELADON RIVER
TARONA
NOMAD LANDS
VIRIDIAN RIVER
N
E
S
W

CHAPTER 1

CADENCE

"Where are my books? I put them right here!" I spoke aloud in my frustration, although I was alone.

Swiveling, I glared around the room. I specifically remembered putting my small collection of precious books on the side table in front of me. They were my only remaining link with my home and parents, and I was sure I wouldn't have forgotten where I left them. I had kept them safe for this long, but there was no sign of them now.

Stomping around the room, I examined both desks, the other side table, and even looked beneath the sofa. Only after I had checked the entire room did I stop in front of the single bookcase which held a small portion of Evermund's book collection—the overflow from his main suite.

With a strangled groan, I spotted my missing volumes neatly lined up with the others. Pulling them off, I muttered irritated accusations at my absent sister. But really, I only had myself to blame. I should have known when I agreed to temporarily share a room with Airlie that she would compulsively tidy my possessions.

I took a moment to flick through some of the pages, my

fingers lingering over the illustrations in my favorite. The royal residence they portrayed didn't look like the palace or attached Mages' Guild here in Tarona. Did they resemble the old palace in the Calistan capital of Calinara, then? The one from before the invasion?

I knew I should get on with my packing, but I hesitated another moment, letting myself sink into memories of my mother and the stories she used to tell. She had loved this book even more than I did, and when she talked, it had been easy to imagine myself as a princess in these halls.

The door from the garden opened, pulling me out of the moment. I looked up in time to see Airlie's eyes drop to the book in my hand before flying over to the open bag on my bed. She looked back at me slowly, and I waited in some trepidation for her comment.

She obviously understood the significance of me packing my meager personal possessions for our trip into the nomad lands, but I wasn't ready to answer any questions on the topic. I didn't know myself what it meant yet—I certainly hadn't made the decision to leave Tartora behind permanently. But neither did I feel certain I would return. Zeke had only been gone for a few days, and I already missed him intensely.

With so much confusion whirling inside me about my future, I didn't want to add Airlie's opinions to the mix. But as she came over to join me, her words showed she was thinking about something else entirely.

"I think our grandmother painted those pictures herself."

"Really?" I looked at the one in front of me with fresh eyes. "How do you know?"

"While I was at the settlement, I met an elderly lady who was born there. Nan. Apparently she and our grandmother were close friends growing up." Her eyes lingered on the pictures as mine had done, and I wondered how the memories were colored in her mind. "I visited her quite a few times, and she mentioned that our grandmother was a talented artist. Apparently her parents used to tell them stories about the glories of Calinara before it fell, and Grandmother liked to sketch the scenes."

My fingers tightened around the book which had just become even more precious to me.

"I'm surprised it wasn't Father who loved it instead of Mother, then," I said. "He was the one always telling us stories about Calista."

Airlie frowned, as if considering the matter. "Father wasn't one for dreaming about balls and tapestries. But he always treated the book carefully when it did pass through his hands, and he never stopped Mother treasuring it. I think he must have felt a connection to it, even if he wasn't obvious about it, like Mother was."

I closed it reluctantly, placing it inside a waterproof leather bag along with my other volumes. I didn't want them to come to harm because of my decision not to be parted from them.

As I tucked them away in the middle of the pack, I moved as slowly as possible, hoping Airlie might collect whatever she came for and leave. She remained in place, however, regarding me with a knowing eye.

"It doesn't matter how slowly you go, I'm not losing interest and wandering away, Cadence."

I grimaced.

"We leave first thing in the morning," she added. "You can't put off seeing Hayes any longer."

"This is a bad idea," I muttered, but without much spirit.

I couldn't deny I had initially agreed to see Hayes in case I needed healing. The fact I had since gotten cold feet did nothing to stop Airlie stubbornly holding me to my initial agreement. I already knew it was useless to argue with her.

"No," she said crisply, "it's the opposite of a bad idea. It's essential." She gave me a piercing look. "You know how important this is, Cadence. Who knows what damage you've already done to your body? Messing with wild power killed our grandfather. Father himself was scared enough of it that he rarely used his ability. It's not your fault you used it before you knew any better, but it would be inexcusable not to get yourself checked over now. For all we know, access to a powerful healing mage might have made a big difference to Grandfather and those poor people in the settlement. So we're going to go to Hayes and see what he can do whether you like it or not."

"But what if he can recognize my affinity?" I whispered as I followed her outside, trailing along as she briskly strode across the courtyard toward the healing wing.

We'd been over this conversation more than once, but I couldn't help voicing the question yet again.

A worried line settled on her brow, but she didn't break stride. "Then we'll deal with that when it happens. Your life is more important."

I sighed, unable to come up with an argument against that point. This was why I had agreed to go see Hayes in the first place. But I couldn't help the dread that filled me at the potential consequences. If only Zeke was still here to stand by my side. I knew that no matter what happened in Tartora, he wouldn't desert me.

Thoughts of Zeke made my mind wander. He was only days ahead of us, but the separation felt significant. I trusted him completely, but his entire life stood on the brink of enormous change. Would Zekiel the nomad prince be a different person from Zeke the apprentice, like the difference between Princess Morgiana and Apprentice Gia?

Airlie pulled open a door and ushered me inside one of the Guild corridors. Shaking off my concerns, I took a steadying breath as I approached the door to Hayes's suite. The sound of my rap barely reached my own ears, so I forced myself to knock again, more loudly.

Footsteps sounded behind the door, and it swung open to reveal Hayes, wearing a look of mild curiosity.

"Good evening." He looked from me to Airlie. "Do you need something? Are you both well?"

"That's what we'd like to find out." Airlie prodded me from behind. "Do you mind if we come in?"

His eyebrows rose. "Not at all." He stepped back, gesturing for us to enter his small but neat sitting room.

I cleared my throat, feeling awkward now that I was here and unsure how to begin.

"I'm worried about our exposure to the raiders," Airlie said when I stayed silent. "Cadence told me what happened here with Dara. I didn't see anybody dropping dead at their settlement, but we did engage the General and his mages in battle in order to escape. How can we be sure he didn't do something to us that we can't see from the outside?"

"I—I suppose it's possible." Hayes sounded bemused, but his expression slowly grew more interested, the lines on his forehead deepening. "We never did manage to work out what happened to Dara, so there really is no saying what the beginning of the condition might have looked like."

Airlie nodded. "Exactly. We'd be grateful if you could check us both, to ensure we're in good health."

I bit my lip, hoping her inclusion of herself would be enough to draw attention away from me, but not at all convinced it would be. How could we hide the truth from Hayes when his ability let him send power into my body? As soon as he made contact with me, I would be helpless to hide anything. Even if it was possible to use my own ability to conceal my nature, I had no idea how.

Airlie held out her arm, and Hayes placed his fingertips lightly against it. He closed his eyes, but I had barely completed a breath before he opened them again.

"You're healthy," he said with a smile. "Remarkably healthy, given everything you've been through. You should try for a little more sleep, though."

"You couldn't just top me up?" she asked sweetly, making him chuckle.

"You're not tired enough to need my intervention. And besides." He gave her a stern look. "I've told you before. Intervention from a healer can help in the short term, but in the long term your body and mind both need true sleep."

I looked back and forth between them, feeling guilty. Hayes must have told her that before her capture, when she was carrying the weight of the Guild on her shoulders. I had been wrapped up in my own concerns back then.

Hayes turned to me, holding out his hand, and I reluctantly raised my arm toward him. As I closed the distance, Airlie kept talking, perhaps hoping to keep him distracted enough that he wouldn't consider anything beyond my immediate health.

"I've heard a rumor that you're coming with us. Is it true?" she asked.

My eyes flew up from my dread-filled examination of the decreasing gap between Hayes's fingers and my arm. Hayes was coming with us? She hadn't mentioned anything about that to me. If he was going to be in the nomad kingdom, too, then there was no urgency to complete this examination right now. I felt completely fine. I could hardly be dying.

I glared at her as Hayes turned toward her also, although he was smiling.

"Yes, that's right. I've just had confirmation from Their Majesties. They insisted on the presence of a healing mage, of course. And as you know, I've accompanied Evermund on some of his travels before. In fact, I'm quite looking forward to—"

His words faltered, his attention swinging back to me. I swallowed hard at the look on his face, my eyes dropping to where his fingers had now made contact with my arm.

"Cadence!" He paused as if unsure how to continue.

"What is it?" Airlie closed in on us, seizing my other arm. "Is she dying?"

Hayes shook himself. "What? No, no! It's not that severe..." His brows drew together. "Yet."

"Is it like Dara?" I asked, my breath quickening. "Can you fix it?"

My earlier fear of discovery was gone, replaced with one even more pressing. I'd been impatient with Airlie's obsession about my health—thinking that if the wild power had done me lasting harm, I would have felt it. I'd hardly spent a lifetime manipulating the awful stuff. But now visions of Dara's face—empty in death—filled my mind.

"Give me a moment." Hayes's words were unusually short, his eyes closed in concentration.

Airlie and I exchanged worried looks as the silence stretched taut and thin. The seconds ticked by impossibly slowly as I wondered if I should be feeling something change within me. Were his efforts not working?

I forced myself to draw a long breath, in and out, calming my racing thoughts. Given I hadn't felt any problem to begin with, there was no reason to suppose a lack of sensation meant disaster now.

I tried not to stress as beads of sweat appeared on Hayes's brow. When he eventually let his hand drop, opening his eyes and staring at me, I gulped.

"Will I be all right?" I asked in a voice that betrayed me by trembling slightly.

Hayes forced his face—which was equal parts confused, concerned, and intensely curious—into a smile.

"Of course." He hesitated. "Have you been injuring yourself a lot since you came to the Guild, Cadence?"

"Injuring myself?" I stared at him. "No, of course not. I'm sure you would have heard of it if I had. But why would I?"

"No reason I can think of," he said lightly, but his expression didn't mirror the unconcern of the words.

My momentary relief was swept away in a new flood of worry. He had sensed something inside me that didn't match with his expectations—perhaps something different from the first time he healed me. But the only thing that had changed was Zeke activating my seed.

I swallowed, trying to think of something to say, but he spoke again.

"I can't tell you what was wrong with you any more than I could understand what it was when it killed Dara."

"It was the same?" Airlie asked sharply.

"An earlier version, certainly, but of the same nature." He looked at me with concern. "Something about your insides was very, very wrong, Cadence. But even now—having examined you thoroughly as well as healed you—I'm not sure I could explain it exactly. In a way it was like a disease, I suppose. Although what I felt in you was only a shadow whereas Dara was saturated with it." He shuddered, seeming genuinely lost for words. "There was just something wrong with your insides."

I watched him wordlessly, my eyes wide. I didn't need any more detail. I knew just what he was describing because I had felt that wrongness myself in the wild power.

"Thank you," I whispered. "For getting rid of it."

"It is all gone?" Airlie asked, her words fast and the look she gave him piercing.

He nodded before hesitating again. "I was able to drive it out, but it was difficult. Far more difficult than it should have been given how little of you it had touched, Cadence. That's why I asked if you had experienced a number of healings since our first encounter. Then it was your first healing and easy as any healer could hope. Today I would liken my task to healing a hardened veteran whose body had learned resistance after scores of healings."

I exchanged a look with Airlie, neither of us having to speak to read the other's thoughts. My body had no reason to resist the healing like it might do in my elderly years, so it must be the condition itself. Hayes was one of the Guild's most powerful healers, and yet he had struggled to heal the most mild aftereffects of handling wild power. And if it got harder each time, like regular healings...

I shuddered. Clearly I couldn't manipulate wild power in the expectation a healer would swoop in and fix me afterward. Not even an army of healers would be enough to protect me if I tried to tackle all the wild power still lurking in Calista.

"I can't explain why it was so hard to heal," I said after a moment. "But it wasn't because of previous illness or injury."

He sighed. "No, that would have been far too simple an explanation."

He fixed me with a keen regard that made me want to writhe. I forced myself to stay still and calm, however, doing my best to look innocent—whatever that looked like.

"I would like to check you again in a few weeks if that's all right? In case it comes back. It makes me uneasy not knowing what we're dealing with, or how it might progress. I believe I've eradicated it all, but how can I be sure?"

"I..." I swallowed, glancing at Airlie who gave me an insistent look. I sighed. "Certainly. I mean, of course. Thank you."

His brow wrinkled, his eyes flashing between the two of us. "I don't need to tell you that a healer's work is confidential. I have no desire to pry into other aspects of your life."

Every muscle tightened as I forced my numb lips to thank him. Airlie took over, chatting about the upcoming trip as she shepherded me out the door. We exchanged farewells, and I couldn't tell if they were somewhat strained on his side or if the impression was only an illusion based on my own discomfort.

As soon as the door had closed and we had started down the corridor, I grabbed Airlie's arm.

"What was that about?" I hissed. "Could he tell? Does he know about me now?"

Airlie shook her head. "Of course not! I'm sure he wouldn't have hidden it so well if he did. He could just pick up on your agitation and was giving you a standard healer's reassurance."

I frowned, glancing back down the hall at the closed door. "I don't know. I thought his voice had more weight than that. And the way he was looking at us at the end…"

"I'm sure he was too distracted by your strange affliction," she said stubbornly, fixing me with a look that spoke as clearly as words. She was bursting from not pointing out she had been right about my health.

"Maybe," I said, still uneasy.

Hayes had noticed a difference when he healed me this time. Had it truly just been the aftereffects of my contact with wild power?

"What does it matter anyway?" Airlie's voice was laced with impatience. "He's clearly not intending to say anything to anyone even if he did pick up on something."

"For now," I said, looking back a final time. "He's not going to say anything for now."

CHAPTER 2
AIRLIE

We assembled in the garden outside my suite before dawn. The eastern sky had lightened from inky black to a deep blue, but we would be out of the city before true light. Officially, the delegation heading for the Hidden City would be leaving Tarona in two days' time with a great deal of fanfare—as befitted the first ever Tartoran delegation to visit the nomad capital. In reality, we were creeping from the city under the cover of dark, like thieves in the night.

None of us minded, however. Not if it increased our chances of avoiding a run in with the raiders. By the time the city discovered the scheduled elaborate departure wasn't happening after all, we would hopefully be long gone and well out of the raiders' reach.

Evermund fetched Cadence and me out of our room with a rap on the door. He greeted us with breakfast rolls and a smile —although I sensed it more than saw it in the pre-dawn light.

His upbeat mood eased some of the tension in my chest, increasing my excitement for the adventure to come. In the three days since our return, he had spent most of his time closeted with the monarchs and the Triumvirate, preparing for our upcoming visit to the Hidden City. It had been a struggle to suppress the irrational resentment at their stealing my influencer as soon as I was finally reunited with him.

The resentment had only been amplified by the king's obvious displeasure with Evermund—an emotion I could read even from afar on the few times I had crossed paths with the two of them. Clearly King Marius was still incensed at Evermund's participation in my rescue. Or maybe he was just angry Evermund hadn't prevented the twins from taking part.

King Marius and Queen Celestine were both waiting with the rest of the group in the garden—two more bodies in the gloom. I wanted to stay close to Evermund, but when he moved directly for them, I broke away, stopping beside Renley instead.

Poor Renley looked as if he wanted to fade into the darkness altogether, and I couldn't entirely blame him. He had even less place in the Tartoran delegation than Cadence and me, but he had received his own invitation from Zeke and had requested permission to travel with us. I wasn't sure whether the nomads had invited him for his own power affinity or for his insider knowledge about the raiders, but he insisted he wanted to come with us, regardless of potential dangers.

He greeted me with a nod of his head, and when a sliver of shielded lantern light glanced across his face, I caught the flash of a smile. I smiled in return. Standing next to him gave me a feeling of familiarity and home that was unexpectedly welcome alongside the thrill of the coming unknown.

My eyes followed the lantern—held in the hands of one of the guards—to where the king and queen were talking with Evermund. Their manner surprised me, all traces of previous tension gone. Any animosity the king might still feel toward Evermund seemed to have been superseded by the momentous occasion or perhaps by the feeling of furtive camaraderie created by the darkness.

He stepped close to his nephew, offering his hand to the younger man.

"You'll keep them safe?" he asked, as if he already knew the answer.

"You know I'll do everything in my power," Evermund said quietly back, as Queen Celestine enveloped him in a brief hug.

Gia and Nikolas appeared, and the king and queen moved on to their children, leaving Evermund free to disengage and step away. Warmth filled me when he glanced quickly around, only to move to my side—as if it was me he had been searching for in the darkness. I reminded myself I was his apprentice, so it was only natural. But I couldn't help the happiness it brought to know he wanted to be near me—whatever the reason.

Before either of us could speak, however, Cadence joined us.

"Will we be leaving soon?" she asked in a hushed voice.

Evermund chuckled. "We'll be with Zeke soon enough."

I expected her to flush, thrown off balance, but that was the old Cadence. Instead she just laughed back.

"Not soon enough, by my reckoning. But the more pressing issue is whether we can make it up the river without a run in with the raiders. The whole point was to sneak out of the city *before* it was light, I believe?"

A reprimand leaped to my tongue, but I swallowed it back down. She wasn't a child anymore, needing to be reminded not to draw attention to us. She was the last power mage in the kingdoms, and she had spent longer living side-by-side with Evermund than I had. Certainly his amused words of agreement suggested she had correctly judged how much morning impudence he could handle.

"Will the rest of the guards meet us outside the city?" Renley asked, his uncertain voice and tone suggesting he was conscious of not drawing attention, even if Cadence no longer was.

"This is the full delegation," Evermund replied, his tone giving no indication of his opinion on the matter.

"But..." Renley's clothes rustled as he moved in the darkness. "There must be only—"

"Eight of them," Evermund finished for him. "Including Captain Huxley, who leads them."

"So few to travel with the princess and prince?" Renley asked. "I would have thought..."

"Believe me, the number was carefully calculated," Evermund said.

"I was expecting a bigger delegation as well." Cadence's eyes shone with interest in another flash of the lantern. "I suppose speed is the issue?"

Evermund nodded, and her voice grew strained and apologetic. "I'm sorry. Even if I wanted to, I don't know that the western branch—"

She cut herself off before I could kick her ankle to remind her to watch her words. Evermund might know about her affinity, but the other decision-makers in Tartora did not. No one was expecting her to pull us upriver using the wild power that was laced through both the Viridian River and the eastern branch of the Celadon.

Renley frowned, looking between Cadence and Evermund, but before he could question further, the king issued a general farewell in carefully muted tones, and everyone began to shuffle into something resembling a double line.

The princess appeared at Cadence's side, sliding her arm through my sister's and beaming at us all. Nikolas took the spot beside Renley and, within seconds, I was leaving the Guild for the second time. This time my departure was by choice, but the darkness prevented any sentimental last glimpses of the building that had sheltered Cadence and me when we were alone in the world.

I felt little desire to look back, however. This wasn't a trip to the ocean—the place of most of my childhood dreaming—but it was somewhere nearly as good. To be among the first non-nomads to glimpse the Hidden City was an honor I had never imagined.

The cobbled streets of the city passed silently beneath our feet, the houses and stores slipping past in the darkness. If there were others about at this hour, they avoided a party as large as ours. Even with only eight guards, the presence of Master Augusta and Hayes at our head put our number at sixteen.

"Are you sure it's not too many?" I murmured to Evermund beside me, gripped by sudden nerves.

"We can do it." His calm reply settled me instantly, his presence at my side a welcome comfort, despite the darkness.

I nodded resolutely, although no one could see me. Of course we could do it. I lifted my face slightly, enjoying the early autumn breeze that flowed down the street, darting playfully around the buildings and swirling about our legs as we walked.

Without thinking, I reached for a bit of it, twirling it around me and dragging it with us as we slipped out of one of the smaller side gates of the city. The two guards on duty had been briefed on our departure, and they whisked the gate open for us, closing it as soon as the final guard in our party stepped through.

Outside the city walls, a stronger wind hit us, and I let my small breeze go, setting it free to join the flow of air. The sky had lightened yet again, and I could now make out my companions without the aid of the lanterns, if only dimly. In the distance I felt the call of the Viridian River—the vast accumulation of water an alluring presence. But we had exited the city from a western gate, heading away from Tartora's eastern river.

Quiet conversations sprang up around me now that the stifling presence of the city was removed. Just ahead of us Renley glanced over his shoulder, his eyes latching on to me.

"I don't understand why we're only traveling with eight guards. I'm still learning the Tartoran ways, but I had the impression—"

"We need speed," I explained. "If we travel by more traditional methods, we won't arrive in the Hidden City before the vote. We have to take the river."

"But it's upstream." Renley frowned.

"Welcome to civilization," Nikolas drawled in a superior voice. "We have mages, remember?"

Renley's eyes widened, and Cadence appeared from behind us, poking her head between Evermund and me.

"You're going to push us all the way there?" She sounded worried. "But surely that's—"

"Well within our capabilities," Evermund said calmly. "As long as we take a boat that fits no more than sixteen people. I told you, the calculations were exhaustive. We'll make it."

"There's me, too, remember," Gia said from Cadence's side.

Evermund nodded. "We couldn't do it without you."

I gave Gia a speculative look. Drake had tested the two of us together a couple of days before, and I had been surprised at her strength. I got the impression Drake had been as well. By the end of the session, he was muttering that she might turn out even more powerful than her father, a pronouncement that for some reason had seemed to fill her with gloom.

"Here!" Master Augusta called from the head of the column, and we all pressed forward into a loose clump.

Two wagons pulled out from a minor side road where they must have been lying in wait for our arrival. The drivers—by appearance two farmers of medium affluence—tipped their caps at us.

Without further ceremony, we piled into the back of the wagons which had been strewn with fresh hay to provide a bare minimum of comfort. No one complained, although Nikolas's face held a look of mild disgust as he took a position in one of the corners.

Evermund, on the other hand, looked as unruffled as

always. When he caught me looking at him, he grinned. "Where was one of these when we were heading back to the city?"

"I seem to recall we did manage to hitch a ride some of the way in the back of a wagon," I said with a return grin, wondering suddenly if that had been the inspiration for our mode of transport now.

"Yes, but the onions," Gia said with a groan, and we all chuckled.

"It took three full days to wash the smell out of my hair." Cadence sighed. "I still say we should have walked."

"I kept dreaming about onions," Gia complained.

Renley gave her a confused look. "How can you dream about onions? They don't do anything."

"I didn't say they were *interesting* dreams." Her eyes twinkled at him. "The most boring ones I've ever had. There I was on the biggest adventure of my life, and every night I just wandered through fields of onions. Airlie called down *lightning* for goodness sake, and I just got onions."

She sighed disconsolately as Renley continued to regard her with confusion. When she caught his expression, she winked, and he colored slightly, looking quickly away.

"Leave him alone," Cadence said, throwing a clump of hay at Gia. "He's not familiar with Apprentice Gia yet. He's going to get a very strange idea of princesses."

It warmed my heart to hear Cadence defend him given how uncertain she'd been about him ever since my rescue. And it was nice to see him opening up as well. We would be traveling in close quarters, so it would be easier if everyone was comfortable with each other.

"Apprentice Gia?" Renley looked at me for clarification, but I just shrugged, leaving the explanation to Cadence.

It was Nikolas who spoke, however, his voice tinged with a trace of resentment. "When we're among the apprentices, my sister likes to pretend to be one of them—a delightful game she calls Apprentice Gia."

Gia rolled her eyes and shifted slightly to put her back toward him. "Ignore him. But the basic idea is correct. While it's just us, I'm plain Gia. I won't be able to keep it up all the time at the Hidden City, though, unfortunately."

"I should say not," Nikolas muttered.

"Are you worried about traveling with only eight guards?" Renley asked Gia.

She shrugged. "I don't think it really matters. Most nomad tribes train all their members in basic warrior skills, and while they don't have the formal mage/non-mage divide we have in Tartora through our Mages' Guild, they have a long history of great strength across all three affinities. I don't think eight hundred guards would be enough to stop them if they intended us harm. As it is, I have faith in Evermund and Master Augusta to keep us safe. But obviously an honor guard was needed, at the least."

I frowned. "I believe Captain Huxley is well-respected." I tried to peer past the two horses pulling our wagon to where he sat with Master Augusta and most of the guards in the front one, but I couldn't get a clear view.

Evermund nodded. "That he is. His seed was strong enough that he could have apprenticed into the Guild. But he chose to join the royal guard, instead, and apprentice under one of the old captains." He glanced at Renley. "It's the only other accept-able avenue for young people with strong seeds. But it was his strength of character, not just the strength of his ability, that ensured him a captaincy of his own after his apprenticeship. And once he had the rank, he was an easy choice as Guild liai-son. Under his auspices, more mages than ever have been recruited into the guard."

"So he must be an elements mage then, too, I suppose," Renley said. "Why isn't he helping with our travel?"

I shook my head at the same time as Cadence.

We looked at each other for a moment before I remembered she could now sense people even more effectively than I could. I should have realized she would be able to tell someone's affinity as well as their presence—a skill we shared, although from her description, the process and sensation were almost entirely different.

I referred to it as smelling, although it didn't exactly involve my nose—or at least not a physical scent. But the air I breathed in carried all sorts of information from the world around me, and it included the affinity of those in my vicinity—like a flavor my ability could instinctively recognize.

I hadn't given a lot of thought to Captain Huxley before now, but his presence was familiar, and I knew he didn't have an elements affinity. I left it to one of the two guards at the back of our wagon to reply, however.

"We're not exclusively elements," he said, looking Renley up and down as if he hadn't yet decided whether he should be considered a threat to the group. "We have all three affinities among our number."

"And right handy all of them are," the female guard at his side agreed. "I wish my own healing affinity had been strong enough to qualify me to be apprenticed within the Guild or to one of the captains. A healing mage comes in mighty useful in a guard unit."

"Along with healing, they can also read deception," Cadence explained to Renley. "And if they can get close enough to touch someone, they're the most dangerous fighters of all."

Renley blanched, apparently considering for the first time what sort of damage a healer could do to the inside of a human body.

"Captain Huxley is a plants mage like my brother," Gia said, apparently taking pity on Renley. "But he wouldn't be helping regardless. None of the guards will be involved with our transport. As it is, my parents are concerned about the two strongest of us tiring themselves out with the task. Master Augusta had to have some stern words about her own capability before they would agree to the scheme."

"We can't risk our precious elements mages being out of commission," Nikolas muttered, and I looked him over with narrowed eyes.

Apparently the hope that his arrogant resentment with the world might have sweetened in my absence had been misplaced. In fact, he seemed worse than during my rescue, so I could only assume the last few days hadn't gone well for him.

Gia, however, seemed to take whatever their parents had thrown at them in stride, her normal bubbly enthusiasm as undimmed as ever. She continued to chat brightly with Renley, but I let their voices fade away, turning my attention to the road ahead of us. I closed my eyes and stretched out my awareness—using the extra sense I had possessed ever since Evermund activated my seed. As easy as sight or hearing, my power reached out, rushing eagerly to meet the elements it encountered.

Although the earth beneath us felt as dry and dead as the plants that grew in it, the wind and the air blazed with enticing brightness. I ignored them, however, reaching further, straining to see how far I could go. I was about to give up when I felt it in the far distance, something deep and powerful and cool.

I called to it, but it was too far to respond to my power, and with a sigh I let go, opening my eyes again. Evermund raised a single eyebrow, his eyes on me. I just shrugged.

I had nothing to report. We all knew we were heading toward the Celadon River, and I had sensed nothing untoward on the wind. Apparently our ruse had worked because I smelled no one on the path before us waiting in ambush.

The road that ran west from the capital would deliver us to a ford just below the point where the two northern branches of the Celadon joined into a single river. On our previous journey, we had ridden the eastern branch down from Lake Aterra, but now we would be taking the western branch. The western branch was the main river and marked the border. On its western side, a long stretch of grazing land extended between the river and the sea, while on its eastern side, the land was divided between Tartora in the south and Calista in the north.

The grazing lands belonged to the nomads, and much trade took place across the Celadon. Before departing, the nomads had assured us that the Celadon remained safe from the taint that had been growing in the Viridian. And while we knew wild power lurked in the eastern Celadon as well, we hoped the western branch was still free of it.

"You can sleep if you like," Evermund told me softly. "You'll need your strength once we hit the river."

I hesitated, but he was right. Murmuring agreement, I tried to heap some hay into a somewhat comfortable cushion before curling myself into a ball. The last thing I felt as I drifted into sleep was Evermund's arm holding me steady against the jostles of the road. My sleep was deep and peaceful.

CHAPTER 3

AIRLIE

When I woke, the sun had passed its zenith and started its slow decline. We were stationary, and Evermund was just climbing back into our wagon, while Augusta made her way toward the lead one.

"Is everything all right?" I asked.

He nodded. "We've just changed horses and drivers. We'll likely reach the river about dawn tomorrow, so you might want to take a quick chance to stretch your legs."

I leaped out without wasting time on further words, nearly collapsing in an inelegant heap.

"Thanks," I gasped to the guard who half caught me. "I didn't realize my leg had gone to sleep."

She shook her head admiringly. "You were sleeping deeply. I wish I could sleep in a wagon like that."

"I guess it's a gift," I said lightly.

She had no idea how much lighter I felt away from the walls of the Guild and the responsibility to monitor it for threats. Here, with just the sixteen of us and open skies, I felt infinitely more relaxed. As long as the raiders remained a threat, crowds would remain a stress to me.

I wasn't feeling so light and free by the time darkness fell, though. All of us were stiff, sore, and grumpy, and conversation had fallen to a minimum. Given my long nap, I didn't feel ready for sleep, but somehow Cadence wormed her way over to me and fell asleep with her head in my lap, so I was trapped in place anyway.

I didn't dislodge her, though. For a brief time, while she slept, it was easy to forget everything that had happened and remember the years it was just the two of us. A rush of affection and longing filled me, and I closed my eyes, recalling our small home as clearly as if we sat there now. Cadence and I had shared so many good times, but I had let the memory of the pressure and the responsibilities overshadow them completely.

How strange it all was. Cadence kept saying and doing things that made her seem like a different person—one grown beyond her need of me. And then a moment like this sent me back into the past so forcibly that I had to reach for the wind around us to assure myself it hadn't all been a dream.

"Do you think they'll come for us?" a low voice asked, breaking my reverie.

I opened my eyes. The cloud cover of the night before was gone, and the moonlight gave me a clear view of Renley's worried eyes.

"On the river, I mean," he added.

A particularly large bump in the road made Cadence stir, murmuring something in her sleep as she rolled off my lap. For a moment I thought she would wake, but she seized a clump of hay and held it against her chest, resettling. I pulled my legs up, wrapping my arms around them and resting my chin on my knees.

"I don't know," I said to Renley. "You should have a better guess at that than me."

His face twisted. "The General must be furious. And if he's

heard we're invited to the Hidden City, he'll be…" He shook his head. "I can't even imagine. He doesn't like losing."

"I'm sure he's had word of the invitation by now. The news must be all over Tartora. It's unprecedented. The main question is if he somehow got wind of our travel plans."

"Even if he hasn't heard anything specific, the river's the most obvious route," Renley said, worry in his tone. "And we'll have to travel the entire western border of Calista."

"But it's also the only means of travel that will get us there in time for the beginning of the voting process," Evermund said, unexpectedly joining the conversation. "There's no other choice."

I started at his quiet words, not having realized he was also awake.

"Do you think the raiders will attack?" I asked.

"I'm hoping we'll slip by ahead of anything they might be planning." His voice remained level, but I knew him well enough to recognize a hint of unease behind his words.

And if he was uneasy, so was I.

But meeting his eyes, I understood his unspoken thoughts. Speaking those concerns aloud wouldn't help morale. We had no choice but to proceed with the plan and remain alert.

When I nodded slightly, keeping silent, his eyes warmed with approval. I looked away quickly, my heart rate increasing uncomfortably.

Evermund had always been my biggest support at the Guild. He was far more than just the person who had activated my seed. As well as being my influencer, he was also my closest friend, aside from Cadence.

He had never intended to take on an apprentice, but that hadn't stopped him from being the best possible support for me and Cadence. Despite the preoccupations of his role as Royal Mage—which had prevented him from being the one to actively train me—we had been well provided for from the first day.

The guilt of it was eating me away.

Ever since learning the price he had paid for his loyalty toward me—the way he had stood alone against both the Guild and palace, insisting they keep searching for me—the guilt had been growing. I had tricked him into activating me, and he still didn't know it. He thought I was as innocently caught up in our connection as he was, and the more time I spent around him, the heavier that knowledge sat in my chest—a barrier between us that he knew nothing about.

Cadence stirred again, and Evermund suggested we all attempt to get some sleep. I lay down beside my sister, hearing Renley settling himself not far away, but it was hard to get comfortable in the wagon. Too many disquieting thoughts spun in my mind to allow me more than a few hours sleep before dawn and the river arrived at the same time.

Everyone piled from the wagons with yawns and stretches —and in the case of the older travelers, the occasional audible crack from stiff limbs. No one dared to ask Augusta—by far the oldest of us—about her physical state, however. Her expression challenged anyone to question her ability to keep up with the youngest and fittest.

Just as the wagons had been prepared and waiting for us, so a boat now appeared, traveling slowly downriver. They must have timed their journey exactly, perhaps to avoid drawing attention to a boat anchored at this small, out of the way spot.

We had left the road not long before, avoiding the well-used ford at the end of the western road. So there was no one around as we farewelled the drivers and the two-man crew who had brought the boat this far.

Captain Huxley and two of his guards leaped onto the vessel first, examining it thoroughly, as if checking for hidden surprises. But considering it was an open boat, barely larger than the one they had used in my rescue mission, it was hard to imagine what could be lurking in there.

Within seconds they were waving us all aboard, directing us to one seat or another in an attempt to distribute our weight and balance the boat which contained five plain, wooden bench seats. I ended up at the far end of the third bench, and when everyone else had settled into place, I realized Gia sat beside me and Evermund sat directly behind. So our places weren't entirely allocated on weight.

Gia's breathing sounded strained, and for the first time I wondered if she was nervous. She hadn't shown it earlier, but now was the moment when she had to prove herself able to keep up with Evermund and me. I put a hand on her shoulder and gave it a gentle squeeze, along with an encouraging nod. She smiled back at me, the expression a little set, as she tried to hide the nerves beneath.

Evermund leaned forward, ostensibly directing his words toward me. "Traveling upriver is different from moving downstream."

Gia glanced at me and nodded, as if to back up his advice, but her whole body leaned slightly toward him. She was listening to every word, while trying to appear as if I was the sole target of his instructions. No one had corrected the king's assumption that Evermund and Gia had combined forces to push the rescue boat upstream to Lake Aterra. Gia had supposedly helped with the journey in both directions, while I had only had experience bringing the boat back downstream.

In reality, as both the weakest elements mage and the newest apprentice, Gia had rested on the way back from the rescue and hadn't attempted the feat at all. Evermund's words were more for her than they were for me, although I was still grateful for his instruction on the far more difficult task of moving upstream.

"We'll work together," he continued, "in pairs. That's why it's important there are three of us—we'll each get a chance to rest as we rotate through the roles. This is a considerably longer journey than the one to Lake Aterra."

Gia nodded again, her hands tightly gripping the seat beneath her.

"A strong wind in the right direction will be a significant help," Evermund said, "but the boat will move much faster if it's not fighting the current. So one of us will keep a steady wind blowing upriver, while the other will set a small section of water on the surface of the river to flow in the opposite direction."

"That will be the harder task," I commented.

He made a noise of agreement. "The trick is to keep hold of as little water as possible. We're not trying to reverse the flow of the river here. We've selected a boat with the lowest possible draft—there's hardly anything below water, not even a rudder. You won't need to go down deep. Just take control of a small section of water at the surface of the river and propel it in the opposite direction."

"Just that," I said with a snort.

He grinned back at me. "Just that. I have no doubt you'll be well up to the challenge."

Beside me, Gia gulped. Evermund glanced at her.

"I'll go first controlling the water. Gia, you do the wind. Airlie, you watch how we both do it. After an hour or two, you'll take over from me, I'll take over from Gia, and Gia can rest. We'll just keep cycling around from there."

His eyes flicked from me to Gia as he spoke, and I understood his unspoken instruction. I would be ready to help Gia get past any initial nerves and settle into the job.

But despite the tension in her body, Gia called up a wind easily.

"Whoa," Evermund said softly as the boat lurched and rocked, shooting unevenly forward across the water.

She immediately corrected herself, reducing the intensity of the blast.

"While we want to move fast, we also have to consider sustainability," Evermund said, again appearing to direct the explanation at me. "It can take a few minutes to settle into it, but then it should be easy to keep up the flow. If it's not, we're going to have a problem a long time before we reach the border."

Now that we were underway, I was itching to take my turn. But I had to content myself with examining their efforts. I could at least ensure I was ready to take over as seamlessly as possible when Evermund declared it time to change roles.

The wind rushed around me, pulling at my clothes and sending strands of my hair dancing across my face. Getting a feel for its strength was as easy as breathing, and once I had the chance to experiment for myself, it would take only a few moments to work out what level of power to apply to match it.

The water was less straightforward. I let my hand dangle over the edge of the boat, trailing through the river. I didn't need the physical contact to connect my power with the water, but it did help. Deeper, beneath my hand, I could feel the force of the river's normal pull, a constant counterbalance to Evermund's efforts.

Keeping hold of the necessary section of water would require more concentration than fueling the wind. And it would exhaust me faster, like being engaged in a never-ending game of tug-of-war.

The effort was worth it, though. The boat flew up the river, moving as if it was traveling downriver with a stiff wind at its aft—which from the boat's perspective was exactly what it was doing.

I laughed, a soft sound snatched away by the wind. Glancing back over my shoulder, I caught an answering gleam in Evermund's eyes. It was exhilarating bending the elements like this.

By the time the sun set again, however, the exhilaration had long since faded. I don't know if I could have continued through the stiff aches and exhaustion if not for Hayes. He could do nothing to add to the strength or longevity of our abilities, but he could—and did—reverse the effects of a full day and night in the back of a wagon followed by a full day on a small, wooden bench. Even Augusta, who wasn't being called on to use her ability, lowered herself enough to speak several blessings over him.

"I knew it was a smart idea to bring you along," she told him. "Master Colton wasn't too pleased to lose his second again so soon, but I'll speak up for you if it's needed, down the line."

Hayes thanked her, moving on to Cadence who watched him curiously.

"You didn't give up the second role permanently, did you, Hayes?"

He nodded, offering her his hand which she regarded with a trepidation that I hoped only I could see. After a brief pause, she shook her head.

"I feel fine," she said in a voice of false cheer. "Save your energy for those more in need."

Hayes raised one eyebrow slightly, but didn't challenge her, answering her earlier question instead.

"Actually, I've resigned from the role completely. It's a little earlier than would be the case for a normal stint as second, but I don't like leaving him in the lurch with all my travel. This way he can select his next second immediately, so he'll have someone to help him back at the Guild while we're gone."

"I'm sorry," she said, her eyes shadowed. "I didn't mean to pull you into this."

"Sorry?" He shook his head. "We're going to the *Hidden City*.

This is an opportunity of several lifetimes. They'll probably include our names in history books one day."

"That's assuming there's anyone left to write history books after these rogue protections are done with us," Augusta muttered.

"In the raider settlement," I said, raising my voice enough to be heard across the boat, "they called it wild power."

Augusta fixed me with a piercing look, her eyes slowly narrowing, but all she said was, "Well, it does seem to be that. It certainly isn't protecting anyone."

Guards passed around food, as they did at regular intervals, and Evermund directed us to once again change roles. I refocused on my job, time blurring together. The longer we continued on, the more tired I became, the drain on my ability something Hayes couldn't relieve.

When I wasn't on duty, I slept, losing track of the passing hours as it went from light to dark and back to light again. Only a few moments stood out.

One was when we neared Tartora's northern border. Tension filled the boat as everyone fixed their eyes on the eastern bank. The low, rolling hills themselves didn't change, but the stark contrast as we swept past the border was noticeable anyway. As the eastern bank turned from Tartoran land to Calistan, the grass died off, the clumps of trees became infrequent and twisted, and no animals could be seen.

But as more time passed without incident, the tension eased. We saw no sign of the raiders whose settlement was positioned near Lake Aterra, which was further east than Tarona. We might be gliding past Calistan land, but the raiders were small in number compared to the vast emptiness of what had once been an entire kingdom.

My heart twisted when the hills ceased and a vista was revealed of vast, barren plains. According to my father, they had once been lush fields of crops, and the sight of the empty stretches of dirt and dust were even more confronting than the twisted landscape of the hills.

I met Cadence's eyes across the boat and knew she was thinking the same thing. It was a little easier to understand our father's determination to save Calista now that we were seeing more of it for ourselves.

A stubborn defiance rose up in me. Saving Calista wasn't worth losing Cadence. I wouldn't let her sacrifice herself—that was too great a price to pay. We still had Tartora, and if we could save it and the nomad lands, that would be enough.

When the river plunged into a stretch of dense trees—the start of the great northern forests—it was a welcome relief from the emptiness. The difference between the two banks remained vivid, however. To the west, in place of the vast grazing lands of the nomad herders, healthy trees and bustling undergrowth pressed up to the bank. A few times I even caught sight of a distant campfire or the movement of people and horses.

"They can't all fit in one city," the Master of Plants said, having apparently caught the direction of my gaze. "Each tribe will have sent representatives to cast their vote, while leaving many of their number behind."

"Does that mean they've all already determined who they'll vote for?" Cadence asked curiously. "I thought Annora had to hurry back to finish her campaign."

"Minds can always be changed," Gia said, sounding sour. "That's the nature of politics. The tribes vote for their heads, and those heads then have full authority over the tribe—unless they do something bad enough to be deposed, of course. The heads will all be in attendance and will make the final decision."

I sighed and looked into the trees on the eastern bank. Here the forest stretched out, devoid of all undergrowth or movement. Occasionally I caught sight of a tree so twisted as to have become fantastical in shape, but they were always gone again before I got a good look. A dark pall seemed to hang over the trees on this side, the shadows deep and forbidding, and the shafts of light rare.

My eyes flicked back to the western shore, glad of the relief provided by the healthy scene. My attention caught on something that quickly passed behind us, and I gasped quietly. Twisting, I tried to get a better look at it, but it was almost gone.

"What is it?" Evermund asked.

It was his turn to rest, but he was alert as always.

"Did you see those trees?" I asked in a murmur.

"Yes." He frowned. "They're not the first ones like it we've passed, either."

I felt my cheeks pale. The two trees had been so twisted, they were like a single growth, stripped completely bare of leaves or life. They had belonged on the opposite bank—evidence that wild power was breaking through even here, where the raiders weren't active.

Gulping, I looked between the two sides of the river again. With the wild power expanding beyond Calista's borders, it was terrible timing for instability in the nomad kingdom. I could only hope they chose their next ruler wisely since their monarch had full authority for all nomad dealings beyond their own border. Whatever combined efforts Tartora hoped to bring against the wild power would be done in alliance with whoever won the upcoming vote. If they weren't cooperative, both kingdoms might end up being overwhelmed.

Evermund declared it was time for another change of roles, pulling my mind away from worries about the future. As soon as he took charge of the wind from Gia, she slumped thankfully into an exhausted huddle on the bench beside me, while I took hold of the water beneath us.

I didn't talk again for some time.

By the time the trees began to thin, my ability was drained

almost to the point of exhaustion. I wouldn't be able to carry on much longer.

Thankfully, I didn't need to. It was my turn to rest, and Evermund murmured that he thought my subsequent stint pushing the water upstream would be the last we needed.

It would also be the most difficult, however. The ground was now noticeably sloping upward as we reached the foothills at the base of the great northern mountain range.

"When we hit the base of that first mountain," Evermund said, "we'll be met by nomad guides and continue on by foot."

"We're going to climb those mountains by foot?" Nikolas sounded horrified, the long days of boredom and aching muscles having soured his ordinary unpleasantness even further.

"How exactly we get to the city will be up to the nomads at that point," Augusta said crisply. "Need I remind you that we have never had the opportunity to ascertain the city's exact location? The assumption it is somewhere deep in the mountains is just that—an assumption."

"Your turn, Airlie," Evermund said softly behind me. When I turned to him, he gave me a warm smile. "Not much longer now. And then I'll make sure you and Gia get whatever rest you need before we go climbing any mountains."

I thanked him, too weary to manage more than an absent-minded smile. Didn't the nomads carry their beds with them? I would climb anything they wanted if they would just let me have one night in a bed first.

Thinking of soft pillows and smooth sheets, I stretched out my power toward the river, plunging into the now familiar water that cupped our boat. I took hold of it, feeling the unnatural pull slacken as Evermund withdrew his power. Without having to think about it at this point, I smoothly asserted my own control, gradually increasing my efforts as his dropped away to allow for a seamless transition.

Just before he released the water completely, however, he gave a sharp, wordless cry. My attention sharpened, my muscles tensing as I sensed something unnatural about the water ahead of us.

Somewhere in front of me, Cadence gasped loudly a second before the boat slammed into an invisible wall.

The front crumpled as the back jerked up, flinging its occupants into the freezing depths of the river.

CHAPTER 4
CADENCE

I had been dozing lightly when the sharp blaze of approaching power brought me back toward wakefulness. For one sleepy moment, I thought we must have reached a group of nomad guides.

Evermund's cry brought me to full alert, and I realized the power wasn't on the bank but ahead of us in the water itself. For a terrifying half-second, I thought I was back in the wild power attack on the Viridian.

But this was different. The power was stationary, almost like a—

The boat crunched loudly, voices screaming as the force of the collision catapulted me off my seat and into the air. I spun, trying to catch my breath and make sense of the land, water, and sky that flashed past my eyes.

Before I could work out what was happening, I hit the water hard. The sudden icy cold was like knives piercing every inch of my skin, and only the most basic instinct kept me from gasping lungfuls of water.

Without thinking, acting on the same instinct that had shut my eyes and mouth, I reached for the familiar brightness of my sister's power. The thrashing water pushed me downriver, but she was stationary, above the surface. Had she somehow avoided being thrown free of the boat?

As I latched on to her, the shape of her power became obvious. Instantly, I followed her pattern, as I had done so often with Zeke. Weaving the same forces around myself, I pulled my body toward the surface. I hadn't broken through when she faltered, slipping downward herself, and I realized my horrible mistake.

Letting go of the power I had inadvertently sucked from her, I reached instead for the invisible wall that had collided with our boat. Seizing the power that had created it—power that must have come from unknown elements mages—I thrust that power into the pattern Airlie had unwittingly demonstrated for me.

I flew from the water with almost as much force as I had hit it. The liquid surface of the river hardened beneath my feet, allowing me to stand on the otherwise moving surface as water streamed from my body, clothes, and pack.

Wiping water from my eyes, I looked around. Even in those few short seconds, the current had sucked me downstream.

"Cadence!" Airlie was staring at me wide-eyed.

She took a step in my direction, the water hardening beneath each foot as it touched the surface of the river. Feeling the way she shaped the power, I copied her, dashing upriver to join her and Evermund, who stood further upstream again.

"Airlie!" I flung my arms around her. "What happened?"

"Never mind that!" Evermund called back to us. "We need to get everyone to shore."

I gulped, following his gaze to where several of our group already stood, dripping wet and shivering on the western bank. Only Evermund and Airlie were still dry. Apparently they had reacted with enough speed to catch themselves in the air before they could hit the water. Not even Gia had managed as much, although she had already reached the shore and was holding up balls of fire to warm her shivering companions.

"Get over there," Airlie hissed at me. "For now, they'll be thinking I'm helping you, but I'd rather you were helping me. There must be power somewhere around here that you can feed us. We've all got almost nothing left after pushing the boat here."

"Yes, of course," I said.

"Get onto solid ground first," Airlie said. "After that, the priority is grabbing people. Everyone will assume it's Evermund and me doing all the work."

I nodded, hurrying across the top of the river and onto the bank. While I did so, Renley appeared from beneath the surface, carried in a great stream of water up and out of the river. It dumped him, spluttering and gasping, on the bank before streaming away in all directions.

I turned back toward the river, searching for the others. One of the guards launched straight up into the air on a fountain, only to be caught in an unnaturally strong crosswind and blown over the edge of the bank.

The wind faltered, though, and Captain Huxley leaped forward to catch her, breaking her fall although he staggered backward and nearly collapsed himself under the awkward weight. Evermund and Airlie were losing strength and needing help.

I focused on the river again. The spots of power that burned inside each member of our group were distinct against the rush of the water, and the ones still caught in its clutches were being carried further and further away. I pinpointed the most distant.

Not wanting to mess with both water and wind at the same time, I decided to focus on the water. Seizing more of the power that had fueled the barrier, I shaped it into a whirling tunnel of water that formed around the guard and sucked her back upriver. When she leveled with me, I sent the column of water —and her with it—shooting out of the river and onto the bank. She landed harder than the earlier guard had done, and I winced in sympathy and apology but didn't dare speak.

Instead I pinpointed the next person, who had been swept even further away now, and repeated the same process. When I seized the third and final one in a whirling tunnel of water and dragged him back toward us, I nearly faltered. His power was dimming. How long had he been under the water?

Fueled by my desperation, I propelled the water even faster, ejecting the poor guard from the river at speed. He landed so hard, I heard something crack.

"Hayes!" I shouted, racing to his side and dropping to my knees. "He isn't breathing!"

The healer appeared from out of the huddle of people, still dripping water as he joined me beside the man.

"Hurry!" I gasped, trying to will the flicker of the man's ability to brighten.

He was one of the weakest among the guards, his ability far below that of a mage, so I hadn't noticed how dim it had become until I had him in my clutches. I should have gone for him first.

I stopped the frenzied pace of my thoughts as Hayes's power reached into the man. The guard's lungs seized, squeezing together and expelling the water inside them violently from his mouth. He rolled to one side, coughing weakly and groaning as the stream of water finished.

The movement dislodged Hayes's hand, but he merely muttered soothingly as he reached for him again, healing his broken arm and pushing oxygen back into his bloodstream. The man shook his head, still appearing dazed, and sat up.

I rocked back onto my heels with a sigh of relief. Augusta, an irritated expression on her face, strode up the bank to join the huddle of people around us. In the distance, an enormous vine trailed from one of the overhanging trees into the water. Apparently the Master of Plants hadn't needed an elements mage to save her.

The gray strands in her silky black hair seemed particularly stark, but no sign of age showed in her determined steps.

"What?" she demanded, "was that?"

One of the guards stepped forward, nodding respectfully and holding out a questioning hand. I expected her to bite his head off for suggesting she needed assistance, but instead she nodded regally.

Rather than taking her arm to help her along, however, a small jet of air rushed between them with a whoosh. Augusta gave a soft sigh, closing her eyes for a moment and giving herself a shake. Curious, I examined the power he was using and realized what was happening just in time to see the visible effect as her clothes dried. A handy trick like that must often be in demand—especially since it required so little power that most ordinary people with an elements affinity would be able to manage it.

Between the mysterious barrier and the efforts of my team, plenty of leftover power still swirled around and through this section of river, so I didn't even think before borrowing the guard's pattern and producing my own jet of hot air along with a soft sigh that mirrored Augusta's. The warmth on my skin after the freezing cold dunking was hard to resist.

Airlie immediately appeared at my side, and I playfully directed a stream of the air toward her. She just frowned, however, putting a hand on my arm, and I immediately flushed and let the air dissipate. I knew she was trying to cover for my momentary forgetfulness, but it was hard not to feel resentment at her disapproving presence.

"I assume whatever caused that accident didn't come from you?" Augusta asked, looking between Airlie and Evermund.

Evermund shook his head, his face grim. "I should have seen it coming, though. If I hadn't been so distracted because we were in the middle of changing roles..."

"And exhausted," Airlie said quickly, glaring at Augusta as if the older mage was blaming Evermund for what had happened. "Evermund, Gia, and I are all utterly exhausted. It's true we were distracted by the changeover, but it had a positive effect, too. It meant both Evermund and I were connected to the water when we reached that barrier. If one or both of us had gone under as well, it might have ended differently. As it was, we nearly weren't in time to fish everyone out."

Her eyes wandered over to the guard who appeared to have effected a complete recovery, thanks to Hayes.

"What I want to know," Augusta snapped, "is who *is* responsible? Or, rather, more relevantly, should we be expecting another imminent attack? Are the raiders lurking in wait somewhere?"

She looked sharply in all directions, and my eyes followed, the lingering warmth disappearing instantly. I hadn't even considered the possibility that whoever had been responsible for our mishap might still be lurking nearby.

Evermund glanced my way, the hint of a question in his eyes, and I immediately stretched out my awareness. No one lurked on the other side of the river. On our side, I found a distant clump of people upstream, but they were both stationary and a considerable distance away. I shook my head as subtly as I could at him, but Augusta's eyes still narrowed, her sharp eyes having caught the exchange.

"I think if our attackers were lingering near," Evermund said smoothly, "then they would have struck while we were still fishing ourselves out of the river."

"Was it rogue wild power, then?" Hayes asked, joining us now that his patient no longer needed him. "Just a poorly timed flare from the eastern forest?"

"If I'm not mistaken," Nikolas said in a drawl that suggested he didn't consider such a thing a possibility, "then we've already passed the border. We're in nomad lands now, on both sides of the river."

I swung around to gaze at the far bank. It looked just like our own, the rolling hills just as green as the ones on this side, except for the occasional odd crater.

"I believe you're right." Evermund nodded, but something in his bearing gave me the impression he would have preferred Nikolas not point out that particular fact.

I had my own reasons for knowing it hadn't been an attack of wild power, regardless of the location of the border. It was ordinary power that had created the barrier, although it definitely didn't belong to anyone in the boat. So where had it come from? There was far too much lingering power for it to be leftover from a previous activity. This was a deliberate barricade kept across the river.

Augusta turned to frown out over the water. "I can feel nothing," she said. "But neither can I see any physical impediment. Whatever wall we hit wasn't a physical one." She looked back at Evermund, Gia, and Airlie. "I assume it was something done to the water or air itself?"

Evermund glanced at Airlie. "It felt like the river to me."

She nodded. "I agree. It was like when we harden the water so we can stand on the surface. You only recently showed me how to do that, so I'm not as familiar with the effect as I'd like, but that's how it felt." She wrinkled her nose. "As if the river ahead of us was solid instead of liquid."

Slowly my gaze moved from Nikolas to the far bank and then back down the river, eventually finishing on Evermund who had seemed disapproving of Nikolas mentioning we had crossed into nomad land. I gasped.

"Like a border, you mean?" I asked Airlie. "As if someone

blocked the river passage at the border? That doesn't sound like the raiders, that sounds like..."

Evermund gave a soft, long-suffering sigh, and I realized too late that he hadn't wanted that particular avenue of thinking explored aloud. A moment's thought told me why. It was a political mess, and his delegation was almost entirely made up of youthful and inexperienced members.

I shot him an apologetic look, relieved to see amusement in his eyes despite the disapproving shake of his head.

"It was definitely something purposeful?" Nikolas asked, wrath in his voice.

Evermund glanced at Airlie who hesitated and then nodded.

"I don't see how it could be anything else," she said apologetically.

"I concur," Evermund said shortly.

"What sort of welcome to the nomad lands is this?" Nikolas demanded. "It's outrageous."

He looked around for his sister, as if expecting her to back him up. Instead, a crease appeared between his brows when he saw her slumped against Renley, Renley's arm around her shoulders appearing to be the only thing keeping her upright.

"She just sort of collapsed against me," he said in a strained voice, as if afraid of being accused of laying hands on the princess.

"She's all right," Hayes told Nikolas quietly. "She's just exhausted from expending so much of her ability. There's nothing I can do to help with that, but rest will fix it easily enough."

Nikolas looked between Gia and the rest of us, clearly torn between helping his sister and continuing his diatribe against the nomads.

"It's certainly not what we hoped for," Augusta said briskly. "But events are moving at speed, and the nomad kingdom is in a time of upheaval—and likely some level of chaos—as they prepare to hand over the reins of government. There's every chance this barrier was left in place by accident."

Nikolas crossed his arms, a combative light in his eyes, but she stared him down.

"Most importantly, we have no proof the nomads were behind it." She looked at Evermund. "Is there any further information you can give me about what was done here? Anything at all?"

Evermund sighed. "I wish I could. But our collision with the barrier seems to have shredded it past all recognition. It's no longer in place, so I'm already guessing as to its nature. I only got the briefest sense of what had been done to the water before it broke apart."

I winced. He seemed to be assuming the boat itself had caused the damage, but I was fairly sure that had been me, grabbing wildly at the power as I thrashed beneath the water—and then continuing to help myself to it ever since.

Airlie put a cautionary hand on my arm, and this time I kept quiet. I agreed with her that it wasn't the moment to be bringing attention to myself.

"Very well, then," Augusta said. "We have no evidence the incident even happened, let alone that the nomads are responsible." She turned a stern look on the entire group, fixing each of us with her authoritative eye in turn. Even the guards received the same treatment. "We will not begin this visit with an unprovable accusation against our hosts. As it turns out, no serious harm was done, so we will all pretend that tedium was our greatest trial on the journey here. Do you understand me?"

We nodded and murmured our agreement. I could certainly see her point.

She looked over at Gia, concern on her face. "I think we'll need to make camp here and rest before attempting to continue on by foot to meet our guides."

"Make camp?" Captain Huxley raised an eyebrow, a note of

dark humor in his voice. "With what supplies would we be doing that?"

I gulped, only just realizing for the first time that almost everything we had brought with us had disappeared down the river. Thankfully I had already put the pack of my personal belongings back on before the accident, overeager to reach our destination and be done with the boat. So I had clothes at least, and my mother's precious books were safe. But Airlie's bag was gone.

I looked at her measuringly and realized with surprise that we were almost the same size these days. She could share the clothes I had packed.

Several other packs had also been saved. Two guards had been assigned the task of watching the packs of the twins, Evermund and Augusta, and they had taken their assignment seriously, somehow managing to hold on to all of them. And Hayes had been wearing his medical bag. Everything else was gone, however.

"I did save this," Gia said in a quiet, exhausted voice, that made me look at her in concern. I had never heard her so flat and lifeless. "I pulled it out of the river before I started drying people out."

She reached over to pat a chest beside her, swaying wildly. She would have fallen if Renley hadn't grabbed her.

I hadn't noticed the chest before, although it was both opulent and beautiful, the sleek wood studded with jewels. I couldn't imagine what it might contain, but Augusta apparently knew because she heaved a sigh of relief.

"There are some mercies, then," she said.

"It's our parents' gift to the new monarch—whoever they may be," Nikolas said in his annoyingly superior way, apparently having seen the confusion on my face. "To be presented along with our formal request for an alliance against this...wild power."

"Supplies or not," Augusta said, "we clearly can't go traipsing into the mountains without rest."

"Perhaps…perhaps it's not necessary to go so far," I said timidly, not wanting to say more than I should. I sent a pleading look at Evermund. "Could you check ahead? Maybe if our guides aren't too far up the river, you might be able to sense any campfire they've built? We could all do with a proper camp, so if it's not too far, it might be worth it."

Evermund took one look at the silent message I was trying to send him and nodded. I couldn't tell him outright that I felt someone upriver, but it didn't seem too much of a stretch to guess that our guides might be waiting to meet us. And if they had a fire, food—even tents and beds, potentially—then I would carry Gia there myself.

"She's right," Evermund said after a second. "There's a couple of campfires not too far up the river. I think we can make it that far."

"Well done." Augusta gave me an approving look, although a gleam of interest still lurked behind it, making me uncomfortable.

She turned to Hayes. "Can Her Highness make it, do you think?"

Hayes nodded. "We can help her easily enough. She's in no physical danger from her condition."

Gia tried to straighten, pushing away Renley's support.

"I can make it," she said bravely. But when Renley obediently stepped away from her, she swayed so dramatically that Nikolas hurried over to take Renley's place.

"Of course you can," he said with staunch support, and I once again warmed toward him. If only he showed the rest of the world the same care he showed his twin.

No one argued Gia's fitness to travel in the face of their combined insistence, so we gathered what few possessions we still had and began the short journey. Thanks to those with an elements affinity, we were a dry but bedraggled bunch who made our slow way up the riverbank. And though it wasn't far, we were all relieved to see the gleam of a distant fire as soon as it appeared. It wasn't yet dark, but the day was drawing to a close, and the warmth and security of the flames enticed us all to a faster pace.

CHAPTER 5

CADENCE

The nomads who sat around the fires leaped to their feet at the sight of us, hurrying forward to take Gia from Nikolas's arms since he was clearly ready to drop after carrying her half the distance.

"The princess is merely exhausted from overuse of her ability," Augusta said, making the nomad who held her flinch in alarm at the discovery he was holding royalty.

Certainly nothing in the surprised faces around us suggested this group had been involved in blocking our path. And when I looked at them more closely, I recognized the pattern of the embroidery on their robes. I gave a sigh of relief at the indication they belonged to Tribe Nicabar. I might not be sure about the rest of the nomads, but I did know Zeke and his tribe were safe. If Annora sent these people, then they hadn't tried to sabotage us.

"I thought you were coming by boat?" the eldest of the nomads present asked, concern lining his face.

"We had a small...accident," Evermund said, "and have had to come a short way on foot."

"Not the raiders, I hope!" the man said in alarm.

"We believe not," Augusta replied. "But we would appreciate the chance to rest by your fires, and we will need to beg your assistance in making camp for the night as much of our supplies were lost."

"By all means, please sit." He gestured for us to gather around the two fires, and we pressed forward eagerly. "My name is Roscoe, of Tribe Nicabar, and I have been sent to see you safely to the Hidden City. You need have no concerns about supplies as we will press on immediately now that you've arrived. We can afford to waste no time."

"Immediately?" Augusta frowned. "Clearly that will be impossible."

Her eyes moved meaningfully to Gia who had stretched out on the ground and gone to sleep. When her gaze traveled on to Airlie, I realized my sister looked only slightly less tired than Gia.

"Rest will not be an issue," Roscoe said with a slight grin. "Indeed, you can rest to your heart's content." His smile grew, as if he'd made a joke.

"I don't understand." Captain Huxley's tense muscles suggested he sensed a threat.

"I believe you're already familiar with the method we mean to employ," a new voice said. "But your healer is welcome to examine the brew before any of you take it."

I gaped as a face I recognized stepped out of one of the tents.

"Liara?"

The Nicabar apprentice nodded at me. "Cadence. I'm glad to see you decided to visit after all." She looked around the rest of the group. "Some of you will recognize me from the tour." Her gaze lingered on Airlie with curiosity, but she continued without asking for an introduction. "None of the other members of the tour could be spared, but Annora thought you might like to see a familiar face in case you had any concerns."

She grinned. "Such as whether your welcoming committee were only posing as members of our tribe."

I frowned, startled. The idea hadn't occurred to me, but now that she'd implanted it, I was indeed glad of her familiar face.

"Annora understands what she asks is not a small thing," Liara continued. "But it was necessary in order for Tribe Patrin to agree to your visit."

Augusta's eyebrows rose. "I see. However, I'm still not sure what is being asked of us."

"I can guess," Hayes said. "Does it involve a certain herb developed by Annora herself?"

Liara grinned cheekily at him. "That's the one."

"No, absolutely not," Nikolas said sharply, reminding me that Hayes had used the herb against Gia and Nikolas when the raiders attacked the Guild on the night Airlie was taken.

The memory gave me sympathy for his instant dismissal of the idea, but I also knew it wasn't going to be that simple.

"There was no mention of this back in Tarona," Evermund said, regarding both Liara and Roscoe closely.

Liara shrugged. "Perhaps they thought you would be more easily convinced once you'd already made it this far."

"They wouldn't be wrong about that," Airlie muttered in my ear. "I didn't push everyone all the way here and then fish them out of a river so they could turn around and go home now."

I raised my hand to cover a snort. "Give up the chance to see the Hidden City?" I whispered back. "No one's going to do that. This is all just posturing."

Augusta's eyes narrowed. "I take it we're talking about some sort of sleeping potion?" She looked to Hayes for confirmation.

"A full knock out," he said. "The healing affinity has been considering its potential uses in our healing centers ever since

Zeke introduced us to it. I believe it already sees wide use among the tribes."

"It's perfectly safe," Liara said. "Many nomads have used it. You won't experience any lingering effects."

"We'll just conveniently sleep all the way to the secret location of your city," Nikolas said with a note of disgust.

She smiled at him sweetly. "Precisely."

"And this is the only way we're moving forward?" Augusta asked.

"That is correct," Roscoe said. "I'm afraid on this we cannot budge."

"It makes sense to me," I said cheerfully. Nikolas glared at me, but I just shrugged. "We did all think it seemed a little too good to be true that the nomads were suddenly willing to reveal the location of their hidden capital."

The others might be annoyed, but I was filled with an unexpected lightness at this development. Evermund's words back in Tartora had been weighing on me, the background question of what exactly the nomads might want from me always lingering. But this reduced the compromise they were making considerably, thereby lessening the pressure of what they might want from me in return.

Augusta frowned. "I'm not pleased with the plan or with our having been kept in the dark—especially given our recent less-than-pleasant experience with a similar drug at the hands of the raiders. I hope I'm a reasonable woman, however. I can understand why the tribes have made the stipulation. But how am I to guarantee the safety of my charges if I'm unconscious?"

"Two among your number are excused from this requirement," Roscoe said, and both Evermund's and Augusta's eyes lit up. But the nomad's gaze stopped on Airlie and me.

"Us?" Airlie asked. "Why us?"

"That is the command of the head of my tribe, backed by the newly elected head of Tribe Patrin whose responsibility it is to safeguard the city and kingdom in the king's stead until a new tribe can be elevated to the throne."

So we weren't going to get answers. At least not publicly. I could guess at them, though. Annora knew Airlie and I weren't really Tartoran and that our history with the kingdom was only recent. Did she hope to lure Airlie into joining the nomads as well? I had to admit, the idea of being able to stay with both Zeke and my sister was appealing...

Or perhaps she merely thought the others wouldn't consider me enough protection, and she had picked Airlie as the one with the next weakest link to Tartora after me.

"You must choose," Liara said, sounding almost bored. "Do you trust your safety to Cadence and Airlie? If so, we can all proceed. If not, they may come without you, if they so wish."

I froze, looking at the others with widened eyes. Surely they wouldn't abandon us at this point? I was relying on their presence to make sure I wasn't swallowed up in the nomad's mountains, never to be seen again.

"We're coming," Gia said, pushing herself onto her elbow and talking with a hint of her usual spirit after her brief nap. "Personally, I much prefer the idea of a long sleep to a long hike. And I more than trust Cadence." She glanced at my sister. "And Airlie," she added, a beat too late.

Airlie just grinned at her. "Thanks for the vote of confidence."

Gia smiled ruefully in return and put her head back down on the ground. Evermund, Augusta, and Captain Huxley stepped aside to confer in hushed voices, returning with a mix of responses evident on their faces. Augusta looked offended, the captain anxious, and Evermund intrigued.

They all agreed though, without further demur, and Augusta gave Airlie a stern lecture on the kind of care she expected her helpless body to receive. I listened as well, knowing that I was at least as capable as Airlie, even if the Master of Plants didn't know it.

Eventually Augusta was satisfied, and the drink was handed around. When the rest of the delegation were sleeping peacefully beside the fire, I looked at the nomads with some trepidation.

"What now?"

"Now we begin the journey," Roscoe said.

It took an astonishingly short time for the small group of nomads to pack up the tents, douse the fires, and fetch three large wagons from behind a small hill. When they rolled out, I frowned, glancing from them to the steep, rocky mountains that towered so close now that the screening tree canopy no longer hid them from view.

Airlie also looked at the wagons in surprise, although her astonishment passed more quickly into understanding than mine.

"Tunnels!" she gasped. "Of course. It's the only thing that makes sense."

Liara nodded, only a hint of impatience in her voice as she replied. "Of course. How else would we transport goods and animals with us, let along our young, elderly, and infirm?"

Her voice turned apologetic. "You'll ride in the back of the wagons, and I'm afraid you'll have to agree to be blindfolded. We trust you more than them—but we don't trust anyone that much."

She said it in a matter-of-fact way, different from both the scornful girl I had first met and the obsequious one she had subsequently pretended to be. I liked this Liara a great deal more than either of the other two.

"What's changed?" I asked her, deciding to go for the direct approach.

When she looked confused, I gestured between us.

"Oh." She considered for a moment, eyeing me calculatedly.

"I may not approve of Zeke's choice, but he's clearly made it. I know a lost cause when I see it. We may not be best friends, but you're almost as good as tribe now."

I blinked, startled by her honesty. "Thank you."

"Almost," she stressed, making me blink again, but she followed it up with a wink before disappearing toward one of the other wagons.

Airlie succumbed to her exhaustion and climbed into the closest wagon, settling herself to sleep on a pallet that had been laid along its base. I made myself stay awake and alert, though, watching the others loaded into the second and third wagon. To my relief, the nomads treated them gently and respectfully, and as soon as they were all secured, I climbed up into the third wagon to join Airlie and six of our unconscious friends.

Roscoe himself came to blindfold us with thick lengths of black material. I helped wrap Airlie's eyes while she slept, apparently too tired to be woken by our efforts. I just hoped she recovered herself before we ran into any more trouble.

"I will remain with you at all times until we reach the city," he told me once my eyes were covered and I was sitting on the pallet next to Airlie, listening to the crunch of the ground beneath the rolling wheels of the wagon.

"How am I meant to watch over my friends when I can't see?" I asked, realizing it was a little late to be asking the question.

"You have your other senses," he replied. "If you hear trouble, you have my permission to remove your blindfold. And besides, even with your eyes covered, you're not truly blind. Sight is not a mage's strongest sense."

He stated it as a fact, and I could sense his gaze turning elsewhere, as if to signify he had completed the conversation. But I sat there, unmoving, shocked.

If he knew I could sense my companions from here, then he

knew my affinity. I had known Annora knew it, but I hadn't been prepared for a stranger to reference it so casually.

As the shock passed, I realized the truth of his words, however. Reaching out, I felt the reassuring presence of each of the other fourteen people in our delegation—and even more reassuringly, I found them alone in the trays of the back two wagons. Besides Airlie, me, and Roscoe, the other nomads all rode in the front wagon.

I settled myself down to watch over the rest of the delegation. Having slept most of the journey on the boat, I was ready to take the first shift, while Airlie slept.

Soon time began to meld together, all normal markers lost in the strangeness of my unaccustomed blindness and the rocking of the wagon. For the first few minutes I wondered if I should attempt to track our passage, but I soon gave up on the idea. I didn't have a strong enough sense of direction for that, and the nomads would have their tunnel entrances extremely well concealed.

When I relaxed and limited myself to keeping track of my friends, it was actually quite peaceful. At one point we stopped, and there was some noise up ahead, but Roscoe assured me all was well, and no one approached either the second or third wagons.

As soon as the wagons started moving again, I realized the pause had marked the beginning of the tunnels. It was remarkable how much I could pick up with my eyes covered.

The air quality changed—turning cool and smelling of rock —and the grass beneath the wagon wheels switched to hard stone. I mused idly that they must have their plants mages regrow the grass behind them each time they passed to prevent the creation of a track leading right to their tunnel—like wiping down the snow to erase your footsteps in wintertime hide and seek.

We traveled for an unknown length of time, although even

without the blindfold, I wouldn't have been able to track the passage of the sun. Several times we made turns, and sometimes breezes seemed to spring from cross-tunnels, telling me there were other branchings we didn't take. Occasionally we passed out from the tunnels completely, traveling for brief stretches outside before plunging underground again.

At some point Airlie woke up, expressing her interest in all the things I'd already noted.

Several times we stopped to stretch our legs and eat, and each time we were permitted to remove our blindfolds until it was time to return to the wagon. The first time, I had been eager, full of curiosity, but there was nothing distinctive about our location. We stood in a rough tunnel of gray stone, comfortably wide and tall enough for the wagons and horses, but not wide enough for two wagons to travel side-by-side. The only light came from the lanterns carried by the nomads, and no markings on the walls gave any indication of a guiding route.

"Has anyone ever been lost down here?" I asked, with some trepidation.

Roscoe chuckled. "Oh, aye, I imagine they have. But not an official tribe group like ours. Every tribe has members well-versed in the underground ways, and we would never travel without at least two of them among our number." He nodded toward the small group of nomads in the front wagon.

"Are you one?" I asked.

"Me?" He shook his head. "No, thank you. I prefer the open sky and the changing road. I've not spent much time at the Hidden City."

"It will be a big sacrifice for you if Annora wins the vote, then," Airlie said. "To live down here potentially for decades."

"Bless you, child." He chuckled. "It's a sacrifice for the ruling tribe to put down roots for a generation—but that's why the other tribes swear them their loyalty for that span. The honor can't be won without sacrifice. But it's not so great a sacrifice as that. The Hidden City isn't under here. No one would nominate for monarch if it was." He chuckled again, apparently amused at our ignorance.

Airlie and I exchanged intrigued looks, but the call came for us to replace our blindfolds, so we climbed back into the wagon without asking further questions.

The further we rolled along, the more my thoughts fixated on what was waiting for us at the end of this final leg of the journey—or rather who.

I missed Zeke with an ache that was as much physical as mental. In the shifting sands of my life—a life that no longer seemed rooted in any physical place—he had become my anchor. We had been through so much together, and somewhere along the way Zeke had come to be my safe place. Without him, I felt adrift. I could function well enough, of course, but my thoughts turned away from the people I was with too often for me to feel truly planted.

It had surprised me how little pang I felt on leaving the Mages' Guild. I had thought it had become home, but apparently it had actually been Zeke all along.

So a part of me wondered, as we traveled deeper into the mountains, whether I was about to see my future home for the first time. But even though the thought brought a tingle of excitement, fear rushed in with it. Even if Airlie agreed to come with me, I couldn't see her spending her life in a remote mountain city. The true nomad life would appeal to her more, but if she joined another tribe, it would be little better than having her in Tartora. I would rarely see her.

And what of Gia, and Evermund, and even Nikolas? Of course I knew they were royalty, and we wouldn't always be as close as we were in the artificial confines of our apprentice years. But I didn't want to be cut off from them completely like I would be if I lived in a city that visitors had to be drugged to even enter.

Eventually I shook the thoughts loose. I was running ahead of myself. I hadn't even seen the Hidden City yet.

As if to echo my thoughts, Roscoe gave a pleased grunt, calling for us to remove our blindfolds. We both pulled them off eagerly, only to find nothing but stone around us. My face fell.

"Don't worry," Roscoe said with a grin. "We're here, right enough. But I wanted to bring you the scenic way." He sounded pleased with himself, so I did my best to hide my impatience.

"Come on," he said. "We're going to wake the others. They'll want to see this, too."

A shiver ran up and down my spine, the anticipation building as I hurried to join him. I thought he might be a healing mage, but he merely waved a small bottle beneath the noses of each person in our delegation, one at a time.

Some woke quickly while others took a little longer, but all returned to full alertness in a surprisingly short span. Over and over again, Airlie and I reassured everyone that no one had been near them during our travels.

To my relief, Gia was one of those to wake quickly, bounding from the wagon with a familiar air of excitement and no sign of her previous crippling exhaustion.

"Are we there?" she asked, looking around at the rough stone walls with bemusement. "I feel like I slept for a hundred years."

"Apparently Roscoe wants us all to see it for the first time together," Airlie said.

"That I do." Roscoe stepped forward. "If you follow me, you'll get your first glimpse of the capital city of the nomads, hidden jewel of the mountains."

Airlie and I exchanged a look, surprised at his enthusiasm given his earlier comments. Clearly, regardless of his personal feelings, the city was a source of pride to the tribes.

"Come on, then," Airlie said with a grin, her eyes moving from me to Evermund. "Let's go see what all the fuss is about."

CHAPTER 6
AIRLIE

The tunnel turned sharply ahead of us, and as we approached the bend, I increased my pace, leaving Cadence behind to join Evermund in the lead, Augusta at his other side. He glanced at me, a smile lighting up his brown eyes in a way that made me forget for a brief moment what we were about to see.

I stumbled on a rough stretch of ground, and he reached out instinctively to steady me. I regained my balance easily, but his hand remained on my arm, both of our eyes trained on it.

Slowly, I looked up, my heart fluttering in a strange way as I met his eyes. Then we both turned, not fully conscious of our surroundings, and gave near identical gasps. We stopped, his hand falling from my arm as we gaped at the scene before us.

"What? What it is it?" Cadence's voice sounded behind me, and then she pushed her way to my side, going silent as she took in the same sight holding me spellbound.

Roscoe chuckled. "It's always a pleasure to bring tribe youngsters here for the first time. But they've all heard stories about what to expect. This is even better."

We hadn't just reached the end of the tunnel but the edge of the mountain. Below us, a near sheer cliff face dropped away into a deep valley. At the bottom of it, distant, lush greenery filled the gap that separated the mountain we stood on from its near neighbor.

Not much more than a mile away from us, another mountain reached toward the clouds, its face nearly as sheer. But directly across from where we stood, the rocky facade was broken by an enormous platform. On the platform stood a city, built from the same gray rock as the mountain and looking as much a part of this hidden locale as the mountains and valley themselves.

Tall, elegant buildings lined stone streets, and the same lush greenery as filled the valley floor wove between the structures. An underground river apparently emerged from the mountain into the city itself because on both sides of the platform, thin waterfalls cascaded down in sheets of white foam to disappear into the valley below. As we watched, a shaft of light appeared from behind a cloud, striking the city perfectly and setting rainbows dancing around the waterfalls' spray.

And connecting us with this wonder was a long, arching, impossible stone bridge.

Roscoe chuckled again, apparently pleased with our shock and the heavens' timing. The gasp I had uttered had now been repeated many times as each member of our party pressed forward for their first glimpse of the city.

"It's beautiful," I said at last, turning to Roscoe. "Thank you for bringing us here."

He shook his head. "That wasn't my decision. I'm just doing as instructed."

"Still." I turned back to the vista. "I never dreamed such a city could exist."

Were my eyes shining, reflecting the sense of wonder that was filling me fuller and fuller with each moment I stood here?

"Better than the ocean?" Cadence asked me with an upward tilt of her lips.

I elbowed her. "I'll let you know when I see the ocean to compare."

She grinned, but it didn't quite reach her eyes.

My brow creased slightly, trying to work out why it hadn't been the answer she was hoping for. But Gia pressed forward, looping her arm into Cadence's and exclaiming loudly, and the moment passed.

Once everyone had been given their chance to gaze at the view until they stopped exclaiming, Roscoe indicated for us to proceed onto the bridge.

"Is it safe?" Renley regarded the thin stone with trepidation.

"That is hardly a naturally occurring phenomenon," Augusta said tartly. "It's held together with something far stronger than stone."

I stepped over to him. "Don't worry. If you fall off, I'll have the wind catch you."

A spark leaped into his eyes, and he laughed. "Thanks for the offer, but if Master Augusta declares it safe, I have no concerns. Calistans aren't cowards."

I nodded. "Nan would approve the sentiment, I think."

He gazed over the edge of the stone at the valley below and then back toward the city. "She would love this place."

"Maybe one day you'll be able to bring her here," I said softly, regretting the pain I had brought to his eyes.

He had left everyone behind to help me flee, and I shouldn't mock his courage, or his determination to honor them.

Since the others had already started moving, we joined the group, stepping out onto the bridge in a clump and leaving the wagons to bring up the rear. No one suggested riding in them, and I was glad for it. I'd had more than enough of sitting still and was ready to stretch my legs.

A waist-high stone wall ran along both sides of the bridge, a necessary security measure since the wind gusts grew stronger the further out over the valley we got. While they didn't bother me—in fact I reveled in them—the buffeting was strong enough that it might have put both people and wagons at risk without the barrier.

Unafraid on my own behalf, I walked right alongside the wall, peering over at the long drop to the valley floor below.

"It's incredible!" I said to Cadence when she edged over to join me. "The entire thing!"

"It's beyond beautiful," she agreed. "I certainly never imagined the Hidden City would look like this."

I glanced at her, confused at the slight strain in her voice. Her eyes were fixed on my hand as it trailed along the top of the waist-high wall, and she seemed to be carefully avoiding looking at the drop on the other side.

"I didn't know you were afraid of heights." I couldn't quite keep the amusement out of my voice.

"I wasn't before," she said, the strain more pronounced. "But is it really necessary to walk right by the edge?"

I laughed. "I'm not going to be blown over the wall, Cadie. I'm an *elements* mage, remember? And I won't let the wind take you, either." I considered for a moment before lowering my voice. "Here, let me show you."

I reached out and directed the next gust that blew past, bringing it curving back around to swirl alongside us in a mini twist that kept several leaves circling beside us. For a moment, I felt the wind pull against me in an unnatural move I had learned to recognize as the work of another elements mage. But a moment later, the pull stopped, and instead the circling wind grew stronger as the other mage aligned their efforts with mine.

"That's enough now," I murmured, letting the wind escape and stream away freely before anyone else noticed.

When I glanced back at my sister, she was grinning.

"I've never controlled the wind before," she said. "Zeke is a plants mage, of course, and most of my practice has been with him. And back at the river, I focused on the water. It's fun!"

I smiled back but couldn't help my eyes darting around to check no one was standing near enough to hear her words.

"It is fun," I agreed. "And now you know that if anyone falls off, I'm not going to let them go plummeting down to the valley below. I can't imagine anyone would build such a bridge or live in such a city without a plethora of mages around."

"It's a very defensible position," she said thoughtfully. "All they have to do is destroy the bridge, and they cut off access completely. But then if the other side have strong plants mages, I suppose they could just create a new one."

Evermund strolled over to join me in peering over the edge. "Since no one knows where the city even is, I don't think an attack is their greatest weakness."

"What is it, then?" Cadence asked, but I could already guess what he was going to say.

"At the current rate that abilities are weakening, this city might not be sustainable for many more generations." He glanced at me, something in his eyes I couldn't read. "I'm no longer surprised they're nearly as interested in you, Airlie, as in Cadence."

I grimaced. "I'm not defecting to the nomads, if that's what you're worried about."

Cadence stiffened beside me, but when I sent her a quizzical look, her face was impassive. I looked back at Evermund.

"This autumn only marks a year since I became your apprentice. I still have over a year of my apprenticeship to go. I was taken to the raider settlement by force—I have no intention of walking out on my apprenticeship by choice."

"You're not bound by Tartoran laws here," Evermund said in a carefully neutral voice.

"Neither are you," I shot back. "You could get rid of your troublesome apprentice without hindrance. Are you planning to abandon me here?"

He laughed, clearly startled by the accusation. "No, of course not."

"Exactly." I frowned at him. "You wouldn't walk out on your obligations, and neither would I."

"I'm glad to hear it." A slow smile spread over his face, but I was still feeling irritated.

"I can't believe you would think me so lacking in loyalty! You and Tartora took me and Cadence in when we didn't have anyone, and I'm not going to forget that."

Cadence shifted uncomfortably beside me, her steps veering slightly to increase the space between us. I wasn't sure if she'd done it intentionally, but I knew her well enough to read the discomfort in her face.

"Oh, I didn't mean you, Cadence," I said hurriedly. "You're not bound to a Tartoran apprenticeship. You didn't—" I cut myself off, flushing as I realized I had nearly blurted out my secret in front of Evermund. "You don't owe anyone anything," I said hurriedly, to cover my lapse.

"Don't I?" She sounded weary. "Sometimes being the last power mage feels like owing something to everyone. But I can't be everywhere at once."

My mouth twisted. Months ago, when I'd been activated, I'd felt an incredible thrill. After so many years of knowing I was a disappointment to Father, it had been heady to discover I was special—sought out and admired. But once I took on the task of guarding the Guild, those feelings had quickly faded under the weight of expectation and responsibility. I couldn't blame Cadence if she saw her ability as a millstone rather than a gift.

I slipped my hand into hers. "We'll work it out." I gave her a reassuring squeeze, and she squeezed back.

But a second later she pulled herself free with an excited cry.

"Zeke!"

She ran forward, outstripping the rest of the group to reach the end of the stone bridge and throw herself into the arms of the tall young man waiting there with an equally delighted expression.

I stumbled slightly, shocked at the strength of the empty, bereft feeling that hit me at her departure. I would always do what I could to help my younger sister, but I wasn't the one she would look to when she made this decision. Even if she hadn't recognized it yet, it was obvious to everyone else.

No wonder Zeke looked so exultant to see her here, in his home.

"Don't worry," Evermund said softly beside me. "We're a Tartoran delegation about to step foot in the Hidden City. Times are changing."

I smiled up at him, thankful for the reassurance. And he was right. Even if Cadence decided to stay when I left to return to Tarona, that didn't mean I would never see her again.

I was seized by the sudden desire to slip my hand into his, so tantalizingly close, and feel his solid warmth in place of my sister's presence. But my courage failed me, and in a few more steps we reached Zeke as well. He still had an arm around Cadence, clearly wishing all of us were elsewhere so he could give her a proper greeting.

But he smiled broadly, putting aside his personal feelings as he said, "Welcome to the Hidden City!"

"Zeke, it's incredible!" Cadence said. "I can't believe you never said anything!"

"Not saying anything about our capital city is something of a nomad obsession," Zeke said with a laugh. He looked at the rest of the arriving Tartorans. "My mother apologizes for not being here to welcome you in person, but she is preparing for an important ceremony in the lead up to the vote. You've arrived just in time for it. But for now, if you'll come with me, I'll show you to your accommodations."

Augusta gave him a formal response, and we all turned to

follow him, everyone staying on foot, with the wagons trailing behind. Zeke and Cadence talked at full speed, but too quietly for others to hear, as they led the way, arm in arm. When his shoulders tensed and his steps faltered, I could only assume she was filling him in on our eventful arrival into nomad territory.

Renley stepped up beside me, clearly awed as he looked around.

"These are enormous buildings," he said loudly enough to make Zeke glance back at us.

"Remember that the current occupancy of the city is much higher than in normal times," he said. "Usually it's only the ruling tribe who live here permanently, along with a handful of rotating representatives from each of the other tribes and anyone too infirm for constant travel. Many of the buildings you see are the store houses owned by each of the forty-one tribes. They're designed to hold tribe history and treasures, not people."

He pointed at another large building that differed from the others in that it had broad double doors and many windows. "And that is our main house of healing. Anyone requiring long term convalescence or predicted to have a difficult birth takes up temporary residence there where they are tended by Tribe Patrin healers."

"It must be a complicated process to turn over the administration of the city to a new tribe following the death of a ruler," Cadence said, her eyes focused on the healing building.

Zeke shrugged. "Both the departing tribe and the new ruling tribe will cohabit the city for several months for a handover period. It's a well-established procedure at this point. Ah, here we are."

He gestured for us all to enter a set of open gates that led the way into a courtyard paved with the rough, natural stone of the mountain platform the city had been built on. Two tall, narrow buildings with rows of windows looked down on the courtyard from directly ahead of us and from our left. To our right, a much larger, shorter building stretched away, dotted with only the occasional window.

"This is the central holdings of Tribe Nicabar," Zeke explained. "Although we have several other storehouses within the city, of course. But this is where our city representatives live and where you will be hosted."

The gates swung shut behind the last of our group, and the nomad wagon drivers directed the horses toward the doors of the large building which were slowly swinging open. I watched in interest as the wagons disappeared inside.

"With more of the tribe here than would normally attend the city—even for a vote—some among our number are camping in there," Zeke said when Cadence murmured a question.

"They'll unhitch the horses and take them to the stables in a moment." He indicated a small, squat structure wedged between the closest residential building and the storehouse. "Of course, if we win the vote, we'll all be moving to the palace and the various royal holdings."

"Is it looking like you'll win?" Cadence asked anxiously.

"I certainly intend to do my best," a new voice said from the entrance to the closest building.

CHAPTER 7
AIRLIE

We all swung around to give shallow, respectful bows to Annora, head of Tribe Nicabar. Only Gia and Nikolas remained upright.

"Welcome," she said, as I absorbed the splendor of her elaborate and richly embroidered robes. "As I'm sure my son has informed you, today is an important day in the process of succession. It's unfortunate you did not arrive with more time to prepare, but I'm pleased you've arrived at all."

"Apologies," Augusta said stiffly. "We traveled as quickly as we could."

"Of course." Annora inclined her head. "And I was most disappointed to hear of the trials you encountered." The steel in her voice suggested she was more angry than disappointed.

Zeke shot her a look. "You knew?"

She met his gaze calmly. "I have just been informed." She turned to the rest of us. "Please, follow my assistant inside, and you'll be directed to your rooms. Let her know if you need assistance with fresh clothing given the loss of some of your own luggage. Unfortunately, due to the timing of your arrival, there will not be time for you to have a proper rest before we need to leave."

"We've done nothing but rest," Augusta said sharply.

"Ah yes, I apologize for that as well," Annora replied, her calm unbroken by the implied accusation in Augusta's tone. "I'm afraid it was the only way to receive official sanction of your visit. As you can see, you were delivered here safely, and no harm has been done."

She gestured again toward the woman waiting just inside the door of the building, and Renley was the first to move forward. Gia and Nikolas, along with most of the guards, had already stepped inside when Annora spoke again.

"If I might prevail on you to wait a moment, Augusta and Evermund. I would like a word."

I froze, looking back over my shoulder. Captain Huxley had also hesitated, but after a brief, shared glance with Augusta, Evermund waved him into the building. Perhaps he had been instructed to prioritize the protection of the twins over himself or Augusta.

Cadence gave Annora a curious look but attempted to untangle herself from the arm that was clamping her to Zeke's side. He merely tightened his hold, however, giving his mother a look of defiance.

I immediately stepped back toward them. If my sister was staying, so was I. Evermund had suggested they had an interest in both of us—and their allowing me to travel with only a blindfold backed the idea. I intended to push it as far as it would go.

Annora looked from her son to me before sighing and focusing her attention on Augusta and Evermund. "I truly am sorry about the incident at the river. It should never have happened."

Augusta's eyes narrowed. "You admit it was nomad doing, then?"

Annora hesitated.

Zeke's gaze flicked toward the closed gate, as if wanting to reassure himself we were alone within his tribe space before he spoke, directing his words toward his mother.

"I heard you inform Tribe Patrin that our guests would be arriving up the Celadon yesterday."

"And I heard them issue the instruction that the tribe on duty at the river be instructed to lower the defenses," she said. "What I have only just learned, however, is that Tribe Alia are on duty this week. Clearly I should have had my assistant check the schedule before now."

"Alia." Zeke ground the name out between his teeth. "How could you have predicted that they would dare such open defiance?"

"It is my job to predict all such things," Annora said crisply. "Certainly I blame myself." She inclined her head toward Augusta. "And for that I am truly sorry."

"What can they have been thinking, though?" Zeke asked. "Do they want to catapult us into war with Tartora, on top of everything else? What if someone had died?"

"Naturally Alia are claiming it was an honest mistake—that they never got the message," Annora said. "I don't believe them for a moment, but it would look petty to demand a public truth-telling ceremony when we are the front-runners for the vote. And even if they were forced to confess, they would no doubt say a fuss is being made over nothing—that if Airlie is as strong as is claimed, then there was no real danger. And there are plenty who would be quick to accept that explanation."

She shook her head. "The truth is that Alia is the most aggressive of the faction who are angry about Patrin giving permission for outsiders to come to the city. The last thing they want is for Tartorans—powerful guests of Nicabar, no less—to feel welcome."

"Are we in danger here?" Augusta asked sharply.

"Not within the city," Annora said. "Those who oppose Patrin are a minority, and not even Alia would dare an open attack. At the border there was still a measure of deniability. Under the cover of our hospitality, there is not."

She sighed. "As you know, any tribe may nominate their head for the throne, but traditionally the honor has been shared between only a few of our strongest tribes. That is understandable since in order to secure the necessary votes, a tribe must convince a majority of the other tribes that they have the strength to hold and defend our capital and treasures."

"I remember Tribe Alia's previous rule," Augusta said. "They held the throne before Fenix was elected."

"Indeed. And directly before them was Tribe Patrin's previous rule. Alia consider it to be their turn again, and they have not taken kindly to the appearance of a serious contender—especially not a tribe they consider an upstart to the honor."

I frowned, remembering from our lessons that Tribe Nicabar had not always had its current strength or size. It had been growing steadily for generations and was only now in the position to challenge for the throne for the first time.

"Does that mean you'll be dealing with internal division even if you win?" Cadence asked with dismay, and I guessed she was thinking about the threat of the wild power. We were all hoping for a united front against both it and the raiders.

Annora shook her head sharply. "Nomads value loyalty above all else. If Alia lose the vote, they may hold a grudge—and they'll certainly increase their efforts for the next vote—but they will give full and utter loyalty to the current monarch for the length of their reign. If they didn't, it would ensure they never won another vote again."

Cadence looked relieved, but my stomach still clenched uncomfortably, waiting for whatever was coming next. Annora hadn't held Augusta and Evermund back just to give a more thorough apology for the attack.

Sure enough, Annora spoke again.

"There is not time to discuss nomad politics further at this point. We must move quickly as it would be fatal to be late to the coming assembly."

"I take it you want us to attend with you?" Evermund asked.

Annora hesitated almost imperceptibly before she replied.

"Certainly you must be presented to the tribes. And it would be ideal if you all were present for the occasion. However, a team of elements mages is about to leave the city, and I would like to suggest that your own elements mages accompany them."

"What nonsense is this, Annora?" Augusta asked sharply. "We have only just arrived."

"As I said, the timing is unfortunate. But as crucial as this vote is, we must look beyond it. Our true enemy is not Alia but the fallen kingdom."

Evermund's brow creased, his expression sharpening. "We are in agreement on that. But don't tell me you intend a foray into Calista? It would be folly."

"Not across the border, no. But we have been working on various strategies to protect our lands."

"Like the river barrier?" Evermund didn't sound impressed.

Annora shook her head. "The defenses on the river are there to protect against the raiders. As you have experienced, the rivers are by far the easiest approach to the mountains and this city. But I'm talking about defenses against the wild power. While we haven't yet experienced the extent of the depredations that Tartora is enduring, we have seen the wild power begin to encroach beyond our borders—as I reported in our recent visit. It is a matter of utmost urgency that we find a way to prevent this, and we are more than willing to work with Tartora on this matter and share whatever breakthroughs we might experience. You've sent three of your strongest elements mages on this trip, and the opportunity seems too great to ignore. With the three of you assisting the efforts, they are that much more likely to succeed—and you will also gain firsthand knowledge of the techniques to take back to your own kingdom."

"You want us to separate?" Augusta asked slowly. "With Evermund, Airlie, and Gia to travel immediately back to the border?" She glanced at me as if expecting me to protest, but I said nothing, unsure how I felt.

"We're all of us caught up in unprecedented times," Annora said. "A sense of urgency is not unjustified. I'm not responsible for the expedition to the border, and I have no authority to delay its departure. You either leave immediately or get left behind. It is up to you. Either way, you and your people need to be back in this courtyard within the hour—dressed for travel or for a formal convocation."

"What if we all go on this expedition?" Augusta asked.

"I'm sorry, but that would be impossible. Tribe Nicabar has been granted only six places. I would like to send one or two of my own people but would be willing to give all six places to you if you so desire. I can offer no more than that." She raised an eyebrow. "I cannot believe that you, of all people, Augusta, fear being separated from your elements mages."

Augusta snorted. "Perhaps they fear being removed from me."

Annora laughed. "It is more likely. Either way, I request that you and Cadence remain. Until the moment the vote is cast, Tribe Patrin still rules this city, and they have requested an introduction with the two of you, in particular."

Augusta raised an eyebrow. "You astound me. And here I was thinking I was totally eclipsed by the young." Her caustic gaze flickered to me and away.

"That is the way of things," Annora said. "And yet age and guile may yet win the day. I will see you in an hour."

She swept away, and I immediately turned to Zeke. "Well?"

He shrugged. "This trip to the border has been in planning for weeks—from before King Fenix's death. I only learned of it when I arrived from Tartora, but I was the one to suggest you be included. We may have two or three mages who can rival your strength, Evermund, but we have none as strong as you, Airlie. And we all want this to succeed.”

“What do you think?” Augusta asked Evermund.

He hesitated. “I think I’m reluctant to leave so soon after our arrival. But I cannot fault any part of Annora’s logic. The threat from Calista is the reason we have a pressing need for a renewed alliance with the nomads. To repudiate this offer now would be a poor beginning.”

Augusta sighed. “That it would. But I don’t like how this trip is progressing. At every turn, our hands are tied.”

“Tribe Nicabar are not your enemies,” Zeke said quietly. “That, at least, I can swear.”

“We go,” Evermund said decisively. “And apparently we have little time to lose. I’ll inform the princess.”

“Given there are other tribes involved, I would feel more comfortable if you had one ally with you who knows the people and the land,” Augusta said. “We will leave Annora one place among the travelers. But you will take Hayes and one of the guards with a plants affinity. And we will keep those guards with elements affinities. I would prefer that neither group be left entirely deficient in any area.”

Evermund nodded. “The voice of wisdom, as always, Augusta.”

“Ha!” She snorted and turned for the building. “I suppose I must be grateful my own bags were saved. I’m much too short to fit into anything of Annora’s.”

Evermund followed her, but Cadence reached out to stop me when I tried to go as well.

“Are you sure you’re all right with this?” She watched me with wide eyes. “They didn’t even ask your opinion!”

I laughed. “I don’t think Augusta is in the habit of consulting with apprentices. I feel the same as Evermund—I’m sorry to leave the city, but I trust we'll be back before too long. And if we can find a way to stop the wild power—one that doesn't involve you—it will be well worth the effort."

Cadence chewed on her lip. "I don't want you going just because of me."

I shook my head. "This is for all of us. I just wish I wasn't leaving you behind."

I glanced at Zeke. The whole situation felt too much like what I was most dreading. I wasn't ready to hand my sister over to Zeke and walk out of her life. We had barely had the chance to be sisters without the barrier of deception between us.

I shifted uncomfortably at the thought. If I didn't want any barriers between us, why hadn't I been completely honest with Cadence about everything I'd discovered in the settlement? I still hadn't told her about the paser trees, and the way they could store power, or how their destruction was the cause of the wild power. I couldn't entirely explain my reticence—even to myself.

Zeke sent me a piercing look that made me shift uncomfortably. But it also flashed through my mind that perhaps here was the answer to my reticence. He said nothing, however, and neither did I.

Instead, after a moment, his arm tightened around Cadence. "I'll look after her while you're gone." The glow in his eyes held so much warmth as he gazed down at her that I murmured about needing to change and fled the courtyard.

A nomad appeared while my eyes were still adjusting to the darker light inside. She showed me up the stairs and to my room, pointing out the rooms of the other Tartorans on the way. She left me standing in my doorway, but despite the enticement of a well-appointed room in shades of green with a soft looking bed and several comfortable chairs, I didn't step across the threshold.

After pausing for a moment to consider the matter, I

retraced my steps and knocked four doors down. It opened promptly, Renley looking surprised to see me standing there alone.

"Is everything all right?" he asked.

"Can I come in?"

"Of course." He stepped aside to allow me past.

"The elements mages are being sent on a mission to experiment with ways to stop the wild power," I said, jumping straight in. "We leave almost immediately."

"What?" He gaped at me.

"I was wondering..." I paused before rushing the words out. "Would you like me to activate you before I go? I haven't activated anyone before, but I think I know how."

"Oh." He ran a hand through his hair, looking a little sheepish. "Actually, Evermund activated me before we left Tarona. I'm supposed to be helping Cadence learn how to use her ability, and he thought I might be better able to do that if I had personal experience and not just stories from my parents. Plus he said that on a trip like this, no one should have any part of their personal defenses shackled—no matter how minor my ability."

Evermund's thoughtful consideration brought a smile to my lips. But I shook my head at the same time. "Why didn't you tell me?"

"Sorry." He didn't meet my eyes. "We didn't announce it publicly because Evermund knows I'm not planning to stay in Tartora long term, and he didn't want me locked into an apprenticeship with someone who has no idea how to train a power ability. I was going to tell you, of course, but..." His sheepish expression grew. "I was waiting until I'd had a chance to practice first."

I processed that information for a moment. If I'd thought about it, I knew he intended to find a way back to his family, but it still caused a pang to hear him say outright that he wasn't planning to stay. But I was more than a little relieved not to have to fumble through an attempted activation myself.

"That's excellent news," I said eventually. "And it makes me feel a little better about my second question."

He gave me a curious look, and I blurted it out.

"Will you keep an eye on Cadence for me?"

"Of course," he said quickly, although his eyes gleamed with a look half amused, half quizzical. "Although I think that role is already covered by someone more capable than me."

I shrugged, not sure I could properly explain myself. "I'm not saying I don't trust Zeke. Let's just say we haven't even been here a day, and I'm already sick of being surprised. They're saying Tribe Alia was behind our mishap on the river, and we may have other enemies here as well. There are limits to even Zeke's ability. You might be a stranger to the Hidden City, but you grew up with the General. You know more than me about treacherous people."

A shadow crossed his face. "Not that I proved myself particularly adept at spotting his lies."

I shook my head. "You saw through him in the end. And I'm guessing that only makes you more alert now. I'd just feel better if two people were actively keeping watch on her behalf."

"Consider it done," he said.

"Thank you." I gave him an impulsive hug. "I appreciate it more than I can say. But for now, I need to go beg a change of clothes from Cadence." I paused in the door of his room and looked back. "Stay safe, Renley."

"And you, Airlie," he replied, his eyes serious as he watched me turn and go.

CHAPTER 8
CADENCE

As soon as Airlie disappeared and we were alone, Zeke swept me back into his arms and lowered his lips to mine. I sank into his embrace, the pent-up emotions of the last few days melting away.

When he pulled back, I sighed, going up on my tiptoes to try to reach for him again. He groaned and pressed his lips over mine a second time. But this time the kiss was hard and short, a reminder of everything still facing us instead of an escape.

When we drew apart, I glanced guiltily up at the windows of the two tall buildings, all of which suddenly looked like watchful and disapproving eyes.

"Are we allowed to kiss in the Tribe Nicabar courtyard?" I asked.

Zeke laughed. "I don't know that anyone's ever made a rule on the matter." He tightened his hold around my waist, his eyes gleaming down into mine. "But I dare them to try scolding me about it."

I pushed back, and he reluctantly let go. "I'm trying to make a good impression here, remember!"

But as soon as we fully separated, I shook my head and

rushed back into his arms. He grinned and pulled me close again.

"I know it's only actually been a few days," I said. "But somehow it feels a lot longer."

He frowned. "Well, a lot has happened. And a lot more is about to happen."

I grimaced at the reminder. "Do I really need to get dressed up and attend some formal assembly immediately? Will your whole tribe be going?"

"Not everyone. The assembly hall couldn't hold the current population of the entire city. But as one of the nominating tribes, we'll have a significant presence."

"Ugh. That means I really do need to go and dress." I suddenly remembered what had happened to half our luggage. "And Airlie is probably looking for me right now to borrow something to wear."

Zeke winced. "She lost her bag?"

I nodded. "I can loan her some of my outfits, though. Thankfully I wasn't sure what sort of situations we'd be encountering, so I packed most of my limited wardrobe."

"Hurry back." Zeke dropped a swift, soft kiss on my lips before stepping completely away.

Reluctantly I waved goodbye and dashed inside. Liara appeared from nowhere, the sardonic look on her face suggesting she'd witnessed at least some of my reunion with Zeke in the courtyard. I fought to keep the flush off my face as she took me up the stairs.

"Don't you need to get changed as well?" I asked her. "Or aren't you coming to this assembly?"

"Actually, I'm going with the expedition to the border," she said.

Both of my eyebrows shot toward my hairline. "Annora can only send one, and she's sending *you*?"

"There's no need for all the surprise." Liara flicked her hair over her shoulder. "I was raised alongside Zeke, you know. My mother is one of Annora's staunchest supporters, and I'm well versed in the ways of the various tribes. I may have only just finished my apprenticeship, but I'm one of the tribe's most powerful elements mages." She said it in a matter-of-fact way that made it impossible to disbelieve.

"Oh." I did vaguely remember she had an elements affinity from our conversations on the tour, but I hadn't seen her use her ability, and we'd never discussed her strength.

Sudden resolve filled me. "In that case, can you keep an eye on Airlie?"

Liara's eyebrow rose. "I thought she was the strongest of us all."

I shrugged. "Maybe. But she also has a tendency not to think about her own well-being when she feels a responsibility toward anyone else."

Liara regarded me steadily. "I'm not anticipating any need for valiant self-sacrifice."

"In my experience, such occasions tend to leap out when you're not expecting it," I said wryly.

There was a moment's silence.

"Certainly I'll keep watch over her," Liara said in a dignified tone. "That's what I'm there to do."

I wondered if the words hid resentment. If she really was one of the tribe's most powerful mages, did she begrudge Airlie and Evermund's presence, which relegated her to a babysitter rather than her tribe's primary contribution to the mission?

Or was going at all what she resented? Was Annora sending someone so young because the important action was happening in the city, the more senior mages needed at her side for the upcoming vote?

Whatever Liara's private opinion, I sensed sincerity in her words. Whether for all our sakes, her tribe's, or merely her own, Liara would do her best to bring Airlie back safely.

"Cadence! There you are!" Airlie popped out from one of the rooms, just as Liara was indicating the next door along was mine.

As I had expected, my sister wanted to raid my bag, so we shut ourselves in my room. There was little time to talk, however, beyond the discussion around who would take which of the outfits.

In the end, Airlie took three of the most practical and hard wearing, leaving me one along with several more formal garments. I had both an elegant pale blue tunic and a full-length ballgown gifted to me by Queen Celestine the day before we left, and I chose the tunic for the ceremony.

I had time to complete only the most elementary wash before pulling it on, but when I examined myself in the mirror, I decided that—thanks to the tunic—I would disgrace neither Tartora nor Tribe Nicabar. Which had no doubt been the intention of the queen when making the gift.

Given my delay in getting upstairs, I was one of the last to arrive back down in the courtyard. It was the first time I had seen Gia since learning the news of our coming separation, but I barely had time to embrace her and wish her well before we were both being hurried out into the street.

For a second, I paused to watch Liara lead Airlie, Gia, and the others back toward the stone bridge. But I couldn't pause for long. A nomad I didn't recognize gestured for me to join the group already moving in the opposite direction, heading toward the palace that rose in the center of the city, the sheer mountain face at its back.

Annora and Zeke strode side-by-side at the front of the clump of people, Zeke now dressed in robes almost as impressive as his mother's. Nomads surrounded them on both sides, so I made no attempt to join him. This was Tribe Nicabar's moment, and I was a mere guest here.

Instead, I fell into step beside Nikolas. He had a closed look on his face that I couldn't read.

"Was Gia all right about going to the border?" I asked. "I didn't have a chance to talk to her."

"Gia?" He gave a laugh that didn't sound at all amused. "Are you joking? Given the option between a formal meeting where everyone stands around and says things everyone else already knows and an adventure into the unknown? Do you have to ask?"

"Fair point." I frowned up at him. "Would you have liked to go too?" Something had certainly put him in a bad mood.

"Of course not," he said stiffly. "I, at least, understand the importance of ceremonial occasions."

Too late I remembered Nikolas's sensitivity about his affinity. Once again, his sister had been favored over him just because she had been born with an elements seed. I immediately grasped on to his words, trying to refocus the conversation.

"I didn't get as far as asking anyone what this assembly is about. It's not actually the vote, right? That's not for days yet."

"This is the nomination ceremony," he said. "All the tribes will be in attendance, and any tribe wishing to nominate their head for the crown will have the chance to do so."

"Oh, I see." That made sense of Zeke's comment about Tribe Nicabar being a nominating tribe.

But it also explained why Gia would consider it boring. I didn't mention that to Nikolas, however. And for myself, I was curious to see representatives of the tribes gathered together, as well as to have the chance to witness one of their formal ceremonies. The tribes might all know, but I had no idea who meant to nominate beyond Nicabar and Alia, so it wasn't old news to me.

"I'm sure Gia and the others will be back soon," I said instead.

Nikolas nodded stiffly, and after a pause, spoke again. "They're going to fight wild power. They should have been permitted to take more people with them."

I instantly felt guilty for assuming his bad mood was entirely due to his own jealousy. If he was worried for his sister, I could understand that.

"They'll look after each other," I said, injecting more confidence into my words than I felt.

Nikolas just looked at me contemptuously and fell silent. I sighed internally and turned my attention back to the city around us.

Everywhere I looked, I saw gray stone and lush green plants. It was a beautiful effect, somehow evoking both enduring solidity and constant, living growth. It was all too easy to imagine making this place home—it took an effort to remember that being raised to a roving lifestyle might make a life here stifling.

More people joined us on the street, all moving toward the palace. In physical appearance, they were as varied as possible, but their style of clothing tied them together. The robes, which included a wide range of colors, all bore similar intricate embroidery which I knew would communicate more than just their tribe to a knowledgeable viewer.

The air of excitement was subdued, as befitted an occasion of some solemnity, but it buzzed below the surface. Smiles lifted many faces, and as new groups merged onto the road, those already there called pleased greetings to friends from other tribes.

No one called to Annora, however. Instead she received respectful nods or calculating looks. She responded to both with the same calm dignity, and I wished I knew what was going on in her head. Did she really have the utter confidence in victory that she portrayed externally? Or did she worry constantly that years of work was about to come to nothing?

Unless there was some unlikely and tragic accident, this was her one and only chance for the throne.

When we reached the palace, I discovered it was instantly distinguished from the palace in Tarona by having no wall. Instead, the palace seemed an extension of the city itself—perhaps, in normal times, when most of the residents belonged to the ruling clan, it was.

The crowd completely ignored the great steps that led up to the beautifully carved wooden doors. Swerving left, we all moved along the front of the building toward enormous doors that opened into the north wing.

The doors had been propped open, allowing free passage inside what turned out to be an enormous, circular hall. The ground—which appeared to be the natural stone of the mountain but polished smooth rather than rough like in the tunnels—dropped away in wide tiers. Each level had elegant wooden balustrades stretching around it with gaps for normal sized stairs that had been carved into the stone to allow easy access to lower tiers. Collected behind the balustrades were groups of people clumped together in scattered positions around the room.

As those entering from the city reached the top tier, they split away, no one slowing or hesitating as they beelined for different levels and positions. Clearly each tribe had an assigned position within the hall, and everyone already knew their places.

Nikolas and I kept close to the Tribe Nicabar representatives, although my eyes darted rapidly from side to side, taking in as much of my surroundings as possible. The crowd entering with us seemed to represent the bulk of the remaining tribes, places around the circle filling up fast.

Some clusters had fewer than ten people, while others, like the crowd from Tribe Nicabar, must number at least a hundred. If the size of the group indicated their intention to nominate, it looked as if at least ten tribes intended to do so. My mind spun at the thought. Somehow I had been imagining a direct contest between Tribe Nicabar and Tribe Alia. But it looked as if it was going to be far more complex than that.

Captain Huxley appeared, gesturing Nikolas and me to a position at the rear of Tribe Nicabar's massed group. His remaining six guards had formed a loose circle with Augusta and Renley at the center, and he thrust both of us in to join them.

"Shouldn't you be up the front somewhere?" I asked Augusta and Nikolas. The prince was tall enough to see over most of the heads, but Augusta—who was one of the shortest women I knew—had even less chance than me.

Before either of them could reply, a Nicabar tribeswoman appeared from within the clump of people, pushing toward us. It took me a moment to place her as Liara's mother. She seemed to be looking for us, suggesting I was right in assuming the important visitors would be given a place closer to the front.

She stopped next to Captain Huxley, but her eyes were fixed on me.

"Annora requires your presence."

"Should we take up a position closer—" I began to say, a little confused, but she cut me off.

"She wishes you at her side, Cadence."

"Me? Just me?" I looked toward the others, but she seized my arm and towed me forward.

"Zeke is waiting for you."

I frowned back at the captain who seemed torn as to whether he should be intervening. I caught a single glance of Augusta's eyes—narrowed to near slits—and then they were all cut off by the crowd of Nicabar tribe members.

As soon as I was deposited beside Zeke, I grabbed him in alarm. "What's going on?" I hissed. "I shouldn't be singled out like this! Augusta's already been wondering what's going on. Now she'll be—"

But Zeke didn't have a chance to do more than look at me with concern in his eyes when a loud bell chimed. Instantly all conversation ceased, and everyone turned toward the middle of the room.

A middle-aged man in a midnight blue robe devoid of all embroidery descended the steps, walking through the unsettling silence to stand in the empty floor at the center of the circle. I recognized the significance of his robe from a book I had read in the Guild library. He was in deep mourning, suggesting he was a member of Tribe Patrin. Given his age, I suspected he was one of the sons of King Fenix—likely the one who had been elected to clan leadership in his father's place.

"Welcome, tribes of the kingdom," he called in a deep, carrying voice. "Tribe Patrin is honored to host you again for the last time under the reign of King Fenix. We stand together to choose a new monarch."

A sudden great sound swelled in the room, as the crowd echoed in chorus, "We stand together."

"And once the voting is complete, we will stand together behind a new monarch."

"We will stand together," the crowd chorused.

The man waited until complete silence had fallen again before continuing. "Any tribe who wishes to stand for the crown must speak now." He took a step back, as if ceding the floor, and looked up expectantly at the crowd.

For a moment there was only the rustle of clothes as everyone turned and twisted, trying to gaze in every direction at once. Then an older man from the direct opposite side of the room pressed forward against his balustrade and spoke in a voice nearly as loud as the Patrin host.

"Alia stands for the crown."

So that was Tribe Alia. I regarded them carefully, trying to keep my dislike from my face. They had as many members present as Nicabar, if not more, and those I could see had a haughty bearing.

A brief murmur had broken out at his declaration, but it quickly faded. After another drawn out moment, a woman from the highest tier also pressed herself forward and declared loudly, "Esterla stands for the crown."

The clump of people behind her were substantial, but noticeably smaller than our own representation, and the murmurs in response to her declaration were louder and longer.

After another pause, a man stepped forward and cleared his throat. "Darshan stands for the crown."

As with Tribe Esterla, the size of this group of people had made their nomination less obvious, and some in the crowd seemed surprised at his declaration. His face remained impassive, however.

The crowd had hardly quieted when another man spoke. "Talman stands for the crown."

This candidate I had at least guessed, based on the size of the group behind him which was similar to that of Tribes Nicabar and Alia. They were located on the second tier and halfway between us and Alia. And as with Alia's declaration, they received only a slight ripple of interest.

Silence fell again, but now most heads swiveled in our direction. I could feel a bead of sweat forming under my hair and wished I could slide back into the crowd behind me. Many speculating eyes were on not just Annora, but Zeke and me, as they waited for her declaration. Still it didn't come.

Eventually the silence stretched on for so long that the man from Tribe Patrin stepped forward again. Two steps from the middle of the room, however, his progress was interrupted by Annora, as she took a half step to press herself against the balustrade. The whole room, already poised for her movement, focused back on her before she opened her mouth.

"Nicabar stands for the crown."

It was a well-orchestrated move. Alia might have begun proceedings, but there was no question who had dominated the moment.

A soft sigh, almost like a release, swept the room. Clearly no more nominations were expected. The man from Tribe Patrin barely hesitated before resuming his walk toward the middle of the room. But he had only just reached it, when Annora once more raised her voice.

"By gracious permission of Tribe Patrin, Tribe Nicabar has welcomed the first ever visitors to observe our august proceedings. Please allow me to introduce my guest," she turned to me, and I froze, horror washing over me, "Cadence of Calista, last of the power mages."

CHAPTER 9

CADENCE

Not a murmur but a roar burst forth, the sound swelling to a shocked crescendo. I managed with some effort to keep my mouth closed and some semblance of calm on my face, but it was only Zeke's arm around my shoulders that kept me from fleeing the combined weight of hundreds of eyes.

Only Tribe Nicabar and Tribe Patrin refrained from joining the hubbub, their restraint revealing who already knew the truth of my affinity. I was in too much shock to know how long the noise took to die down or what formalities the host recited to finish the meeting.

One moment I was standing there, trying to keep my legs from shaking, and the next I was being hustled down the street. Now it wasn't just the Tartoran guards forming a defensive ring around me, but the entire complement of Nicabar tribe members. They formed a ring of bodies that prevented anyone else from getting near enough to speak to me—something a number of the other tribes seemed intent on doing.

We had made it halfway down the street when I remembered the presence of the remaining Tartoran delegation members. I hadn't seen any sight of them since being pulled up to the front to stand conspicuously at Annora's side, but they must be with us somewhere, and they certainly would have heard her announcement.

Which meant it was only a matter of time before all of Tartora knew the truth about me as well. It didn't matter where I went now, my secret had been revealed.

When we stepped through the gates of Tribe Nicabar's headquarters, a momentary surge of relief rushed through me, strengthening my shaky legs. I'd never felt more in need of a haven.

But a moment later, the trembling returned. This time it was anger, not shock, that fueled it. The people closest to me had kept my secret because they knew it would be dangerous for me if it got out. Even Evermund had done so—although whether for my own sake or Airlie's I wasn't entirely sure. But Annora hadn't hesitated to throw me to the wolves for her own political gain—and my friends along with me, depending on how King Marius responded to the discovery of our joint deception.

Annora looked just as regal as she had done inside the assembly hall, but she clearly knew the chaos she had caused. Without pause, she led Zeke and me directly into a large sitting room on the ground floor of the leftmost building. Liara's mother followed us, and several moments later Augusta, Captain Huxley, Nikolas, and a very reluctant looking Renley were ushered after us. I had a glimpse of the Tartoran guards taking up places in the hall outside before the door closed.

The second the latch clicked, Zeke turned on his mother.

"What have you done?" he asked in a terrifying voice of icy fury. "How could you?"

Annora met his anger with the same maddening calm. "I did what I've always done—I worked to ensure the future of this tribe and our family. I didn't discuss the matter with you ahead of time because you've made it clear your top priority has changed."

She spoke the words in a matter-of-fact manner, but I caught the barest hint of pain and hurt when she glanced at me. Guilt tried to latch on to me, but I shook it off. I wasn't the one who should be feeling guilty right now.

"Don't you care at all about how this affects me?" I asked. "Are you totally heartless?"

She gave a long-suffering sigh, evoking the uncomfortable feeling that I was a toddler having a tantrum, needing to be pacified by my elders.

"Of course I care. But I'm acting as a leader must act and considering the good of all and not just one."

"Mother!" Zeke hissed, but she held up a hand to stall him.

"Tribe Alia went as far as sabotaging the Tartoran delegation's arrival in their determination to undermine us and reject a future alliance. Do you really think they're the rulers we need given the crisis we're all facing?"

"You think you're the ruler the nomads need?" I asked.

"Yes." She looked straight back at me, not showing even a flicker of uncertainty. "And I promise you that when I'm queen, my sole focus will be on finding a way to defeat the wild power and free Calista."

"Free Calista?" I was startled enough to forget my anger for a moment. "Not just protect the nomad lands?"

"I don't believe any of us will be truly safe until the problem is eliminated entirely. And so far, events seem to be proving me correct."

"Do you really think it's possible?" I asked. "Because if you think I have the capacity to—"

"I think you are a key element, certainly," she said. "But naturally you cannot single-handedly remove the wild power."

"So you intend to keep me here and force me to help you?" My earlier outrage surged back.

Zeke stepped forward slightly, his expression threatening, and Annora looked between him and me.

"Of course not. I can't imagine any good would come of that attempt. As soon as the vote is completed, you will be free to leave—if you wish to do so."

"But until then, I'm a prisoner."

"I would prefer you to think of yourself as an honored guest. But your thoughts are, of course, your own."

"How gracious," I muttered.

I looked up into Zeke's eyes, and a wordless communication passed between us. I didn't doubt for a second that Zeke had known nothing of her plan. Once again, Annora had cut out her son when she considered it beneficial for her plans. I glanced back at her.

Despite the fury I felt on a personal level, I did believe her assurances. She had surprised me, and it felt like a betrayal, but she had never actually promised me anonymity here—that had been my own assumption. And I couldn't look into her face and believe her lying now. She truly did believe she was acting in the best interests of everyone—the monarchy as much a stepping stone to eradicating wild power as it was a goal in itself.

I sighed, my shoulders slumping. I didn't like her methods, but I couldn't afford to repudiate such a valuable ally. After the last year, I was just as dedicated to the mission of defeating the wild power as Annora herself.

"Very well, then," I said. "I'll remain here until the vote. After that...no promises."

She inclined her head. "Thank you. I hope I may yet convince you of the value of staying and working with us for a longer period of time."

Her eyes strayed to her son, and it was easy to guess she considered him her primary tool of persuasion. But from the simmering fire in his eyes, I suspected she would find him less cooperative than she anticipated.

I turned, suddenly intensely weary and wanting my room, only to find myself face to face with Augusta. The Tartoran Master of Plants had been so uncharacteristically silent that I had forgotten her presence. I started violently, my face going pale as I took in her expression.

"It seems," she said, "that we need to have a chat. Would you like to come to my room, or should I accompany you to yours?"

"There is no need for you to go anywhere," Annora said. "We will leave you the use of this sitting room." She gestured to her deputy, and the two of them crossed toward the door.

Augusta's reply made her halt before exiting, however.

"And are the rest of us to consider ourselves prisoners as well?"

Annora looked back at her. "By no means. I would never presume to hold captive senior members of another kingdom's royal family or government. You are free to leave whenever you wish to do so. Naturally I hope you choose to stay and observe the vote as you were invited to do—followed by a discussion of an ongoing alliance with the new monarch. I won't do anything to force that course of action, however."

"Except holding hostage the only living power mage," Augusta said quietly, her eyes not leaving Annora to find me.

The ghost of a smile flitted over Annora's face. "Except that."

"And, of course, half our delegation are conveniently absent —preventing an immediate departure or even a significant show of displeasure at your actions."

"That is certainly convenient for me, yes." The hint of a smile on Annora's face grew stronger. "And I hope by the time they return, any immediate feelings of shock and outrage will have tempered, and a desire for mutual assistance will once again be the primary feeling between us."

"That's why you sent them away!" I gasped. "You were

getting rid of Airlie before the meeting. You must have known she would be furious on my behalf."

Annora's eyes flicked over Augusta's shoulder to meet mine. "The task they are attempting is vitally important, and every reason I gave for their inclusion is valid. It's always best to seek a solution that solves as many problems as possible."

"Cadence isn't a solution," Zeke said. "She's a person."

"Certainly she is a person—as are we all. Personally, I strive always to be a solution. It strikes me as a far better option than being a problem."

Not waiting for an answer, she gave a shallow bow and left the room, closing the door firmly behind her.

"And that," said Augusta, almost admiringly, "is that. It's a quite unarguable point."

Her eyes moved to me, narrowing as she regarded me. A heavy silence fell over the room. Captain Huxley had taken up a position near the door, clearly interested in the proceedings but unwilling to intervene in any way. But to my surprise, Renley drew a deep breath and strode over to stand beside me, flanking me on the opposite side to Zeke.

Augusta's eyebrows rose. "Clearly you were aware of this situation, young man."

Renley met her gaze without flinching. "Yes, Master Augusta, I was. Cadence is an old family friend. And," he continued staunchly, "I also have a power affinity."

This time both her eyebrows went flying up. "Are you telling me Cadence is not, in fact, the last of the power mages? Is there a whole army of them lurking somewhere?" Her gaze sharpened. "Or perhaps a whole settlement?"

"Unfortunately, Renley's ability is weak," I said. "As far as we're aware, I'm the only one with a strong enough ability to qualify as a mage."

"And you're already activated?" she asked.

Zeke took a half step forward. "I'm her influencer."

Augusta snorted, looked around the room, and then stalked over to the closest armchair, sinking into it in a dignified way.

"Of course you are," she said when she was settled. "What a mess."

She sat in silence for a moment, clearly running over the past in her mind.

"Evermund knows, of course," she said briskly after an interval of silence. "And Airlie." Her eyes fastened on Nikolas. "And since you're not ranting and raving about being kept in the dark, I can only assume you and your sister knew as well."

Nikolas stiffened at her harsh words but didn't actually protest. Augusta looked at Huxley.

"Captain, if you tell me you were also informed, I may have to go into hysterics."

A restrained smile flitted across his face. "Then I'm pleased to be able to inform you that I was not aware of Cadence's affinity, nor did I even suspect it."

"Hmph." Augusta looked back at me. "And so you've chosen the nomads then, girl."

"No." I shook my head firmly. "I've spent many months in Tartora now, and it seemed only reasonable for me to visit the nomad lands as well. But I've made no decision about my future." I straightened. "And I wouldn't advise anyone to try to push my hand. They might not like the consequences."

"Oh, I'll be bound," she said ruefully. "Annora's certainly made it clear you've a ready haven here for as long as you might want it." She leaned forward, pinning me with her gaze. "I can't answer for how King Marius will take the news. And unlike Evermund, I won't be keeping any secrets for you."

"Of course not. I wouldn't expect as much," I said.

"Evermund's a young fool," she said softly. "It won't be just the king with questions for him after this. Drake and Colton won't take it any better. To sit on something this big...To let you blithely walk into the nomads' arms." She shook her head.

"I hope he won't be punished for wanting to protect me," I said quickly. "He's always considered me his responsibility because of being a dependent of his apprentice."

Augusta snorted. "As if he needed the excuse. You were a youngster in distress, and he could never resist assuming responsibility for anything and everything that crossed his path. That boy has always had a sense of responsibility big enough to envelop the kingdom. I'm sure he took one look at the two of you out there in the wilderness and had no intention of leaving you, regardless of how matters played out." She frowned. "But he'll have some difficulty talking his way out of this one. It is vitally important that both the crown and the Triumvirate trust the Royal Mage."

"I believe he means to resign," Zeke said quietly, entering the conversation for the first time.

Augusta looked up, the surprise in her eyes quickly replaced with resignation.

"Yes, that makes sense," she said slowly.

"Resign?" I gasped. "He can't do that! Not because of me." I stared at Zeke, appalled. "How do you know?"

He shifted, looking uncomfortable. "We discussed it on the way back from rescuing Airlie. I wanted to know what he intended to do now that he knew the truth about you."

I stared at him. "You talked about him resigning?"

Zeke shrugged. "He said that it wouldn't be reasonable to ask the Triumvirate and the king to continue to place their trust in him after having kept such a secret, but neither was he willing to betray that secret—not when he couldn't be sure how they'd react."

An indignant sound from Augusta made him look in her direction.

"Well? Was he wrong? Can you truthfully state that Tartora would have left Cadence free to make her own choices—to come here if she wanted to do so—if they'd known the truth?"

Augusta paused, a rueful look filling her eyes. "Of course I can't do so. As you must well know." She sighed. "That has always been Evermund's problem. Somehow both idealistic and realistic at the same time."

"That doesn't sound like a problem to me," I said.

"No." She sighed. "But then you're young."

A burning feeling pushed its way up my throat. "So that's it? I've single-handedly destroyed Evermund's career?"

"I don't know that I'd say single-handedly," Augusta muttered, eyeing both Zeke and Renley.

I turned on Zeke. "You should have…"

But my words trailed off. Should have what? Insisted Evermund tell King Marius the truth? I hadn't insisted on that myself—and could I truly say that I would have done so if I'd known the cost of his silence?

Zeke looked back at me with a stubborn light in his eyes. "Of course I wasn't going to tell him to do anything that might hurt you. Evermund is an extremely powerful mage with both experience and connections. This is hardly going to destroy his life. Especially not now with the increasing danger from Calista. Tartora can't discard one of its most powerful mages. They have just as much need of them as we do ours."

I bit my lip but didn't argue. How could I?

"So Colton didn't recognize your affinity." Augusta's sudden cackle nearly made me jump. "He's going to have trouble living that one down. He had you right under his nose and dismissed you without a second thought. Of course all our attention was on your equally remarkable sister. So tell me, how did such a talented family manage to hide in plain sight for so long?"

"Actually," I shifted uncomfortably, "we weren't really hiding in plain sight. I grew up in Calista."

"In Calista?" Augusta rocked backward in the chair. "Don't tell me the destruction of the fallen kingdom is another deception! I saw it with my own eyes on the journey here."

"Oh, no, no, not at all. It's just as barren as everyone says." I hesitated. "But it turns out wild power is repelled by the presence of people with a power affinity. My father had a power seed like me, so he lived across the border his whole life."

"Power mages repel wild power." She tapped a finger against the arm of her chair. "Your value only grows, young Cadence. No wonder Annora was willing to break the nomads' immutable rules to get you here. We couldn't understand the reason—even Airlie's power didn't seem enough—especially when they were willing to allow Evermund and me to accompany you."

Her hand suddenly stopped its movement, her eyes jumping back to me. "The attack on the barges? It ended awfully abruptly. That was you?"

I nodded slowly. "I'd never actively fought it off before, so it took me some time to work out what to do."

Augusta stood in one swift motion, no longer looking either weary or discouraged. "But you can fight it off? You can drive it away?"

"No," Zeke said firmly. "She can't."

Augusta looked between us.

"I can," I said, giving him a look. "In the sense that I'm capable of directing and even using it—or some of it, anyway. But I couldn't possibly handle as much as is swirling within Calista's borders, and I don't know how to destroy it at all. So I'm not much help, I'm afraid." I tried to keep the dejection out of my voice, but it leached in.

"I don't know that I would call that no help," Augusta said. "And perhaps your capacity to manage it will grow as you come into your powers. You're still just an apprentice—"

"No," Zeke said, even more firmly. "What Cadence hasn't mentioned is that connecting with wild power is incredibly painful for her. If you'd seen her do it, you wouldn't suggest she try it again. It's a futile and deadly endeavor."

"Deadly?" Captain Huxley asked, interjecting for the first time.

"Deadly," Zeke repeated. "You no doubt remember the raider who dropped dead at the Guild. Hayes couldn't understand what was wrong with her, but she had a power affinity too—and she had been messing around with wild power."

"Hayes?" Augusta frowned. "Does he know of this, then?"

"I..." I hesitated. "I haven't told him. But..." I looked nervously at Zeke. "He did examine me just before we left. And he'd healed me before, when we were attacked by the General on our way to the Guild. He might have noticed a difference. So while he doesn't officially know, I couldn't say what he suspects."

"That would be right," Augusta said with resentment. "Always the healer discretion. Hayes takes it to an unnecessary level."

"I'm not sure I agree there," Zeke said, looking unimpressed.

"Naturally not," Augusta snapped, out of patience.

Zeke looked unimpressed, but he also examined me, a crease between his brows. "There's something you're not telling me. Why did you see Hayes? Was it to get checked out like Airlie wanted?" He sucked in a breath. "Did he find something?"

I winced. "Apparently, yes. But he healed it," I added hurriedly.

Zeke still swept me into his arms, anyway, pressing me tight against his chest. Over my head, he said firmly to the room, "No more messing around with wild power. Cadence is not the answer to destroying it."

Gratified as I was by his reaction, I gently pushed him away, disentangling myself from his arms.

"Actually," I said, "I agree with your mother on that one. I'd very much like to be a solution. I just have to work out how to do that without killing myself."

CHAPTER 10

AIRLIE

T turned away from my final glimpse of the Hidden City with a pang. I hoped to be back soon, but I hadn't expected to be leaving it already.

"You weren't forcibly resting for our journey here, like the rest of us," Hayes said, stepping up beside me. "Are you tired?"

Evermund immediately looked back over his shoulder, concern in his eyes, but I shook my head.

"Being conscious only increased my tedium, not my energy output. We were in the back of a wagon the whole way. I even slept." I smiled at Hayes. "But thank you for the thought."

He rubbed the back of his neck. "I'll confess I was looking forward to the end of traveling—at least for a short while."

I grimaced. "I'm sorry you got pulled into this. Master Augusta was being overly cautious."

"Was she?" He cocked his head, eyeing the nomads ahead of us. "Perhaps. But, then again, perhaps not."

I glanced backward, although all I could see now was gray tunnel. "I hope the others are going to be all right."

"I'm sure they will be," Hayes said bracingly before he grinned sideways at me. "Your sister certainly has an enthusiastic protector."

I nodded, trying to put the city out of my mind. We didn't know what we might encounter, and it didn't seem like a good idea to be distracted.

Hours ago, I had also been ready for a break from the monotonous travel, but the thrill of exploring somewhere new was already resurfacing. I was just surprised they hadn't produced blindfolds yet. Or worse—the drug. Without Cadence, I couldn't be sure I'd be excluded this time.

But as the older man at the head of the group took us sharply left at the first tunnel opening, heading south away from the main tunnel and the city's bridge, he made no mention of needing to obscure our vision. He had introduced himself as Gideon of Tribe Calahan, but otherwise seemed uncommunicative, so I didn't question him, merely thankful to be left the use of my eyes this time.

We didn't walk far before the faint sound of distant thunder reached our ears. I glanced up uselessly at the rock ceiling above me, a frown on my face. There had been clear skies above the valley, and no hint of a storm on the wind.

But it didn't take long for the sound to grow, revealing itself to be not booming thunder, but the constant rumbling rush of water. No sooner had the thought occurred to me than I could sense the water. It had been pressing against my distracted awareness for some time.

To my delight, we moved closer and closer to an underground river that ran extremely close to the tunnel in this stretch—separated from us by only a few feet of rock. I was just wondering if the tunnel intersected the river at any point when a dark, gaping hole appeared in the wall ahead of us, and the rushing of the water grew louder.

Gideon stopped by the gap, and I leaned forward in an attempt to get a better glimpse into the darkness. My ability told me it was a river of significant size, but I itched for a closer examination.

Gia appeared at my elbow, holding my arm for balance as she leaned out even further than me. When she glanced back my way, her eyes were gleaming with the same interest I felt. But Mila—the Tartoran guard with the plants affinity who had been chosen to accompany us—whisked her back, looking horrified.

The river had carved a tunnel of its own through the rock, one that had no light source and was filled almost entirely with pounding, foaming water flowing past toward an unknown location. I could understand why the guard was having night-mares about the princess tripping and falling in.

Liara stepped up beside us, a gleeful look on her face. "Have you been wondering why we haven't put blindfolds on you this time?"

I had but chose to stay silent.

She nodded toward the opening, her smile growing. "It's because we're taking that route."

"Yes!" Gia exclaimed, at the same moment as Hayes yelped, "What?" from behind us.

"We don't get to go down the mountain with only elements mages often," Liara said, "but when we do, this is our route. It's the best. Only an elements mage can make it down, and I don't think even you could come back up using this route, Airlie. Thus no blindfold."

I grinned back at her, gripped by excitement, but behind me, Hayes took a further step back.

"I am not an elements mage," he said firmly. "And I have a strong objection to dark, enclosed spaces without air."

"Don't be silly." I leaned forward, once again trying to see into the darkness. "Of course there's air. We're only just heading into autumn. The river won't be at its peak capacity, so it won't be entirely filling the tunnel. There has to be some air in there along with the water."

"Strangely that doesn't fill me with relief," he said dryly

before glancing at Gia. "What about you? I thought you had a dislike of dark, enclosed spaces yourself, Your Highness. You could back me up."

She laughed. "This is completely different. It's not enclosed —it's full of water!"

"Elements mages," he muttered sourly, while I ignored them both, considering the problem posed by Hayes and Mila.

I frowned as I thought through the logistics. "I could get you down, Hayes, but I'm not sure about two of you." I glanced across at Evermund. "What do you think? Could you get Mila down?"

"Get her down?" asked an incredulous voice behind me. "Are you serious?"

A young man who looked to be a similar age to Evermund stepped forward. He examined my face while I gazed back at him in bewilderment.

"You are serious," he said after a moment, shaking his head. "You're ready to step straight off that platform and take someone else with you. We'd heard stories, of course, but I wasn't sure..."

He stuck out a hand. "I'm Paxton, from Tribe Callen."

I shook it, quickly performing introductions for both myself and the four Tartorans. Paxton blinked twice at Gia's title but didn't comment aloud.

"I don't understand," I said when I'd finished. "I thought Liara said..."

"We're going down there," Gideon confirmed, pushing into the center of the group. "But we're not just jumping in."

He nodded behind him to where the rest of the nomads were divesting themselves of bulky packs. I had wondered about them, given we had all been instructed to pack light for fast travel, but it turned out they weren't bags at all.

Moving with quick, efficient movements, the nomads unfolded a collection of coracles. The small boats were longer and narrower than the circular ones I was familiar with—just large enough for a person to lie flat, as long as they weren't too tall. The interwoven wood that formed the shell was impossibly flexible, allowing it to fold into the shape of a pack but now springing open to form a boat with enough rigidity to hold its cargo.

Mila gave a soft sigh, her round eyes fixed on the closest one. When the nomad who had unfolded it turned to assist one of the others, she snuck out a hand to stroke the wood almost reverently.

"I'm assuming a plants mage must have been involved in crafting that?" I asked.

She nodded. "A master mage at that—probably more than one. It's beautiful."

I smiled. "I thought plants mages preferred living plants."

"I love to be surrounded by living greenery," she said, stepping back from the boat. "But many plants mages are employed as carpenters and weavers and the like. Our affinity is useful at the crafting stage as well. In fact, I inherited my affinity from my parents who are shipwrights."

"That definitely makes you the expert, then. To be honest, I've been so busy trying to learn about my own affinity, I haven't had much time to study the others."

"That's why I'm here," she said cheerfully, surprisingly undaunted by being the lone guard accompanying two senior Tartorans on a potentially dangerous mission. "I was nearly accepted for a Guild apprenticeship with a plants proficient, but someone turned up with a slightly stronger seed and won the place instead. I would be a shipwright right now if one of the guard captains hadn't offered me an apprenticeship."

"So you're glad to be here and not at home?" I asked.

She grinned at me. "I've been to the Hidden City and seen wonders like this." She gestured at the coracles. "It's better even than being a mage."

I smiled back, her enthusiasm contagious, but a moment later I counted the boats and frowned. There were two fewer boats than there were people.

"There aren't enough," I said.

Evermund looked at Gideon. "We're not leaving Hayes and Mila behind. We were given permission for them to accompany us."

Gideon shrugged. "Every tribe was instructed to send elements mages. I have no objection to Tribe Nicabar choosing differently, but only a strong elements mage can safely steer a coracle down that. I'm not saying they can't come, just that they don't have the necessary ability to take their own boat down. If you want them with us, you get them down the river. If you can't, they need only follow this tunnel back to its end and turn right to find the city. They can't possibly get lost."

He turned away to speak to one of the other nomads who had started stowing a pack in the foot of each of the boats.

"They'll have to double with one of us," I said to the other elements mages. "It'll actually be easier than trying to control two boats at once."

"It'll be a tight squeeze," Liara said doubtfully, eyeing the closest coracle. "And if they move unexpectedly and unbalance the boat, it might be enough to make you lose control."

I glanced at Hayes and Mila—one of them looking horrified and the other excited. "I don't think they'll be throwing themselves around in there. We'll probably be wedged in so tightly neither of us can move."

"Hayes can come with me," Evermund said. "And Mila can go with you, Airlie. Gia, you're on your own."

Her brow creased. "Are you sure, Evermund? I'm smaller than you, and I'm fairly certain I could keep the coracle afloat with two of us in there."

"Fairly certain?" Hayes said incredulously. "I'll stick with Evermund, thanks."

"Fine." Gia laughed. "I can't say that I blame you in the circumstances."

"Blame me?" Hayes shook his head. "Someone should be giving me a medal for this."

Paxton checked that the pack at the bottom of his coracle was tightly wedged in and then hefted the whole thing into the water. It bobbed up and down but stayed in position, obviously held there by his ability. He grinned over his shoulder at us and slipped in, lying on his back with his feet facing downriver. He had to bend his legs slightly, too long for the boat, but he showed no sign of discomfort. Lifting his hand in some kind of salute, he released the boat to disappear into the blackness, swept away by the water.

The next nomad stepped forward to take his place, and I slipped up beside her, dropping to my knees and dipping my hand into the river while she got her coracle into place.

"Goodness!" I said after sending my awareness down the river. "It's a long way." I looked over my shoulder. "It's likely to be pitch dark within seconds, too. Are you going to panic when the light goes, Mila?"

Despite my own thrill, it was easy to imagine how terrifying the prospect of entering that black tube must be for someone without a connection to the water and air.

Mila just chuckled, though. "Guard sergeants don't take kindly to panicking. If I was prone to it, I wouldn't have made it past basic training."

I stepped back from the river as one by one the nomad mages disappeared into the dark hole, swept away by the rushing water. Liara gave us a final look and a shrug before she stepped into her coracle, leaving only Gideon behind.

"Annora told us you could handle this, no problem," he said. "I trust she's right, but I'm not risking getting my own coracle caught up in it if anything goes wrong for you." His eyes lingered on Hayes and Mila.

"That's fine," Evermund said coolly. "Go ahead. We don't mind bringing up the rear—as long as you're waiting for us at the bottom."

Gideon gave a crisp nod. "We'll be there. This is the Upper Viridian, so we'll be riding it all the way down to the border. A fair distance is above ground, though, so you should be able to see us easily enough when it's time to leave the river."

I nodded energetically, trying to conceal my rising impatience. I was ready to stop talking and step into a boat myself.

"Airlie, you and Mila go first," Evermund instructed as soon as Gideon had disappeared down the river. "Then Gia. Hayes and I will bring up the rear."

His eyes conveyed his unspoken intention. We would sandwich the princess between us, ready to intervene from either direction if she ran into trouble.

I grabbed one of the three remaining coracles and hefted my small bag over my shoulder, lugging both toward the river.

"I'll take the bag," Gia offered. "I can take all five bags, since you're carrying double."

"Thanks, that would be great." I handed over my bag with relief. Both Mila and I had obeyed the orders to pack light, but we would have no extra room in there with two of us wedged into a single person boat. And Evermund and Hayes would have even more trouble. One of them was surely going to end up half hanging out.

I pushed the coracle into the water, resisting the pull of the current with my ability, so that it floated in place beside the hole. The river was running fast, but its liveliness filled me with an answering energy that only strengthened my focus and control. The boat barely even rocked.

"You first, Mila." I gestured the guard forward, and she clambered awkwardly into the small boat without hesitation.

"There's not much room in here," she said breathlessly, attempting to squish herself against one side with little success.

"Sorry!" I winced as I squirmed over her, both of us barely fitting in the confined space.

"Oof!" she exclaimed quietly as my elbow landed in her stomach, and then again when I accidentally kicked her knee.

"Sorry! Sorry!" At last I stopped moving, wedged in at an awkward angle and protruding slightly above the sides but secure enough for our purpose.

I would have raised an arm in the salute Paxton had given except I couldn't move either arm given one had ended up under Mila and the other was crushed against the side of the coracle. Instead I called a breathless farewell and let go.

We shot forward at breathtaking speed, surprising an exhilarated whoop from both of us. Within seconds, the light behind us had entirely disappeared, and we were surrounded by utter black.

Mila gave a slight intake of breath, more felt than heard in the close confines, and then I was concentrating so hard I nearly forgot her presence entirely.

While my eyes couldn't see the path before us, my ability could feel it, the water mapping it out for me all the way to the foot of the mountain. As we barreled around turns and dipped down sudden, sharp drops, water bubbled over the sides and splashed back from the rocky roof just above our heads.

At first, I pushed the water away from both my face and Mila's, but in less than a minute I grew frustrated with the inefficiency of the approach. Instead, I pulled at the air around us, creating a bubble that repelled all water.

We swung sharply right, only for the tip of the coracle to drop down, pulling the rest of the boat after it down an almost vertical drop. My stomach fell away, and I sucked in a deep breath just before the river leveled out somewhat, sending our boat plunging beneath the water.

I pulled it back up to the surface, glad for the protection of the air bubble which had kept us dry as well as ensuring we could breathe.

We swung left next, moving in a more gradual arc, our pace slowing enough that I suddenly remembered I was supposed to be keeping an eye on Gia as well.

In a panic, I sent my ability racing back up the river. When I found no sign of her, my panic grew, but just as I was about to say something to Mila, I sensed a disturbance in the water a long way behind us.

With a deep sigh, I sent my power surging through the area. I didn't have the ability to feel either Gia or her coracle, but an air bubble clearly enclosed something that was moving unnaturally along the top of the water. It had to be her, and from the feel of the water around her, she seemed to be in control.

Before I could disengage my mind, my own coracle dropped sharply. I squealed, my attention dragged abruptly back to our boat. But it didn't matter. Gia was fine.

Most of my muscles were aching by now, protesting the cramped conditions, but Mila lay perfectly still, causing me no trouble. In a normal situation, our combined weight would have dipped us dangerously low in the water, but my ability easily kept the boat afloat.

A particularly violent turn tried to throw us up the rocky side of the tunnel, endangering the thin base of the coracle. I pressed down with my ability, holding us to the main surface of the water despite the strong forces trying to whisk us upward.

I had just checked on Gia again, when I felt the water ahead of us foaming and bubbling. Without even the hint of a plants ability, I couldn't sense the obstruction that must be causing it, but the water told me clearly that something was there.

"Rock! Up ahead," Mila gasped, her first words since we entered the river.

I nodded, remembered she couldn't see me, and spoke aloud.

"I see it." The words weren't strictly true, but most of my attention was on the upcoming stretch of river.

As we neared the rock, easily big enough to tear open the bottom of the coracle, I grabbed an entire section of the river and pushed both it and us up the side of the tunnel, as the river had tried to do to us before.

It was still dark, but now that we were close, I could sense the rock with the same awareness that told you someone was standing behind you, or you were about to stub your toe in a darkened room. Instinctively, I sucked in my stomach and held my breath as the tip of the rock passed just beyond the end of my nose.

As soon as it was gone, Mila let out a breath of relief, and I guided the boat back down to the main surface of the river. Neither of us had much of a chance to catch our breath, however, before another drop opened in front of us and we were falling again.

It was an exhilarating ride through the darkness. The rest of the world had ceased to exist—it was just Mila and me and our coracle, caught in an endless dance with the rushing, foaming water.

At one point, a faint light appeared, and for a brief second, I thought we were nearing the end of the tunnel. But I could still feel the river snaking ahead of us, confined to a small tube of air in the midst of the empty blankness that was how I perceived the stone stretching in all directions around us.

To Mila, it must be the opposite, the mountain alive to her plants affinity, while the water itself was a blind spot.

We both tried to turn our heads toward the light as we passed it, but only I was high enough up to get any sort of view. Another opening flashed past, like the one we had used to access the river.

"Beautiful," Mila breathed, despite being below the edge of the boat, and I realized the eerie glow on the distant walls of the tunnel must come from some sort of plant that she could sense.

Within another breath it was gone, however, and we were surrounded in darkness again. The rest of the journey passed all too quickly, and when light began to grow again, it progressed too rapidly toward brightness to be anything but the end of the mountain.

We shot out of the surrounding stone abruptly, the sky opening above us and the river settling out into a broader, flatter bed. Mila gave a strange groan, half of relief, half disappointment, and I found myself sighing in sympathy.

"Sorry in advance," I said, before pushing myself up and out of my cramped position in one big movement.

Mila gave a strangled yell as I leveraged myself off her at multiple points, rolling straight over the side and into the river. She yelled again when I disappeared over the edge, sitting up so fast that the boat rocked even more violently than at my exit.

When she peered over the side and saw me hanging on and grinning up at her, my body pulled along by the boat, she gave an enormous sigh and then scowled at me.

"A little warning, please."

"I did warn you!" I protested. "I even apologized."

She shook her head, clearly unimpressed, but busied herself crossing her legs and scooting down as far as she could go until she was sitting upright in the front half of the coracle. When she'd finished, she leaned forward and held out a hand to help me back in, but I ignored it. Using the water around me, I pushed myself above the level of the river, stepping easily over the edge into the coracle to take my seat in the back half.

It was still squished, but now that we could safely sit above the level of the boat, it fit two a great deal more comfortably. I gave the shoreline on either side a cursory glance, but there was no sign of the nomads yet. Craning my neck to stare backward, instead, I looked toward the spot where the river emerged from the mountain.

I felt Gia's presence before I saw her, her coracle shooting out into the sunlight before bobbing wildly as she scrambled into a sitting position. We couldn't get a proper look at her from our distance, but her enthusiastic wave in our direction suggested she must be unharmed.

Mila, who had also been watching behind us, let out a soft sigh, her expression turning wry as she watched Gia's boisterous attempts at long distance communication.

"It's a good thing you two are elements mages, or just changing positions would probably have overturned these boats."

I grinned. "Probably. But overturning isn't a problem you tend to have with an elements mage at the helm. I'm sure the captains who commission your parents' boats all have an elements affinity."

She nodded, her gaze leaving the princess to focus on the river ahead of us.

"Any sign of them?" I asked, examining the low hills on either side of us.

"No, I can't see—wait." She leaned forward, squinting. "There might be something up there."

I followed the direction of her pointing finger.

"It might just be the trees," I said doubtfully. "The northern forest extends all the way between the two rivers. There are even pockets of it to the east of the Viridian. And it comes further north on this side than it does back by the Celadon."

Mila leaned back, disappointed. "I think you might be right. It's just a clump of trees."

"Wait, no. You were right," I said after another moment had passed, and the distant sight came into better focus. "I'm sure there's movement. I think they've gone ashore just at the start of the trees."

I drew the boat toward the shore, ready to pull us all the way out of the river when we reached the distant group. But as we got closer, all thought of the nomads was driven from my mind by the scene that confronted us.

My mouth dropped open as the gentle, rolling hills, covered in tough grass, transformed. Deep gouges broke the surface of the ground, leaving dark patches of brown dirt against the green. Trees had fallen, snapped in half or withered unnaturally in place, while others bent at odd angles, somehow clinging to life in impossible positions.

A bird cried, its harsh call grating on our ears and drawing our eyes to where it beat its wings, struggling to leave the branches of a dead tree.

Mila swallowed audibly. "There's something wrong with that bird." Her voice shook.

I just nodded wordlessly as the creature finally managed to take flight, only to go plummeting back down out of sight in the canopy, listing to one side due to one enormous, out of balance wing.

Alarmed cries broke through our horror, and I finally saw the waving arms of the people beside the river. Startled, I wrenched the boat around too quickly, and water sloshed over the side, nearly swamping us.

"Sorry," I muttered, using my power to fling the water back out and send us gliding more smoothly across the river and straight up the bank onto the sandy ground.

Mila stepped out, but her knees were shaking slightly. I followed her, trying to lock my own trembling legs.

"I thought we were going to stop on the nomad side of the border," I said, proud that my voice didn't echo the tremble in my legs.

"We did," Gideon said grimly. "This is nomad land."

CHAPTER II
AIRLIE

I gulped, looking around again. "But it can't be," I said, feeling particularly stupid. "This is what it looks like in Calista, but it shouldn't look like this on your side. There are still some protections on the border. Aren't there?"

"We certainly thought there were." Liara didn't even try to hide the fear in her voice.

"We were coming here to try to strengthen those protections," Gideon said. "Tribe Calahan had a theory that maybe we could use the river. The wild power seems to focus around the two rivers, so we thought if it was coming up them, maybe it could be stopped at the river, like we stop boats." He grimaced. "That's why we sent elements mages."

Gia arrived, her boat shooting out of the river so quickly that Mila and I had to dodge to escape being knocked over. The princess tumbled out of it, her head whipping in all directions to gape at our surroundings.

"It looks like we're too late," an older woman said. "The wild power is already here."

"We're on the nomad side of the border," I told Gia, who was looking confused.

She swallowed, glancing around again, as if seeing it all with fresh eyes.

"Wild power has been here," she said slowly after a moment. "But is it still here?"

"What do you mean?" Gideon jumped on her words.

Rather than answer, she twisted back to the river, waving for the final boat to join us. Evermund and Hayes—who was looking slightly ill—shot across the water impossibly fast to pull up alongside the bank where we stood.

Hayes stumbled out, looking as if he never wanted to leave solid ground again. Evermund followed, leaping out in one fluid movement. A gentle wave lapped behind him, nudging his coracle just high enough up the bank to be safe from being dragged back into the river.

I hid my grin behind my hand as I saw how many of the nomads were regarding Evermund with interest and respect, but the amusement fell away when I saw the bright gleam in Liara's eyes as they lingered on him.

Gia, however, remained focused.

"Evermund!" she cried. "What do you think?"

"About what?" he asked, admirably concealing his impatience.

"We're on the nomad side of the border," she filled him in breathlessly. "Obviously the wild power has been here—but is it still here?"

Evermund's brow creased, his eyes flashing with concern as he regarded his surroundings.

"Where exactly is the border?" he asked.

"It's beyond the trees." Gideon pointed downriver. "We wouldn't have stopped here if it hadn't been for..." He waved an arm at the devastation around us.

Evermund ran his hand through his hair.

"Well?" Gia asked. "What do you think? This was obviously caused by wild power, but it's not like the attack on the barges."

"No, it's more like the aftermath," Evermund said slowly.

"Exactly!" She pounced on his words. "I don't know if we can say for sure if wild power is still here."

"Perhaps not." Gideon's voice sounded heavy and defeated. "But it's obviously been here. Which means the border is in much worse state than we thought. We hoped to get ahead of the problem, but it's clearly far outstripped us already."

"I'd still like to know what we're dealing with." Paxton looked at me. "You're the most powerful of us. Can you feel if it's in the river still? We've already checked, and the damage is definitely centered on the river. It lessens the further away you go."

I hesitated, wishing desperately that Cadence was with us. She could have answered his question and a lot more besides, although it would have been difficult to explain how she knew so much. So maybe it was for the best she hadn't come, after all.

"I can try," I said at last.

It was true I had felt something strange in the waters of Lake Aterra, a faint sensation that something about the water wasn't as it should be. But according to Cadie, the lake was teeming with wild power—so much so that she had to keep herself constantly shielded or she'd feel too ill to function. If I'd only felt the faintest trace of it in the water there, would I feel anything here?

I slid off the edge of the bank, finding purchase on a spot where only my legs were immersed. I didn't need contact with the water ordinarily, but I needed every advantage I could get now.

Closing my eyes, I immersed my ability in the river, feeling the cool strength flowing around and past me. Some of the tension eased out of my shoulders and stomach. There was nothing like the water to remind you that seasons—good and bad—come and go, and life keeps flowing on.

But not all the knots inside me eased. And gradually, the

more I concentrated, the more the old tension returned. I thought—but couldn't be certain—that something was wrong in the river here.

Something brushed against my legs, making me flinch and shudder. Normally the movement of the water gave me warning about an approaching aquatic animal, but right now I was too focused on something else to be paying attention.

The contact gave me an idea, though. Looking back at the group, I waved.

"Hayes! Come over here for a moment."

He came quickly, although he didn't step down to join me, eyeing the river in distaste instead.

"I think there might be something here," I said. "But it's hard to tell. Water is water. But I'm wondering about the fish and anything else that lives in here. Could you tell if they're being actively affected by wild power?"

His expression brightened, his professional interest over-riding his uneasiness about the river.

"Probably. But it's hard for me to tell. Unlike you, I need direct contact to use my power on them."

"But you can detect deception without contact," I pointed out. "So you have some ability to sense living creatures even without it."

"That's true," he said slowly. "I've never really done much work with animals. Those with a healing affinity tend to specialize with either humans or animals from the beginning. But I can try."

Reluctantly he stepped down to join me.

A minute passed and then another. I was bursting with curiosity, but I made myself wait patiently. Something else brushed against my leg, and then a second in quick succession. When I felt a third touch, I spoke.

"Are you attracting the fish?"

He grinned at me. "Those with a healing affinity often

attract animals—although I've never experienced it with fish myself."

"Can you get a better sense of their health when they brush against you?"

His smile disappeared. "Let's climb out. I can tell everyone at once."

We both scrambled up the bank, me slipping slightly until Evermund appeared and offered a hand to haul me the rest of the way up.

"Are you all right?" he asked quietly before dropping my hand.

I smiled, but it didn't feel entirely real. "I think so? If you mean from the trip down, that was the best thing I've done in a long time. But this..." I let my words trail off, my mouth twisting.

For a moment I could see the same pressure in his eyes, and then it was gone, replaced with the usual confidence he projected to the world.

"We'll find a way," he said quietly before strolling over to join the main clump of mages.

"I was able to make contact with a number of the fish," Hayes said. "I only got glimpses of a connection because they brushed past so fast, but I can definitely say that some seem totally normal while others..." He grimaced. "Let's just say, they're not normal."

"And I *think* I can feel something in the water," I added. "But it's hard to tell. I'm inclined to agree with the princess, though. I think wild power swept through here but has now died back down to what are probably normal levels." I looked around, my nose wrinkling. "Leaving its twisted mark behind."

A notable easing of tension swept over the group, shoulders relaxing and quiet murmurs of conversation starting up. My stomach rumbled, and I was wondering who had brought the food, when Evermund spoke, an urgency in his voice that seemed at odds with the rest of the group.

"The question we really need to be asking ourselves is what caused this attack?"

Instant tension seized me, and I kicked myself for not immediately thinking the same thing.

"He's right," I said. "The attack Evermund and Princess Morgiana experienced on the barges wasn't chance. The raiders sent the wild power against them, like a weapon."

Paxton surveyed the damage on either side of the river. "Why would they want to send an attack here? The tribes have been avoiding the Calistan border for a long time now. They can't have been targeting anyone because there wouldn't have been anyone here."

"Which suggests this might not have been a targeted attack," Evermund said. "But that doesn't mean it wasn't an attack at all." He looked around at the gathered nomads. "Those who live in the Tartoran border regions don't have the option of avoiding the border, and we've been the object of the General's attention for some time now, so we have more experience with the raiders."

I looked away. I hadn't known it until recently, but Cadence and I had been the reason for the General's focus on the Tartoran border regions. How many people had been hurt because of our presence there?

"You have a theory, then?" Gideon asked.

Evermund nodded slowly. "I'm sorry to say I do. I can't be sure, of course." His eyes flickered briefly sideways to me. "We've discovered that when the raiders cross the border, they pull wild power with them in an effort to inflict general damage and incite fear."

I froze, my eyes latching on to his face. That made sense. Far too much sense.

"You're saying the raiders are here?" Liara cried. "On our lands?"

Evermund hesitated. "They might have left again already. We don't know when this happened. And I could be wrong. I'm merely saying I think we need to consider the possibility that there could be raiders somewhere near."

An angry mutter swept through the nomads, many of them turning to scan the hills around us or peer toward the trees.

"If they're here," Paxton said, fury in his voice, "then we'll find them and drive them out."

Evermund nodded. "I think that would be a very good idea."

Only minutes had passed, but the mood of the entire group had done another about-face. Everyone looked tense, some looking to Gideon for guidance while others looked poised to go sprinting off in search of raiders. Once again, I wished for Cadence. If she was here, this whole process would be a lot easier. My own ability to smell people on the air was little use away from familiar environments and people—everything more than a short distance away was a muddle of unfamiliar impressions.

Could Renley sense the presence of other people like Cadence could? Now that his power seed was activated, it seemed likely, although no doubt with a much smaller range.

I shook myself, letting the thought go. Renley was no more here than Cadence, which made the matter irrelevant.

"Is there any way to determine when the wild power attacked this area?" Gideon asked, looking between me and the four Tartorans.

I exchanged a look with Evermund before shrugging. "Not that I'm aware of. I don't even know how we'd go about attempting to work that out."

"I don't know much about wild power," Mila said slowly, "but I might be able to help."

We all turned to stare at her, making her flush slightly, but the arm that pointed toward a nearby tree remained steady. The one she was indicating grew right on the edge of the forest, one of those that was still living but twisted into an unnatural state.

"Some of the shoots on that tree look like they must have grown after it was bent like that. I know I'm not a plants mage, but I do have a plants affinity. I might be able to work out how old they are."

"By all means," Gideon said, while Evermund smiled encouragingly.

"All right." She sounded a little embarrassed. "I might just go a bit closer."

She moved away, keeping her gaze fixed on the tree and walking steadily until she reached it. Plants mages didn't need contact the way healers did. Was she just giving herself space from the pressure of the group?

"I think I could bring a second person down," Paxton said thoughtfully, watching Mila. "If they were on the smaller side."

Gideon gave him a skeptical look, and he shrugged.

"You have to admit, it's already proven helpful having non-elements mages down here."

"It was deemed too dangerous two generations ago, and we've only gotten weaker since then," Gideon said repressively.

"Yes, but the coracle design has changed significantly since those days," Paxton pressed. "Tamara's ability might be weaker than her grandparents', but she's a genius with any kind of woodwork."

Gideon rubbed his fingers up and down his jaw, considering the matter. When his eyes moved to a particularly deep gash in the earth nearby, they darkened.

"You may well be right," he said. "Times are changing, and a fast route down the mountain may be more important than ever in the coming weeks. As long as you can find someone willing to ride passenger, I can't see anyone trying to stop you."

He glanced at one of the other nomads. "Only those who are

completely confident in their ability to bring a heavier, unbalanced coracle through should try it, though. This isn't the time to get cocky."

"Of course not," Liara said indignantly. "Do you really think any of us would risk killing one of our tribe?"

Mila rejoined us, cutting off the need for Gideon to reply.

"That growth is fresh," she announced. "No more than a day. I would guess it's been a maximum of two days since this happened."

CHAPTER 12
AIRLIE

The tension of earlier—which had ironically decreased at the sign of a brewing conflict between the nomads—returned.

"They could have reached the mountains by now, if they've had two days." Gideon turned to look at the vast peaks of stone behind us. "But they won't get far among them. Even those tribes with knowledge of the mountain trails spend little time in the high mountains."

"The General's no fool," Evermund said. "I can't see him setting off blindly into the mountains. It's possible they intended to set up camp here and wait for someone to appear, hoping to follow them."

I looked around in all directions. "In that case, they'll have taken shelter in the trees, surely?" I hesitated. "I think if I get inside the tree line, I might be able to identify if there are any people nearby." I looked at Gideon. "You're sure there wouldn't be any nomads in the area?"

"Not this close to the border. It used to be a popular route back before Calista fell, but now..."

"It wasn't just Calista," an older woman said. "We might still be coming this way if we hadn't lost the main tunnel route in this direction. But as it is now, none of the tribes travel through here."

"The raiders couldn't have found an entrance to the tunnels, could they?" Gia asked with concern. "I saw a weird light in a side tunnel part way down. If the tribes don't come this way—"

"That wasn't the raiders," Liara said. "There are several types of lichen within the mountains that glow."

"Oh, that's good." Gia subsided, looking slightly abashed while Gideon focused on me.

"None of us can smell people on the air—we don't have the strength. So we'll be relying on you. If you think being in the trees will help, we'll head there now." He looked around at the other nomads. "Leave the coracles. They'll be collected later."

Mila looked at them with a wistful air before taking several determined steps over to Gia and stationing herself beside the princess.

"Are you sure about this?" Evermund asked me quietly as I led the way toward the trees, the others following in a tight clump. "If there are raiders about, we need to find them, but..."

I shrugged. "I can't guarantee it will work, but I definitely think it's worth trying."

As soon as we stepped among the trees, entering the forest near the one Mila had examined, I stopped and breathed deeply. It didn't matter that the information didn't actually come from my nose, it still helped somehow. I needed to tell my mind which smells were normal, so I could identify those that weren't.

I closed my eyes as well, trusting Evermund to keep me safe, and poured all my attention into sorting out the bits of information coming to me through my other senses.

I'd never spent time in a forest, but we'd traveled a fair way up the Celadon through a different section of this one. And though I hadn't been paying attention to it at the time, somewhere in the back of my mind, I'd been registering the different smells and impressions. Now that I was concentrating, my current surroundings registered as faintly familiar, bringing with them a memory of cramped exhaustion and connection with the river.

So what was different now? A dissonant note—more an echo than anything—caught my attention. But when I focused on it, it reminded me of the faint sensation of wrongness in the river. I couldn't be sure, but I thought it was the lingering effect of the wild power which had twisted this section of forest. I was looking for something different—something warm and alive and buzzing with power.

"There!" I said the words aloud, my eyes flying open. "I can smell a group of people. Mages, too."

"The General?" Evermund asked urgently.

I hesitated then shook my head. "They have someone with an elements affinity, but I don't think it's the General. Whoever it is isn't strong enough, and..." I hesitated again. "I think I would recognize the General. He's familiar enough, especially after our fight when I escaped. I'm not smelling anyone from that—Wait!" I looked at Evermund, concern in my eyes. "Lawson is here. I'm sure it's him."

"Who's Lawson?" Liara asked, sounding worried.

"He's a raider plants mage," I replied. "A very strong one. The General likes to send him on difficult missions."

"It's definitely the raiders, then." Gideon made a couple of hand signals, and the nomads drew in around him in a circle, the Tartorans following several beats behind.

"How many are there?" Gideon asked me.

"Only eight." I did a quick count around our group, reassuring myself about our superior size.

The nomad group had already numbered twelve before the six of us sent by Annora had joined them. At eighteen we far outnumbered the raiders.

"Eight close enough for you to sense," Evermund murmured.

When Gideon started issuing orders to the other nomads, including that we were to seek to capture not kill, Evermund pulled me urgently back a step, whispering in my ear.

"Do any of them have a power affinity?"

I glanced around the group, but only Liara was watching us with a gleam of interest. "Yes, two," I whispered back.

Annora knew about Cadence, but I had no idea how much the nomads knew about the Calistan settlement. They might not know others with a power affinity still lived, and I wasn't going to be the one to tell them, even if a few of those with a power affinity had sided with the General.

"They may still have wild power with them," Evermund said more loudly, addressing his comment to the whole group. "We can't be sure exactly how it works. So don't let our superior numbers make you careless."

I was nodding guiltily when I suddenly froze, slowly turning my head toward the southeast.

"They're moving," I said shortly. "Coming this way."

"Then there's no time for anything but to hope we take them by surprise," Gideon said. "How many of you are confident climbing a tree?"

I expected everyone to nod—after all, heights were a great deal less intimidating when you could control the air. But only about a third of the nomads present stepped forward. Mila gazed at the nearest tree with a longing expression but stayed firmly where she was.

Gia, however, threw her a look.

"Surely you can climb a tree, Mila? You've a plants affinity."

"Of course, Your Highness," she said, a little stiffly.

"In that case..." Gia stepped forward, Mila quickly shadowing her with a grin.

"I can climb a tree if that's where you want me," I told

Gideon, but he immediately shook his head. "I want you front and center. You're not only our most powerful mage, but we know the General has a personal interest in you and has targeted you before. Hopefully seeing you here will draw them all out and bring them straight into the center of our position."

I nodded agreement before giving a warning. "We've probably only got a couple of minutes until they arrive."

"Into the trees!" Gideon immediately barked, and mages scattered in all directions.

Evermund, however, stepped up beside me.

I threw him a sideways glance. "There's no way you're unable to climb a tree."

"I'm not going anywhere," he said firmly, and despite my nerves, a slight smile crept up my face.

I didn't have time to consider the matter further, though. A flicker of movement in the trees ahead of me caught my eye, and all other thoughts disappeared. Without conscious thought, I sparked fire in both my fists, ready to throw fireballs at the first person who attacked me.

But as the first person stepped between the trees, coming into full view, my fire sputtered and died.

"Airlie?" She stared at me, her eyes wide in her pallid, drawn face. "What are—"

Someone behind responded to her words, however, cutting her off with a frantic call for the others to come, and quick.

I tried to step forward, but vines sprang from the earth on all sides of me, wrapping around my lower legs and holding me in place. My fireballs sprang back to life, and I sent them against my own legs in a fury. The vines ignited, burning to ash along with the bottom of my gown. With a hiss, I dumped water on it, dousing the flames before they could incinerate my entire outfit.

When I looked back up, the first person hadn't moved, but

others had appeared to surge around her. I ignored them, still looking at her.

"Marissa?"

She started at her name, looking at me with a frenzied expression I couldn't understand. "What are you doing here?" she asked. "You weren't supposed to be here!"

I couldn't tell if she was horrified or excited by my presence, but I certainly couldn't account for hers. Marissa had been a close friend of Dara. She hated the General and would never serve him. If she was out here on a mission with Lawson—one of the General's most trusted lieutenants—then something was very wrong back at the settlement.

I tried to walk toward her, but Evermund gave a shout, and a wind whipped in front of me with so much force that it blew me several steps backward. It caught at a person I hadn't seen approaching from my left, sending him tumbling to the ground.

"A healer," Evermund ground out between his teeth. "He was going for you."

I paled. If a healer had managed to establish physical contact with me, I would have been unconscious or dead a moment later, depending on this group's intentions.

"How did you know?" I gasped out, staring at the man who was still lying on the ground, frozen in place, his terror-filled face staring at two menacing balls of fire that now hovered just above his head.

A look of confusion crossed Evermund's face. "I...I don't know. I could just...smell it on him?" His eyes widened as we stared at each other.

"You can smell people's affinities?" I asked. "Why did you never—"

"I didn't know." He looked down at the man. "I don't think I've ever done it before. I saw him coming for you, and suddenly I just *knew*..."

"Look out!" I screamed, thrusting out my hands instinctively and sending a rush of air with them.

The force of the wind slowed the fall of the enormous tree that was crashing directly toward Evermund. He ducked to the side, and the tree landed with a mighty thump that shook the clearing. It cut me off from Marissa who still hadn't moved. She was stuck in place, still staring at me as if she didn't know what to do.

I looked left to where two raiders were being whisked from side to side by a mini tornado. A flash of metal in the clutch of the wind was the only warning before a knife blade plunged into the arm of one of the raiders.

He screamed and fell to his knees, but the other gave an outraged cry and sent water spraying out in all directions.

A second, more startled, cry sounded, and a woman fell from a nearby tree, hitting several branches on her way to the ground. Understanding of the team's earlier reluctance dawned. It was one thing to climb a tree in normal times, but quite another to keep your balance while both creating attacks and defending against them.

The tornado died, and the uninjured raider gave a triumphant cry, leaping on the downed woman.

"Evermund!" I cried just as another set of vines sprang from the earth to ensnare me.

When he looked my way, I pointed to the woman.

"I see them!" He sprinted off, and I screamed my frustration at being once again bound in place.

The vines holding me back withered and fell off as I sucked every drop of moisture out of them.

When I looked up, I caught a glimpse of Marissa through the branches of the fallen tree. She appeared shocked, but I couldn't worry about her now. Somewhere Lawson was lurking and clearly targeting me. If I wanted to end this, I had to find him.

I darted right, toward the river, and found two of the nomads. They stood back-to-back, pelting a group of three raiders with floating balls of water which kept rising out of the lake. They worked in perfect unison, their spheres never colliding, and the constant bombardment prevented the raiders from using their superior numbers to overwhelm them.

Somewhere in the back of my mind, I was impressed. Those two had been so quiet during the conversations so far that I had marked them in my mind as likely to be among the least powerful of the group. But a quick glance told me none of the three raiders was Lawson, so I couldn't stop.

A scream that sounded frighteningly like Gia made me abandon caution and run full tilt around the roots of the fallen tree, dashing past Marissa—who had retreated to stand with her back to the horizontal trunk—and toward a tight clump of trees just beyond it.

Two swaying figures wrestled at the base of one of them. As they spun around, I realized with a lurch that one was Lawson and his opponent was Mila. Her left arm hung at an unnatural angle, and vines were sprouting out of the earth on all sides, reaching for her.

Gia lay dazed on the undergrowth, slightly to one side. A broken branch beside her looked as if it had been cleanly shorn from the tree. I dashed toward her, but before I could reach her, she shook herself and stood up, fury on her face.

An enormous force of wind howled from the depths of the forest, gathering strength as it came and making the trees in its path creak and groan. It was a gale few among our group could call into being, and its existence was a mark of Gia's strength. But she was only recently an apprentice, and I didn't know if she could control so much force.

For a moment, I froze, not sure what to do, and then I remembered the two mages at the river's edge, offsetting their weakness by working together. Reaching for Gia's wind,

I directed it with a finesse that was even easier to achieve than usual given I didn't need to feed its strength at the same time.

I wound it around the two fighters, wrenching them apart and sweeping them all the way off their feet and into the air. Mila screamed, and I winced for her broken arm as I sent soft gusts to cushion her, wrapping around her and carrying her gently to the ground out of reach of the angry gale that whipped at Lawson.

He shouted, enraged rather than pained, and something smacked me in the side of the head. For a second, everything went dark.

I staggered, dropping to my knees before my vision returned, a fierce ache blossoming from the left side of my head. A thick branch lay on the ground beside me, and a similar one lay beside a prone Gia.

Mila was already up, though, rushing to stand guard over the collapsed princess. I took two steps toward them, but Gia was stirring and sitting up. Mila, who was looking at something over my shoulder, turned her gaze to me.

"Quick!" She pointed with her good arm. "He's escaping!"

I spun around to see Lawson's back as he fled toward the river. He gave a great shout as he ran, and two raiders darted toward him from the trees. They both looked battered, and one dripped blood from his arm, but they were still on their feet. As they neared the river, the three raiders I had seen earlier managed to break away and join them.

As the last one passed the tree, he growled something inaudible, and Marissa emerged from between the branches, trailing behind them. She threw a glance over her shoulder at me as they reached the river, and for a moment I thought the water had them trapped.

But from behind a tree, the eighth raider stepped out, both hands gripping the side of a boat. As I called out a warning to the other nomads, the raiders threw themselves into the vessel and let the current catch it.

I reached out, intending to turn the water against them and bring the boat surging back, but it was picking up speed, flying unnaturally fast. Obviously one of them had an elements affinity of some strength.

I gripped the water around them anyway, moving quickly before they escaped my range, but the water sucked away from me, gathering into an enormous wave behind them. It fought my efforts, driven by yet more elements power, this time coming from the nomads.

One or more of my companions had decided to capsize the boat and drive its occupants underwater.

"No!" I screamed, my eyes fixed on Marissa who was sitting in the rear of the boat, looking back at me. I'd fished people from the water before, but never when other elements mages were actively working to keep them submerged.

I let go of the water under the boat and seized the wave instead, my power fighting against what I suspected was more than one of the nomads. I gritted my teeth and pulled with all my strength, driving the wave back upriver before flattening it. A ripple spread over the top of the water, but it wasn't enough to topple the boat which was now only a distant dot.

I reached for the boat again, but when I tried to grab for the water around it, my grip was too weak. A moment later, the boat had whisked out of reach of either my eyes or my ability.

"Why did you do that?" Paxton demanded from just behind me.

I whirled on him. "We were supposed to capture them alive, not kill them!"

Gideon stepped forward to join Paxton. "That was because we wanted the chance to question them, not let them escape."

I drew a deep breath, reminding myself they knew nothing of the raiders and the settlers.

"One of them wasn't a raider," I said in a calmer voice. "I don't know what they did to get her here, but she did nothing to attack any of us, and if she's serving the General, it's not by choice."

Gideon's brows lowered. "A hostage, do you mean? Was she Tartoran?" He glanced at Gia and Evermund who had appeared to flank me.

I hesitated. "No, she's Calistan. Many in the raider settlement don't support the General. They've been there since before he was born—he merely seized control of their settlement. But it's a new development that he's forcing them out on raids like this."

"If they're not hostages, then they're confederates of the General," Paxton said stubbornly. "You shouldn't have interfered with me."

"And you shouldn't have interfered with me!" I snapped back. "I would have pulled their boat back and delivered all eight into your hands if I hadn't had to stop to keep you from sinking them."

"Oh." Paxton looked somewhat abashed. "It didn't occur to me you might have the strength for that. I thought they were as good as gone."

"This is the problem with cross-tribe missions," Gideon muttered.

"What do you mean?" Gia asked. "Don't you usually work together?"

"Now we do." Paxton sounded bitter. "But once it wasn't necessary. Individual tribes had enough strength that when an issue arose, the crown could assign one tribe to handle it. It's much easier that way because we train with others of our tribe. We know each other's strengths and weaknesses, and it's easy to work as a team. Together we're stronger than individually." He sighed. "And we don't undermine each other."

I glanced at the two mages who had been pelting the raiders with river water, and Paxton followed my gaze.

"Yes, exactly. They're both from Tribe Talman. They didn't send any of their strongest elements mages, but combined those two can match any of us for strength." He glanced at me and Evermund. "Any of us nomads, anyway."

"It's an effective strategy," Evermund said. "And one I'd like to do further training in myself."

"Me too," I agreed. "But for now, what's the plan? They'll be well into Calista at this point, so there's no question of going after them."

"Certainly not," Gideon said decisively. "But we can't return to the City and leave the way clear for them to come straight back, either."

His gaze roved over the collected mages, stopping at a small huddle who stood to one side. Hayes was at the center, his hand on the arm of a relieved looking nomad who was warily eyeing a blood-stained hole in the side of his tunic. He looked up and said something to Hayes who smiled and moved on to Mila, who was patiently waiting her turn, her left arm cradled protectively in her right.

"You should see Hayes yourself," Gia murmured beside me, but I shook my head.

"It's a headache and some bruising, nothing more. There are worse injured, and he needs to conserve his energy."

Apparently Mila agreed with me, because as soon as her arm returned to its normal shape, she stepped away, shaking her head vigorously when Hayes pointed toward a bruise already blossoming along her neck.

"We'll need to send someone back to warn the City," Gideon said abruptly. "I don't want anyone traveling alone, so it had better be you two." He gestured at the Tribe Talman mages. "Tell them what we've found, and that we're staying to guard the border against further incursions. Some reinforcements would be appreciated."

"We'll be there as quickly as possible," one said. "But we'll have to take the long route."

"Yes, of course." Gideon looked frustrated, but I didn't think it was with them. "Just move as quickly as you can. With luck you'll run into some latecomers heading into the mountain for the vote, and you can borrow horses."

They both nodded, each scooping up a small pack from the ground before diving into the river. In only a handful of swift, sure strokes, they were on the western side and loping off into the distance.

"What now?" Evermund asked.

"Now we split up and patrol as much ground as we can," Gideon said. "We'll have to abandon our original mission to focus on the more direct threat. At the least sign of raiders—or another wild power attack—send a wind to alert the other groups." He looked around at us all. "You feel something tugging at you—pay attention! And follow it as fast as you can move." His eyes narrowed. "Don't get all heroic and get yourself killed. If the attack is more than you can handle, you'll better serve our people by running to warn everyone else than dying."

Evermund glanced from me to Gia and then opened his mouth to speak, but Gideon cut him off. "Don't worry, we won't be splitting you up. We'll go in our tribes. If you're the only representative, pair with someone else who's also alone."

He glanced around, nodding as the nomad mages began to drift into pairs or threes.

"With any luck, we've given them enough pause that they won't be back—at least not until our reinforcements have arrived. In the meantime, everyone, try to stay alive."

CHAPTER 13

CADENCE

I stared at Renley in frustration, trying to keep the worst of my emotion from my face. I knew it wasn't his fault that we weren't making more progress in training our abilities, but I couldn't help feeling increasingly irritated with every session.

"Power mages used to be revered," I said, some of my emotion bubbling out. "They were so revered that the king of Calista went to great lengths to lure all of the families with power mage bloodlines to his kingdom. But they didn't even have wild power to combat back then! They wanted them for what they could do with regular power. So why can't I do anything? What am I missing?" The words got faster and louder as I went on, culminating in a deep sigh.

"I'm sorry." Renley sounded miserable. "I really hoped I could help you, but I always assumed I'd be at home when I was finally activated. There are plenty of people with power affinities there, so getting training would have been easy. It never occurred to me to ask my parents for specifics of how they used their ability."

I groaned. "No, I'm sorry. It's not your fault, and I shouldn't be venting my frustration at you. I just wish I'd had more time with your mother."

As soon as the words were out, I wanted to bite off my tongue.

"Sorry," I said quickly. "I didn't mean..."

"It's all right," he said heavily. "Nothing of what happened was your fault."

I wished I could tell him it wasn't his fault either. But from what Airlie had told me, that wasn't true. So instead I tried to redirect the conversation.

"I haven't had a chance to read any of the books on the power affinity in the forbidden section of the Mages' Guild library, but Zeke has skimmed a few. He assures me they're full of references to power mages doing all sorts of things from healing people to controlling storms. But if there's a manual in there on *how* they did it, it wasn't one of the books he read."

"Maybe that's an advantage to having your ability exposed?" Renley asked hesitantly. "Now it's out in the open, you could ask to do a proper search."

"Yes, I suppose so. But I don't want to just wait until I get back to Tartora." I didn't add that I still didn't know if I would be going back to Tartora.

"Do they have a library here?" Renley gazed out the window into the Nicabar courtyard. "I don't know if the nomads have central resources like that, or if each tribe would store their own books and records. We could ask, at least."

"I already did," I said glumly. "The tribes keep their own libraries, and apparently the power mage families who left must have taken their records with them. From what I can gather, if they did leave anything behind it wasn't kept—or at least, Nicabar doesn't have anything, and none of the other tribes are openly acknowledging it if they do."

"Wasn't kept?" Renley sounded horrified.

His ancestors had been wrenched forcibly from their homes

and heritage and forced to flee with almost nothing. I could only imagine he had been raised to value history and records.

"The nomads prize loyalty," I said. "They must have been disgusted with those who chose to abandon their tribes and relocate to Calista."

"If that's the case, I'm surprised the Calistan king succeeded in luring them all over," Renley said.

"It wasn't just one king. It was an effort across generations. According to the nomad legends, they targeted the younger family members. For some it might have been mercenary, but I'm sure they found other ways to draw them in. Apparently many of them fell in love with Calistans who were then pressured by the Calistan royals to reject the option of joining the tribe. Instead the nomad had to leave the tribe and move to Calista."

I paused, struck suddenly by the similarities between the Calistan plan and Annora sending Zeke to Tartora in search of me. Had she been studying the histories? My stomach churned at the casual manipulation, making me want to instantly reject the idea of remaining in the Hidden City.

But the situation wasn't so simple. Zeke hadn't been part of his mother's scheming, and the Tartorans weren't innocent in their desire to use me either. Having now lived it myself, I could see how the Calistan strategy had been successful.

"But there's always someone," Renley objected. "At least one or two who won't bend and can't be bought."

I shrugged, trying to refocus my mind on ancient history. "According to the nomads, suspicious accidents eventually took out the few who resisted. But only those who are long dead really know the truth of it."

Renley was silent for a moment. "It's uncomfortable, isn't it?" he said at last. "Knowing Calista behaved in that dreadful way. It was easier when I was growing up and thought of us as the victims."

I sighed. "It's always easier to think of ourselves as the victims. But life is rarely so black and white. At least where kingdoms and politics are concerned."

Renley gave me a knowing look, as if he knew exactly what I was thinking. It wasn't only old history that disturbed me but current behavior. How was I supposed to decide who to ally myself with?

With reluctance, I forced my attention back to the issue at hand.

"I suppose we should try again," I said, but I couldn't force any enthusiasm into my voice.

"Where's Zeke, by the way?" Renley asked. "I expected him to be here helping us make no progress whatsoever."

His depressed tone showed he was irritated with the situation rather than Zeke personally.

"I don't know," I admitted. "I was expecting to see him here."

"Did I hear my name?" Zeke appeared in the doorway, a grin on his face.

His presence instantly lightened the mood, and I smiled back reflexively, struck by how long it had been since I'd seen his usual grin. It was a relief to see him looking more like his normal self despite the stress of the vote and the disharmony I had brought to his relationship with his family and tribe.

"You didn't miss anything," I said, carefully keeping the depths of my negativity from my tone.

"I was thinking," he said with a familiar twinkle. "This is your first time in the Hidden City. We should go exploring."

"Exploring?" I stared at him.

He gave me a challenging look. "Aren't you getting sick of staying in here, not making any progress on your training?"

"What would make you think that?" Renley asked dryly. "When it's so much fun."

I snorted. "Forget fun—I thought I wasn't allowed to leave

the Tribe Nicabar buildings. Something about being mobbed on the streets." I let my tone convey my suspicions about this excuse.

"Officially, perhaps," Zeke replied. "But my mother happens to be in a meeting with several other heads of tribes. A meeting that is likely to take many hours." He gave me a significant look.

"Somehow I don't think the rest of the tribe will just look the other way while I flout her restrictions."

"Well, then I guess it's a good thing I've often visited the Hidden City with my mother, and I know Nicabar's holdings very well," he said with a wicked grin.

I brightened instantly. "You know an unobtrusive way out."

"Several." He laughed.

I glanced at Renley, who was looking between us hopefully, although he obviously didn't want to intrude by asking outright if he was included in the invitation. For a moment, I selfishly wanted to stay silent, eager to have Zeke to myself. But I overrode the instinct.

"Would you like to come, too, Renley?"

He looked toward Zeke. "Are you sure?"

A flash of disappointment in Zeke's eyes was gone within a breath, replaced with his easy smile.

"Of course. The more, the merrier. You've been stuck inside as well which is no way to treat our guests."

"Not all your guests have been buried here for days," I muttered, and Zeke chuckled.

"No," he agreed, "and I don't envy Augusta having Nik for company on her excursions. He's been in a foul mood ever since he was excluded from the mission for elements mages."

"Better Augusta than us," I agreed, unapologetically. "And since Nikolas is not only a prince but a plants mage and her apprentice, she can hardly say no to his joining her as she meets with plants mages from across the tribes."

I hurried over to his side. "But never mind Nikolas. Let's get out of here. I'm desperate for some time outside these four walls."

Zeke stuck his head out into the hallway, his exaggerated furtive movements making both Renley and me chuckle. When he gave me a grin over his shoulder, I knew he was doing it to bring a smile to my face, and my good mood grew. Despite all the complications that had so far arisen from coming here, Zeke made everything worth it.

"This way." He led us along the hallway at a brisk pace.

We followed close on his heels as we ducked down a side corridor and then onto a narrower back staircase. At its base, a door opened outside, but not into the central courtyard. A narrow alley separated us from a high wall, and Zeke led us left along it until we found a door in the wall.

The door had an elaborate lock keeping it closed, but Zeke triumphantly produced a key, and within a minute, all three of us were standing on the other side of the door as he dutifully re-locked it.

I took in a deep breath of free air. It smelled and tasted no different from the air on the other side of the wall, but it felt different all the same. I knew in my head it had only been days, but knowing I was virtually a prisoner—combined with the frustration of our training—made it seem far longer.

Taking my time, I gave a long look both up and down the street. Zeke had been the focus of my attention on the day of our arrival, but this time I took the opportunity to absorb my surroundings more fully.

The platform the city stood on might have been carved from the mountain itself, but the buildings had been crafted more traditionally. They still looked a part of their surroundings, though, having been made from the mountain's stone. And clearly ancient plants mages had been involved in the process because their smooth lines were beyond the scope of ordinary builders.

I had a vague memory of elegant, even beautiful, designs from our arrival, but most of my current view was hampered by high walls. We'd emerged into a street that seemed to be more back alley than main thoroughfare, and Nicabar must not be the only tribe with holdings backing onto it.

"Come on." Zeke strode forward, and I had to scramble to catch up. "There's nothing interesting here."

Renley kept pace more easily with his longer stride, and his presence was surprisingly reassuring. At least, I appreciated not being the only one gawking in all directions.

We both stuck to Zeke's side as he ducked through an archway into another backstreet, taking several turns without taking us onto a main road. My guess that he was leading us to the palace was soon proved incorrect as we skirted around it, instead moving closer and closer to the mountain face that towered over the city. A few minutes of brisk walking—welcome exercise after the last few days inside the Nicabar holdings—brought us onto a street that ended abruptly in a dead end created by the steep rise of the mountain.

Seeing it from afar, I'd imagined a sheer rock face, but while it was steep, it wasn't sheer, and enough dirt clung to the uneven surface to allow a few stunted plants to grow. Zeke took us all the way to the end of the road, and he didn't stop there. Using his hands as well as his feet, he scrambled up something that looked like the barest of goat paths.

Renley and I exchanged glances before Renley shrugged and gestured for me to precede him. A momentary surge of anxiety gripped me, but I took hold of the first obvious hand-hold and pulled myself upward, the next coming into view as I did so.

I kept moving, handhold to foothold, until I had to pause, unable to find the next step. I peered further upward in time to see Zeke extend a hand down to me. I grabbed his arm, and he hauled me up onto a small platform that had been invisible from below. As soon as I stepped back from the edge, he reached down to offer his help to Renley.

I turned away from the mountain face and gasped. From here, we could see the whole city stretching out below us. And beyond it, the elegant span of the bridge looked even more delicate and impossible from this distance. I couldn't clearly see either waterfall, but I could hear their thunder and even feel the faintest mist from the closer of the two.

"When I imagined the nomads' Hidden City, this isn't what I pictured," I said breathlessly.

Zeke laughed. "Were you imagining us huddled underground or something? I think the hardest part of keeping this secret through the generations is knowing how much more glorious it is than anyone imagines. But that's precisely why we haven't risked exposing it."

"Until now," I said, his words immediately sobering me.

He paused, gazing down at the buildings, his face thoughtful. "The hills, and the desert, and the fields, and the forests of Calista have done nothing to stop wild power. We have no reason to think the mountains will be enough either. Wild power isn't an enemy we can hide from which means the time for hiding has ceased." He glanced at us. "To some extent, at least. We're not planning to lay down a path of arrows through the tunnels."

I snorted. "No, I imagine not. Even Airlie and I had to wear blindfolds."

From up here, the unusual nature of the buildings was more obvious, and I regarded them thoughtfully.

"You certainly wouldn't want the raiders knowing the route here. Given the number of storehouses, the city must house many treasures."

Zeke followed my gaze, nodding. "Much of it is kept hidden away, of course, accessible only by the tribe that owns it. But each tribe has one building designated as a museum or gallery of sorts, where other tribes can view items of artistic or historical value. If mother ends up as queen, I'll be spending more time here, and I hope to get the chance to thoroughly explore them all."

He looked sideways at me, but I kept my eyes forward. Was it truly a casual comment, or was he beginning his campaign to convince me to stay?

"Could we see one now?" Renley asked eagerly.

They both looked at me, and I shrugged. "It's all right by me, if any of them are open?"

"Of course, they're always open," Zeke said. "And even more so now with so many people visiting the city. Every tribe is hoping to impress the other tribes and win allies with the quality and value of their exhibits. Here, follow me."

He backed off the ledge, calling instructions on how to get past the difficult first section. For a moment I thought I wouldn't manage it, given our significant difference in height, but my foot managed to find a purchase, and soon I was standing safely on the road again.

This time, Zeke led us along proper streets, and we soon crossed paths with other pedestrians. Some of them hurried forward with determined strides, clearly intent on some errand, but most took the time to look around, almost as interested in their surroundings as we were.

We were an obvious source of interest and curiosity, their gazes quickly moving from Zeke—who seemed to be a widely recognized figure—to me. As we passed each group, we received openly assessing looks and left behind ripples of murmurs, flowing outward.

It didn't take long for the first group to approach us.

"Tribe Orelie extends greetings to you, Zekiel of Nicabar and Cadence of Calista."

"This is Renley, also of Calista," I said, gesturing at our companion. "It's a pleasure to meet you."

I couldn't remember ever hearing anything about Tribe Orelie. They hadn't been one of the tribes to nominate for the crown, so I wasn't even sure of their size.

"Is it true you can drive back the wild power?" one of them asked, looking at me intently.

I opened my mouth to give the same answer as I had given Augusta, but Zeke spoke first.

"She can. I've seen it myself. She defeated a wild power attack the raiders sent against us while we were traveling on the Viridian."

More mutterings swept through the group of eight people who now looked both suitably shocked and impressed. Reluctantly I nodded my agreement before Zeke gave a polite farewell and ushered us on down the road.

"Why did you say that?" I protested, as soon as we were out of earshot.

He didn't quite meet my eyes. "What do you mean? You did drive back that attack."

"Zeke!" I put my hands on my hips. "You know perfectly well that was misleading."

He grimaced. "They asked a specific question, I answered. This vote is important, and it's not as if I lied to anyone."

I wanted to argue that he was just making excuses, but I didn't see the point. This was politics. And could I even complain? If the reputation of my abilities was enough to assist, then surely that was a painless way to contribute.

The next group stopped us only moments later, and another group a minute after that. Zeke responded to them all with courteous patience, turning their questions aside with a politician's skill. By the fourth group, I was in awe.

At the Guild he had charmed everyone, his natural magnetism winning him friends on all sides. But now I saw the full extent of the training he had received from Annora and the preparation for this moment.

Zeke belonged here—he belonged in the palace that would soon be vacated by Tribe Patrin. But where did that leave me? I had never considered myself shy, but I felt awkward and bumbling in the face of the intrusive questions and searching looks. Airlie would have done better in my place.

"You get used to it," Zeke said in a brief moment of peace.

I grimaced. "Do you?"

"This is good, even if it's tedious answering the same questions over and over. It's easy to see from their reactions that Mother is right."

"Right?" Renley asked.

"He means about announcing my identity." I couldn't quite keep the sour note from my voice.

Zeke glanced at me with concern in his eyes but responded to Renley. "I was actually referring to her reports of the result. She said that Cadence's presence with us has overwhelmingly turned tribe opinion toward Nicabar, and—"

"That's obvious from this?" I stared at him. "They're friendly enough, I suppose, but not exactly fawning!"

"You're the first foreigner they've ever seen in the streets of the Hidden City," Zeke said. "And a significant minority were strongly opposed to you being given entry. But we haven't had a single angry look or rude comment. I think we can consider this a very friendly reception."

"I suppose I hadn't thought of it like that," I said slowly, re-evaluating all the introductions.

"Here comes another lot," Renley said in a resigned voice. "I think it's pretty clear we're not making it to any exhibits. We've barely made it down one street. As soon as this group go, we'd better duck back into one of the alleys and head home."

Home. My mind latched on to the word. Where was that exactly? It wasn't the Tribe Nicabar holdings—at least not yet. And even if I decided to stay with the nomads, those buildings wouldn't be a long-term home. Either Annora would win the vote and move into the palace, or she would return to her usual nomadic life with the tribe.

The thought was reassuring since I was rapidly coming to loathe the sight of the buildings.

"You might be right." Zeke eyed the nomads currently walking in our direction. "And I just recognized one of that group. They're from Tribe Alia. Let's not wait."

He turned sharply and put a hand on the small of my back to usher me along with him. I went eagerly, moving just short of a run in my hurry to avoid a meeting that would probably demonstrate how warm and inviting the previous ones had been.

Renley trailed behind us, looking back over his shoulder. "They don't look happy that we're leaving."

"Too bad." Zeke sounded angry. "They left that barrier in the river. One of you could have died. They've lost all respect as far as I'm concerned—and that's quite aside from being my mother's main rivals in this vote. I'm not standing in the middle of the road chatting with them."

We stepped off the main street, and out of sight, but Renley was still trailing us, the gap widening as he continued to crane his head to peer backward.

"They really do look angry." He sounded concerned. "And they're coming this way."

"They're coming after us?" Zeke hesitated, glancing back as well, as if he wanted the chance to confront them. But after a moment, he shook his head and seized my hand. "Come on. I'm not letting them catch us—not when it's just the three of us out here."

He started to run, pulling me with him. Renley's footsteps pounded behind us as he picked up the pace as well. We ducked into another side alley as the sounds of a larger group reached the backstreet we had just left. After that, there was a dizzying sequence of turns before Zeke paused in front of a door. I didn't know how he could tell it apart from the others that dotted the street at intervals, but he didn't hesitate as he produced his key and let us in.

As soon as we were safely shut inside, he locked it behind us, pausing for a moment to stare at the solid wood. When he turned to me, I caught an unfamiliar guilty look in his eyes.

"I'm fine," I said firmly, and he managed to smile, but I knew we were both thinking the same thing.

Annora's excuse to keep me confined to the Nicabar buildings hadn't been a fabrication after all. I had refused her offer to accompany her on a visit to an allied tribe, convinced I didn't want to be paraded around. If I went out, I wanted to be free to roam. But one trip had cured me of that desire.

We walked slowly along the wall, crossing between two buildings to appear in the main courtyard. A small group of tribe members had gathered in it, their concerned, angry voices overlapping. I had time to glance apprehensively at Zeke before his mother appeared.

"There you are," she said, her voice frosty.

Zeke, despite his apparent earlier misgivings, met her eyes directly, keeping his shoulders straight and steady.

"Here we are."

Annora shook her head slightly but didn't press him for more information. Instead of relief, her restraint filled me with foreboding. If they weren't worried about our disappearance, what had everyone so perturbed? My heart began to race faster than it had during our flight through the streets.

Zeke, knowing his mother better than me, stepped forward in concern.

"What is it?" he asked quickly.

"We have just heard that word has arrived from the border." She paused.

I stepped forward as well. "Airlie? Were they successful?"

"They didn't even have a chance to try. There had already

been a wild power attack. And when they went to investigate, the raiders themselves attacked."

"What?" I gasped, frozen with horror. "Are they all...Did anyone..."

Annora looked at me, sympathy lurking in her eyes. "No one was seriously harmed, and they were able to repel the raiders. For now. They've sent word back to send reinforcements while they themselves stayed to guard the border."

"We'll send mages, of course," Zeke said urgently.

Annora's mouth twisted slightly. "Patrin have already organized and dispatched a team."

Zeke's eyebrows rose. "They didn't ask us to contribute anyone?"

I looked between the two of them. Tribe Patrin, the outgoing rulers, had always seemed highly supportive of Annora.

"I believe they were attempting to assist us by not doing so," Annora said. "They hoped to bypass an issue but have not been successful."

She turned her head to look at me, Zeke slowly following her gaze, the shadow in his eyes deepening.

"You don't mean..."

Annora nodded. "Following the news, Tribe Talman announced they are withdrawing their nomination and will no longer challenge for the crown."

I relaxed slightly. Talman had been the third large tribe to nominate, along with Alia and Nicabar. Their withdrawing sounded like a good thing, not a bad thing. And it had nothing to do with me, which was a relief.

"Have they...?" Zeke left his question hanging, but again his mother nodded, and I noticed neither of them looked relieved.

"They've declared their support for Alia, and now, together, they're calling for Cadence to be sent to the border. They want her to repel both the raiders and the wild power being dragged across the border with them."

"Out of the question," Zeke ground out. "She's one person. She can't fend off attacks like that single-handed."

I expected Annora, or one of the small crowd gathered around us, to protest that I'd done it before. But Annora merely nodded her agreement.

"Cadence certainly cannot be wasted in such a way." Her eyes seemed to communicate something to Zeke that I didn't understand. "The risk is far too great."

For a moment there was silence, my mind scrambling to absorb everything that had been said. Slowly understanding dawned.

Annora had won favor with the tribes from my presence because I was seen as protection against some distant threat. But now the threat had arrived, and she wasn't sending me against it.

Talman had already sided with Alia. When the rest of the tribes learned Annora wasn't dispatching me to deal with the raiders, how many supporters would she lose?

CHAPTER 14

AIRLIE

I yawned and rolled off the bed I had made for myself out of leaves. The growing bite in the air wasn't pleasant, but at least the newly fallen leaves made sleeping without a pallet more comfortable.

"Any sign of anyone nearby?" I asked Evermund.

He gave me a wry look. "Yes, the raiders swung past, but you looked tired, so I let you sleep through it."

I rolled my eyes. "Sorry. I can't help but ask."

Stretching, I reached for the sky, rolling each of my muscles. In the course of the last week, we had all caved and let Hayes treat our bruises and other minor injuries from the battle with the raiders. But sleeping on the ground for so many nights had created new aches.

I yawned again. Due to the size of our group, we had been assigned the section of the border immediately beside the river since it seemed by far the most likely approach of the raiders. We had set up a watch schedule to cover all hours, but Evermund and I had insisted on splitting the night watches between the two of us. As the only two who could smell someone's approach, we were far more effective in the dark than the others.

When I finished shaking myself loose, I strolled over to stand beside him, gazing out across the river. We stood in companionable silence, and I tried to stop myself from glancing sideways at him. The informal atmosphere of our unexpected camping trip made it hard to remember that the barrier of my deception still stood between us.

It was hard even to remember that he was my influencer, and I was an apprentice. Since the unexpected discovery that he could smell people on the air, I'd been helping him develop the skill until he could use it almost as effectively as me. For the past week, I had been the teacher, and he had been the student, and he was a charming and attentive pupil.

Seeing his skill grow made me excited for the day I would take on my own apprentices, although I suspected they wouldn't all be as easy to teach as Evermund.

The beauty of the sun sparkling on the water and the presence of the man at my side sent a flash of contentment through me that was immediately followed by guilt. We were only here because of a frightening attack on the nomads, and I had no business treating our guard duty like a holiday. But still I smiled at Evermund.

I was about to ask if anyone had started cooking breakfast—a meal which would no doubt consist of fish—when I stiffened. Turning upriver, toward the mountains, I stared into the distance.

Evermund reacted a breath later, staring in the same direction. After a moment, his stiff posture relaxed.

"I don't think I'd have caught that if you hadn't put me on guard with your reaction," he said ruefully.

I glanced back, noting the hint of worry in his eyes.

"That's because it's just one person," I said reassuringly. "And they're still far away. You've gotten good at recognizing groups or individual people closer in."

He sighed. "No amount of practice or study lets someone

with a weaker ability catch up to someone else's superior strength. I'm just not used to being the weaker one in that scenario."

I gave him a sympathetic smile. "You never know. You thought you couldn't do this, either, until a situation of high enough stress brought out the ability."

He frowned but didn't answer. I knew he was still unsatisfied with how a new level of strength could emerge so long past his apprentice days, but I was more interested in our new arrival.

"Paxton's coming," I called back into the trees.

Gia bounded into view, a grin lighting up her face. Unlike me, she had been bored since the second day, eager for action—or at the very least an update on the situation with the other groups.

"Does that mean reinforcements have arrived?" She followed our gaze back upriver toward the mountains.

"One person isn't my idea of reinforcements," Mila muttered as she took up her usual place at Gia's side.

"We don't know how many they'll have been able to send," Evermund said. "And the other groups are in much greater need of bolstering than us." He frowned. "Although we can't stay here forever. We need to be getting back to the Hidden City before the vote, and it must be happening in only a few days."

"Tomorrow, actually," Liara said, joining us. "I'm sorry, but there's no chance we'll make it back in time, even if Paxton is here to tell us relief is on its way. Since we have to go the long route back, it'll take awhile. And we can't leave until the reinforcements are actually here." She looked apologetic, although I couldn't tell if she was disappointed on her own behalf or just anticipating our displeasure.

"Miss the vote?" Evermund frowned. "But that's the whole reason for our visit."

"I'm sorry," Liara repeated. "But guarding the river is too important."

Thoughts of the vote made Cadence's face flash before my eyes. How was she coping in the city? I hoped the complicated politics wasn't making her life too painful.

Paxton called a greeting, waving his arm at us in an uncharacteristically enthusiastic gesture.

Liara sniggered. "He doesn't want you to mistake him for a raider and attack."

"If raiders are approaching us from the mountains, we've failed our job." Hayes watched Paxton approach with a crease in his brow. "I hope you're right, and we're going back, though. I don't like our delegation being separated for so long."

He glanced at Gia, and I wondered if he was thinking about the fact he'd been sent as healer for two royal children, not just one.

As Paxton neared, I examined his face, deciding he looked tired but reasonably cheerful.

"What news?" Liara called as soon as he got close enough. "Have the reinforcements arrived?"

He nodded. "Each of the larger tribes has sent a team comprised of one mage from each affinity." He glanced at Evermund and Gia. "The smaller tribes didn't bring their strong mages to the City—they left them to protect their people—so they weren't able to contribute. But they're talking of setting up a proper patrol along the whole length of the border, so all the tribes will be involved soon enough."

"So that means we're relieved?" Hayes asked, a sharp note in his voice which was unusual for the healer.

Paxton nodded. "I'm supposed to help Liara guide you back to the city."

Liara snorted. "I don't need help."

Paxton raised an eyebrow. "You know the rule."

"Rule?" I looked between them.

"No one enters the tunnels alone. None of you count since you don't know the path at all."

"So the tunnels go the whole way?" Gia asked, eagerly. "When we were woken in the wagons, it seemed the easiest way to explain their ease in transporting us, but I wasn't sure..."

Liara started, going a little pale and glancing at Paxton, but he seemed unbothered.

"Yes, it's tunnels all the way." When Liara hissed slightly, he glanced at her. "Don't worry. Patrin's new head knows we can't get them back drugged when it's just the two of us. Since they helped defend the border, they've all been given permission to make the journey by blindfold."

"Not on foot, I hope," Evermund drawled.

Paxton chuckled. "Thankfully not. There are horses and wagons waiting for us just inside the start of the tunnel. The reinforcements left them there for us. We'll all be able to get a ride up."

I let out a relieved breath. Our first journey in had been long enough that I didn't fancy the idea of walking that far. Not when so much of it was uphill, anyway.

"That's excellent news!" Liara exclaimed. "We might make it back for the vote after all."

"Do we have time for breakfast first?" Mila asked. "I've nearly finished roasting the fish."

"Yes, please," Paxton said quickly, and I wondered how long it had been since he'd eaten a hot meal. "We can eat first, and I'll tell you the news."

An unpleasant, cold sensation ran through me when his eyes flicked tellingly toward me at the end of his words. What news from the Hidden City could relate to me? Had something happened to Cadence?

I could barely contain my impatience as we gathered around the remains of the fire and Mila distributed the fish.

"Sorry," she said to Paxton as she handed him his portion.

"You've had the bad luck of turning up when it was my turn on cooking—I'm not the best at it."

He responded politely, his mind clearly elsewhere.

"Well?" Liara asked before he could take a bite. "What's the news?"

I could have hugged her for speaking the words in my mind.

"They've completed the nomination convocation," he said slowly, his eyes once again moving toward me.

"Yes, of course. We know that," Liara said impatiently. "It was happening just after we left. Did someone unexpected nominate?"

Paxton shook his head, then paused. "Well, yes, Darshan nominated, but that's not—"

"Darshan?" Liara sounded contemptuous. "They won't get far. That's hardly newsworthy."

"No, I know." Paxton glared at her, out of patience. "It was what happened after Nicabar nominated that has everyone talking." Now he was definitely staring straight at me. "Annora introduced your sister as her guest—and the last remaining power mage."

"What?" I shrieked, startled into losing my calm.

Mila, who was bending awkwardly as she retrieved another piece of fish, started so violently that she stumbled and nearly fell into the fire. Evermund's expression froze, giving no indication of the thoughts below the surface, but Hayes slowly raised both eyebrows, turning slowly to look at me.

"Interesting," he said.

"Interesting?" Gia leaped up, arms crossed. "That's a betrayal!" She glared at Liara as the only representative of Tribe Nicabar present.

A stubborn look came over Liara's face, but she said nothing.

I opened my mouth to agree with Gia, only to stop at sight

of Evermund. He had gone to significant lengths to protect Cadence, so if he wasn't protesting there must be a reason.

I considered what it might be. Annora's actions were a betrayal, there was no doubt about that. We had come here trusting that whatever the intentions of the nomad kingdom as a whole, Zeke and his mother would do their best to keep us safe.

Instead, Annora had betrayed us. She had compromised Cadence's freedom and even her safety. And I was stuck here at the border, with no idea how the other nomads had reacted.

Had that been her intention? Fresh fury swept over me, nearly overriding my decision not to speak. Annora had separated us and then—

I cut off my own thoughts. This news was days old. What had happened at that assembly had already happened, along with whatever immediate fallout it had prompted. Paxton wasn't reporting that Cadence had been attacked or locked away or any other dire consequence. And if we were going to keep her safe in the longer term, Zeke and Annora were still crucial. I couldn't risk alienating Tribe Nicabar—not without talking to Cadence first.

"Sit down," I said shortly to Gia, giving her an intense look that I hoped she could interpret.

The face she turned on me was indignant, but as she absorbed my expression, she went silent and slowly sat. I gave an internal sigh. Some of her initial reactions were off—worryingly so for a future monarch—but she was intelligent, I would give her that much. She only needed a hint.

"So you did already know," Paxton said, finally taking a bite of fish. "I thought surely you must, but—"

"Of course Tartora knows," Evermund said in a firm voice. "And we will take any attempt by the nomads to claim Cadence extremely poorly."

Paxton held up both hands. "I'm just a junior member of Tribe Callen. Don't look at me."

I stood, the rest of my fish forgotten. "We need to get back to the Hidden City. I'm going to gather my things."

I strode away from the fire, my mind whirling. What was happening back at the Hidden City right now? My earlier contentment with our week at the river was shattered, guilt rushing in to take its place. While I'd been idling here, enjoying myself even, Cadence had been facing the full gathering of nomad tribes.

Clearly Annora cared about nothing but her own power and couldn't be trusted to have either honor or...I stuffed items into my bag, barely seeing them. Zeke had told his mother about Cadence—had he known she was going to do this?

Did it even matter? He had told her, and she had announced it to everyone. The outcome was the same.

I secured the bag with abrupt, rough movements. Thank goodness some instinct had kept me from telling anyone—even Cadence—about the paser trees. If Annora knew there was a way to store power, she would pursue any possibility of finding the remaining seeds as relentlessly as the Calistan king had built up his own orchard of power. I'd seen the way Cadence looked at Zeke. If I told her, she would tell him, and he would tell his mother, and...

"Are you all right?" a quiet voice asked from behind me.

I stilled and then slowly rose, slinging my bag over my shoulder before turning to face Evermund.

"*I'm* fine," I said. "It's Cadence I'm worried about."

Evermund gave a rueful shake of his head. "Why does that not surprise me? You're always thinking about someone else, Airlie. But I can tell you're upset."

"Of course I'm upset!" The words burst out of me. "I thought I could trust Zeke and even Annora. And now..." I shook my head angrily. "I feel like a fool, and I hate being a fool."

"You're not a fool." The words were low and urgent. "You just judge people by your own standards, so it's natural to be disappointed when they let you down."

The steady intensity of his gaze, focused on me, calmed the swirl of emotions inside. I even managed a weak chuckle.

"I do sound a bit insufferable when you put it like that."

"That's not what I'm saying!" He took a step toward me before stopping and giving a reluctant smile. "Why is it that I can talk to kings and master mages with ease, but somehow I feel like a fumbling apprentice with you?"

"It's because I'm so advanced," I said with a straight face. "I have so much to teach you."

My mask cracked, and I giggled before he had time to reply. He shook his head, his eyes gleaming as he took another step forward.

"That must definitely be it," he said somberly.

"Not that it's an accurate picture of your behavior," I said. "I've never seen you fumble in your life." I sighed. "Not like me. I keep messing up over and over, and it wouldn't matter if it wasn't my sister who keeps—"

Evermund laid a hand on my arm, stopping my flow of words.

"Cadence will be all right. We'll make sure of it."

His calm certainty was exactly the balm I needed. I looked up at him, my eyes beseeching.

"You'll help me? You'll help Cadence? I know I don't have a right to ask it. You've already done so much for us. But none of this is Cadence's fault, and she needs…You never asked for an apprentice, let alone one responsible for a younger sister, but Cadence at least—"

"Airlie." He spoke my name in a deep, almost breathless voice, and my faltering flow of words failed me. "Of course I'll help your sister. I know how you feel about her. I kept her safe for you this long, and I'm not going to stop now."

"Of...of course." I swallowed, trying to break free of the magnetism in his gaze. "I'm your apprentice, and I know you take that responsibility seriously. It's why I feel bad asking."

"Airlie, no," he said, so quietly I almost couldn't hear the words. "I don't do it because you're my apprentice."

For a single, heady moment I read in his eyes that there was nothing he wouldn't do for me.

Everything in me wanted to accept the comfort and support he was offering. How easy it would be to close the small distance between us—to lose myself in his arms. To accept the emotion I read in his eyes.

I jerked backward, breaking our contact.

"You don't have to tell me you're just as prone to taking responsibility for everything and everyone as I am," I said, trying to keep the trembling out of my voice. "I worked that out in the first few days after you activated me."

I hoisted my bag higher on my shoulder. I would accept Evermund's help for Cadence's sake—I had to. But all this was happening because I had tricked him into activating me, and I couldn't let myself forget it.

He thought I was so admirable, so selfless, but I had selfishly forced him into upending his whole life, just for us. He wouldn't look at me like that if he knew the truth—his own integrity would be repulsed by my deception. Which meant I couldn't afford to tell him the truth while Cadence was in danger.

Evermund stiffened, something I couldn't read crossing his face. "You overestimate me," he said, in a strangely formal voice. "But you can count on my aid with your sister."

I paused, my eyes drawn back in his direction in spite of myself.

"Thank you," I said softly, and a spasm almost like pain twisted his features before swiftly disappearing.

Unable to help it, I stepped back toward him. A fresh wind

caressed me, and I had to concentrate for a moment to be sure I hadn't called it into being with my erratic emotions. But once I was paying attention, I could tell it was a natural breeze. The wind must have changed direction.

I looked back at Evermund before something on the air caught my attention, making me freeze. As I spun around toward the river, he was already stepping forward to my side. Whatever complicated messiness lay between us, it was mutually forgotten in more urgent demands.

"Did you smell that?" he asked, his words tight.

"It's them." I started running. "They're back."

As I reached the doused fire, I called loudly for the others who came streaming from all sides, their packs over their shoulders.

"Raiders?" Mila asked, the one word strained.

I nodded.

"How far from the border are they?" Liara asked. "How much time do we have?"

"No time." I moved toward the coracles, the others hurrying with me. "They're already past the border—well past."

"What?" cried several voices as I slung my pack into the closest boat and pushed it into the water, holding it in place with my power.

"Put your packs in here." I gestured at the floating coracle. "We have to move fast."

"But I don't understand," Paxton said, although he obediently dumped his pack on top of mine. "Haven't you all been keeping watch? How are they already past us?"

"They didn't come up the river," Evermund said. "They're a long way west."

"Why didn't you sense them sooner?" Liara was looking at me, an accusation in her voice. "I thought you used to monitor your Guild for intruders all the time—even when you were sleeping!"

The others pressed in close, throwing in their packs as I tamped down my impatience. "That was a much smaller, enclosed environment. I set up my own winds to flow constantly throughout the Guild and back past me. I can't do that out here, let alone across the whole border. We're lucky the wind changed, or I would have missed them altogether."

As the last pack landed in the coracle, I turned to Mila. "Get in. And you, too, Hayes." I shoved a second coracle into the water and held it steady as well, pointing at it.

I ignored the others. They were all elements mages and could get across a river on their own.

As soon as Mila and Hayes were sitting, I stepped onto the surface of the river between them. Evermund followed me.

"I'll take Hayes," he said, and I nodded, starting to run across the surface of the water.

The coracle with Mila and our packs bounced across the surface of the river along with me. I shot it out of the water on the other bank with more force than necessary, sending it skidding several feet across the grass. As soon as it came to a stop, Mila scrambled out, looking slightly ill.

"Sorry," I said, but she shook her head, looking around for Gia and beginning to gather the packs.

"We're going after them, of course?" the princess asked, appearing at my side.

I hesitated, looking toward Evermund and then across at Liara. "The raiders are northwest of us, heading toward the mountains. But I can also sense a second group." I glanced back toward the forest, although the people I could feel weren't among these trees but within the forest some distance west.

"More raiders?" Paxton asked sharply.

I hesitated, turning my face into the wind and concentrating. "I don't think—no! I can sense Gideon. Those are definitely our people."

I looked between the trees and the mountains. "But they're

170

right in the path of where the raiders most likely emerged. I can tell they're there, but not what state they're in. They may be injured and needing help."

Hayes stepped forward. "We could split up. I could go to check on the other nomads, if Liara or Paxton came with me—"

"No." Liara harshly cut him off. "We all stay together, and we go after the raiders."

"No?" I stared at her. "But they're your people! They might be—"

"She's right," Paxton said, although he clearly didn't like it. "Of course we want to help them, but Gideon would be the first to tell us we have to pursue the raiders—all of us. There are too few of us already. We can't risk letting the raiders get loose in our kingdom just because we sent some of us in the opposite direction."

"I thought they couldn't get into the mountains or find the Hidden City?" I asked.

"They can't. But this is an unusual time. Whenever there's a change of monarch, there's a lot of movement as all the tribes converge on the mountains. Tribes split up since we can't all be accommodated in the city at once, so the raiders could easily find vulnerable nomad groups if they start roaming these hills. Right now, we know where they are, and we have the chance to stop them before they slip through our fingers."

I glanced at Evermund who reluctantly nodded. "They're not wrong about the potential threat a raider band could pose. This is their kingdom. If that's what they want to do..."

"It's not a matter of want," Liara snapped.

"Want or need is irrelevant," I said. "We have to get moving if we're going to have any hope of catching them."

CHAPTER 15

CADENCE

I flopped into a chair at the enormous dining table with a sigh. Nikolas gave me a questioning look from the next seat but wasn't curious enough to vocalize a question. From the appearance of his plate, he'd been here a while and was enjoying his breakfast, but I couldn't muster the energy to do more than poke at the food I had just collected from a long side table.

Glancing around the dining table, I saw only tribe members. The rest of the Tartoran delegation had either already finished or were yet to appear. I looked back at Nikolas with another sigh.

"You clearly want me to ask what's wrong," he said, his focus still on his plate, "so consider this an official inquiry."

For a moment, I considered remaining silent, but then the words came tumbling out. Gia was the one I really wanted, but with my best friend still absent, her brother would have to do.

"It's been days since we heard about the attack, and nothing has changed. Our sisters are out there risking their lives, and we're just sitting here day after day."

"*You* might just be sitting here," he said.

I growled under my breath, wondering if not throttling him qualified me for a medal. It should.

He finally turned to give me a proper look, raising an eyebrow when he saw my face. "You're in an unusually bad mood."

I groaned again. He was right. I was stomping around ready to snap at anyone who would speak to me.

"Sorry," I muttered. "I just don't like being stuck here doing nothing. I've spent far too much of my life in that state, and I've always hated it."

He watched me quietly for a moment. "I assume you're not making progress with your ability, then?"

"It's that obvious?" I heaved yet another sigh and loaded up my spoon with porridge.

"I thought that Calistan was supposed to help you."

I glared at him. "Don't pretend you haven't learned Renley's name by now. What's your excuse for the bad mood? Aren't the nomads being nice to you?"

"Nice to me?" He looked disgusted. "I'm a prince here on a diplomatic mission. It's not about being *nice*."

I rolled my eyes. "Are they failing to show you proper respect, then?"

He hesitated, and I was already starting to shake my head when he spoke. "Actually, it's been fascinating."

I froze, staring at him.

"Abilities are the same whether you're Tartoran or nomad, of course, but some of the nomad plants mages are using their abilities in ways we don't get taught at the Guild. The nomads we're visiting aren't a problem." He gave me a wry, sideways look. "But, no, I don't appreciate Augusta treating me like an unwelcome apprentice instead of a prince."

"Are you seriously trying to tell me the Master of Plants is treating King Marius's son with disrespect in front of foreigners? Because I won't believe you."

174

He frowned. "It's not anything she says...Nothing that others would notice, I don't think. She just..."

He didn't finish, and I didn't try to help him find the right word. We both knew what it was, even if he didn't want to say it aloud. Augusta's respect was for his position and family, not for him—a situation Nikolas was desperate to change since winning the respect of the Triumvirate was his only hope of ever inheriting the crown.

"Well," I said after a minute had passed in silence. "I'm glad someone is learning something. Maybe this trip won't be a total waste."

Nikolas glanced down the table, lowering his voice. "So it's true that public opinion is turning away from Nicabar and toward Tribe Alia? Master Augusta has a strict rule that we're not to talk local nomad politics while we're visiting other tribes, so..."

"That's what Zeke says." I kept my voice equally quiet. "This raider attack couldn't have come at a worse time. Tribe Alia have played the whole thing masterfully. They've completely undermined the advantage Annora got from my presence."

"Are you glad about that?" he asked. "You didn't come here to be her pawn. Or are you disappointed Zeke might not become a prince, after all?"

I considered the question. "No, I didn't come here to be a pawn. And I was furious when she told the whole nomad kingdom about my affinity, but...Annora understands the threat from the wild power and the General. And she's dedicated to fighting it. She'll put the whole of the nomad kingdom behind that effort, and I'm not at all convinced Alia would do the same." I gave him a repressive look. "Zeke being a prince isn't even a factor. Not everyone is obsessed with being royalty, you know."

As soon as I'd said the words, I felt a flush flood my face. I didn't usually speak my thoughts so openly to Nikolas.

He stiffened but then relaxed with a visible effort.

"What do you think?" he said to someone over my shoulder, and Zeke stepped into view, sinking into the seat on my other side.

For an awkward moment, I thought Nikolas was going to repeat my words about royalty, and insist Zeke weigh in, but he merely said, "If Alia win the next monarchy, will the nomads still unite with Tartora to fix the fallen kingdom?"

"Perhaps you should ask Alia that question," Zeke replied, his face carefully devoid of emotion.

"Perhaps I will," Nikolas said. "But for now, I'm asking you. Come on, Zeke, don't pretend you don't know as much about what's going on here as you always seemed to know about the Guild."

Zeke relaxed, grinning at him. "I know more, I assure you."

Nikolas gave him an expectant look, and Zeke's expression grew serious.

"I'm sure any nomad ruler would take a threat to our borders seriously," he said slowly. "But I doubt Alia would take the long-term view that it's necessary to clean out Calista completely to ensure our ongoing safety." He hesitated, glancing sideways at me. "Not all nomads have a good opinion of Calista or Calistans."

I didn't take offense. "How could they have a good opinion of Calista? It's a wasteland populated only by dangerous raiders."

He gave me a quick grin. "That's straight talking. Perhaps I should say they don't have a good opinion of the original kingdom of Calista."

I sighed. I could hardly blame them for that, either, given everything the last king of Calista had done. He had brought conflict to the kingdoms, and his people had paid the price. Still, it seemed foolish to allow opinions about the distant past to influence current strategy.

"You know, Cadence," Nikolas said slowly, giving me a calculating look, "sometimes I hear things when we're visiting the local plants mages."

I frowned at him. "What sort of things?"

"The nomads might not have a power mage of their own, but apparently one of the tribes has a history expert who specializes in knowledge about them. He's nearly reached his hundredth year, but he's still mentally sharp. He even helps the other historians of the tribe run their exhibit. Maybe you should talk to him."

I stared at him, feeling the first bubbles of excitement that I'd felt in days. Was it possible the key to unlocking my ability really was here in the Hidden City?

"What's his tribe?" Zeke asked, his voice laden with suspicion.

"Alia," Nikolas replied in an innocent tone.

"Impossible," Zeke said shortly.

I whirled to face him. "Impossible? Surely not! It's inconvenient he's from Alia of all possible tribes, but this isn't about the election. If I can use my ability properly, maybe I can find a way to save us all. That transcends the question of who wins the throne."

"The fight against wild power might be more important to us," Zeke said, "but that doesn't mean Alia thinks that way. If they did, would they have left the river barrier in place when a historic delegation from Tartora was expected?"

"You think he'd refuse to speak to me?" I asked.

"I think you shouldn't even try. My mother has forbidden anyone in the tribe from talking to anyone in Alia before the vote. Do I need to remind you they're the ones clamoring for you to be sent out—potentially to your death? If it's true they're experts in power mages, that makes it even worse! They must know one power mage, however strong, isn't enough against the General—not when he's armed with an entire kingdom full of wild power."

I winced. His point was a good one. Alia's past and current actions toward me were hardly suggestive of a desire for us to work together. But did that really matter? If I had a chance, surely I had to take it.

"My own safety isn't as important as finding a way to clear Calista of wild power forever," I said.

"We'll have to agree to disagree on that." A dangerous note sounded in Zeke's voice.

I looked at him for a long moment and then sighed. Clearly arguing the matter wasn't going to get me anywhere.

"I'm full," I announced, although I'd hardly eaten anything. "If you're looking for me, I'll be with Renley. For all the good that will do."

I stood up and walked out without looking back.

Had that been our first fight? I knew Zeke only wanted to protect me, but it still didn't feel good.

In my mind, I was planning to join Renley in our usual training room, but my feet took me in a different direction. By the time I realized what I was doing, I was standing by the door in the back of the building, near the gate that gave onto the alley.

Startled, I froze. I shouldn't do anything rash. But the thought was already there, worming its way in. This was my ability, and if I was ever going to master it, I might need to take matters into my own hands.

It took most of the day to work out a way past the wall, given I didn't have Zeke's key this time. I would have much preferred to have him by my side, but I also wasn't going to quietly sit behind the walls just because Tribe Nicabar wanted me to. Tribe Alia might be calling on Annora to send me into a dangerous situation, but they were only playing the same political game she was. They were hardly going to murder me just because I turned up to talk to them.

In the end, I left through the front gate, not the side door, slipping out behind the daily delivery of fresh food supplies. No one else was around, so the driver had to get down from his wagon to open the gate, resume his place to drive through, and then dismount again to close it behind him. I slipped through while he was busy driving, and though he must have seen me walking hurriedly away down the street, he made no protest. He wasn't a member of Tribe Nicabar and probably didn't even know who I was, let alone that Annora had decreed I be kept safely inside.

My heart beat nervously anyway until I turned out of his sight. As soon as I was clear, I hurried to make a second turn that led me onto a street even wider than the one that held Nicabar's headquarters.

Up until then, my whole focus had been on getting away, but suddenly it occurred to me I had no idea how to navigate around the city. I didn't even have an address for the Tribe Alia headquarters.

I stopped walking, kicking myself for being an idiot. But I wasn't going to meekly slip back to the Tribe Nicabar buildings at the first sign of adversity.

Looking around, I chose an older lady with a friendly face who was strolling down the street in company with a girl a few years older than me and a boy several years younger.

Crossing over to intercept her, I stopped in front of them.

"Excuse me. Sorry to bother you, but I'm wondering if you can point me in the direction of the Tribe Alia exhibit."

The lady looked me up and down, open curiosity in her gaze, and I realized that my accent must have given me away. I flushed slightly, wondering if she recognized me as the power mage, or only that I was an outsider. Either way, her reply was perfectly courteous.

"You've not far to go. Follow this street up toward the palace, and you can hardly miss it. It's the large building off the square just north of the palace gates."

"Thank you." I gave her as friendly a smile as I could manage.

She looked like she wanted to say something else, but after a moment's hesitation, she just shook her head and gave me a short farewell, sweeping her younger companions around me and on down the street.

I didn't look after them, instead hurrying onward. No one approached me directly this time, although I wasn't sure if that was due to my reversal in popularity or if I simply wasn't recognized without Zeke's distinctive face at my side. Either way, I took advantage of the anonymity, moving as quickly as I could without drawing attention to myself by running.

The woman's directions proved even easier to follow than I had anticipated. I had obviously been too distracted by the palace to notice the square on my last journey past here, but now that I was looking for it, it was obvious.

The first thing to draw my attention was the elaborate stone fountain in the middle, but second was the large building behind the fountain, its facade ornate with gilded carvings.

I hurried across the open space, ignoring the alluring music of the fountain and the smell from a couple of food stalls that were positioned to one side. At some point my friends would notice I was gone, and Zeke, at least, would guess where I'd gone. I didn't know if Annora would risk a scene by coming after me, but I didn't want to waste the time I had.

When I reached the doors of the elaborate building, I paused to catch my breath, eyeing them warily. Now that I was here, uncertainty was creeping over me.

But I'd come too far to back out now. Pushing open the closest door, I stepped into an entry foyer.

In the moment it took my eyes to adjust, a young woman approached me, her expression detached but not unfriendly.

"Welcome to Tribe Alia," she said, reassuring me I was in the right place. "Would you like a tour?"

"Actually," I said, awkward from the realization I didn't even know my target's name, "I'm looking for someone in particular."

"Oh?" The woman's eyebrows rose.

"He's an elder," I said. "But I was told he still worked here. I'm interested in history myself, and I would greatly appreciate talking to someone with so many decades of learning."

I held my breath, wondering if there were multiple elderly men still working at the Alia exhibit.

"You must mean Otto," she said. "He's three decades older than anyone else here."

I let out a soft breath. "Yes, that would be him."

She regarded me with open curiosity. "He'll be finishing for the day soon as he likes to eat early. But I can check if he'll see you."

When she strode off across the foyer, I hesitated. Was I supposed to follow her? Deciding quickly, I rushed after her.

She threw me a slightly surprised look but didn't protest. Opening a plain wooden door in the left wall, she leaned inside.

"Otto?" she called. "Do you have time for a final tour? Someone's requested you, specifically."

A humph sounded, followed by a grunt of effort. I waited in anticipation, trying to keep my eagerness from my expression. When Otto finally came into sight, I nodded respectfully.

His remaining hair, white with age, had been carefully combed, and his clothes were both good quality and neat, despite his unnaturally lean frame. When he saw me, he paused for a moment, clearly surprised.

Had he been expecting someone older? Or did he recognize me?

When he finally continued moving again, I took a rushed step back to allow room for him to exit into the foyer.

"I'll leave you to it, then," the girl said brightly, as if pleased to have escaped doing the tour herself.

The man grunted and made no objection to her whisking the door closed, leaving us alone.

"Well, I can see why you asked for me," he said, answering my earlier question. "But I'm surprised Annora let you out of her sight."

He fixed me with a direct, challenging look.

"She might not know I'm here," I admitted. "But I'd heard about you, and I had to visit."

"Heard about me?" He sounded pleased about that, a slow smile creeping across his face before he looked around the empty foyer. "You'd better come into the exhibit, then."

CHAPTER 16

CADENCE

He shuffled across to open a much more elaborate door than the one to the guides' room. I let him usher me inside, taking a few seconds to gape at the neat rows of plinths. They held a wide variety of items both beautiful and unusual, and together formed an impressive sight.

"I don't suppose you've come here to see those," he said, making me jump and turn back to him.

"No," I acknowledged. "I just want to talk to you. I've heard you're an expert on power mages."

He gave a wheezy chuckle. "I would have thought you were the expert on those. Although I admit I've been burning with curiosity to meet you, ever since I got word of the happenings at the nomination convocation." He shook his head. "A living power mage. I never thought to meet one again."

"I'm not the real expert," I said. "And I can't access those who are. So you're my best hope."

"Can't access them?" His gaze, sharp despite his age, skewered me. "I know Tartora doesn't have any with a power affinity...so it's true there are some among the raiders, then?"

I gulped. I needed to watch my words more carefully. Was this why Annora would never have agreed to the meeting?

"You said meet one *again*," I said, hoping to distract him. "Have you met one before? How is that possible?"

"Easily." He chuckled. "I'm extremely old. When I was a small child, some of my tribe traveled to the capital of Calista to make a trade deal. Despite my young age, Calinara was so new and exciting that it made a lasting impression. As did the power mages I saw in action there. That's what began my lifelong fascination with the ability."

"You visited Calinara before it fell?" I asked, awed. I was used to thinking of what happened then as ancient history, even though the impact of it still affected us today.

"As I said." His eyes twinkled. "I'm very old."

"All I want is to free us all from the threat of the wild power," I said firmly, taking back control of the conversation. "My aim is to help everyone, but I don't have anyone to teach me how to use my ability properly, and it's holding me back. I thought maybe you would have some insights. I know you're not a power mage yourself, but are you familiar with how they used their power?"

His laugh triggered a coughing fit, and I waited impatiently for it to subside.

"I wouldn't be much of a power mage expert if I didn't even know that," he said at last, making my heart leap.

"Well?" I asked.

"Well?" he said back, faintly mocking. "It's a rather broad question. Are you saying you can't use your ability at all? How do you even know you've the strength of a mage?"

"No, I can use it," I said quickly, imagining again what Annora would think of the conversation and wincing internally. "I can drive away wild power, and I can..." I hesitated.

But I'd come here for answers, and I wouldn't get them without being open myself. "I can take ordinary power and feed it into what another mage is doing, strengthening their efforts —even extending them. But the mages of old could do mighty wonders on their own, and I can't work out how. I can't initiate anything myself. I need an existing pattern to join, or I'm useless."

I watched him breathlessly. I'd made my confession, and now I was going to find out if it would pay off.

"Mighty wonders." He sounded amused. "The power affinity was always the least common, you know. By far. I've often wondered if that fact alone was enough to create the air of mystique, or if the power mages actively cultivated it."

His expression grew sad. "We'll never know, of course. You're an unexpected link to the past, but there are many questions you can't answer."

I stared at him. "Do you mean they couldn't perform wonders?"

"I suppose that's a matter of opinion. I certainly consider their abilities wonderful."

I blew out a frustrated breath. "Yes, but could they do things other mages couldn't? Bigger things?"

"That depended not only on their own strength, but on the power available to them. It's true that with enough power, the strongest of the power mages could perform the same feat it would take ten elements mages working together to accomplish. For that alone, they were valuable."

"They could do it on their own?" I asked eagerly. "They didn't have to work with the elements mages?"

"They could work alone," he confirmed, and I stepped forward, my eyes fixed on him.

"How? How did they do it?"

He frowned. "I imagine the same way any of us use our ability. None of the surviving records or accounts include specific, detailed steps. I always supposed it was because there were none. My ability is drawn to the elements. I can sense them around me without even trying, and reaching out to interact with them is as easy and instinctive as lifting my arm to shake your hand. Is it not so for you?"

"It is…" I huffed. "And it isn't. Sensing power—in my vicinity and in other people—is as you describe. Easy. My influencer is a plants mage, so I see it as vines and roots and branches. Everywhere around me."

I glanced around, consciously taking note of the quantities of power gathered in the exhibit for the first time. Either the objects here had been used by mages once, or the exhibit itself had required a great deal of power to create.

"Gathering any leftover power is equally easy," I continued. "And it doesn't take a great deal more concentration to take the power someone else is actively using."

As soon as I said the last bit, I wished I hadn't. Evermund had once said it was one of the most concerning aspects of power mages, and from the strange look that crossed Otto's face at my words, Evermund was right.

"It's using the gathered power that's the problem," I said hurriedly. "That isn't instinctive at all. In fact, no amount of trying has allowed me to do anything with it on my own."

His brow creased, and he gazed off into the hall, although I suspected he wasn't seeing any of the exhibits.

"It's possible…" he muttered under his breath before focusing back on me. "What are you trying to do with it?"

"Anything," I said, keeping the word from becoming a wail with some effort.

"Describe to me exactly what you try." He watched me closely.

"Well, as I said, my influencer is a plants mage," I said. "So I've most often attempted things he practiced himself as a new apprentice. But I start by gathering up spare power around me, of course."

"Spare power?" he asked. "Any spare power?"

I nodded. "Whatever is in the vicinity, generally. At the Mages' Guild there was no shortage—like here." I glanced around again.

"You just gather up whatever lingering power is around you and then attempt to use it?" He sounded amused now.

"Of course," I said defensively. "It seemed better than stealing power that was being actively used."

He shook his head. "But you just gathered it up indiscriminately? And then tried to use it?" He was definitely amused. "That's your problem, then."

"It is?" I stared at him. "Why?"

"That power didn't just appear," he said. "It came from somewhere. Where did it come from?"

For a second, I considered telling him I didn't want to play at riddles, I just wanted answers. But I reminded myself he was an old man—likely working at the exhibit because he'd been forced to give up his nomadic lifestyle due to age—and he was helping me. If he wanted to lead me along with a series of questions, I would follow.

"The power came from other mages."

"Exactly! And what sort of power do other mages have?"

"What sort of power?" My brow creased as I considered what he meant. Power was power. "All power is the same. It's just weak or strong."

"Is it now?" His eyes gleamed. "Then why do we have affinities?"

"Because people have a natural affinity with different aspects of the world. That affinity determines what their power can connect with."

"Exactly!" he said as if proving the point.

"But the power comes from inside them," I said. "It's just power. Isn't it?" Now I wasn't so sure.

"If it's all just the same power," he asked smugly, "why can power mages sense the affinity of someone's ability? You did mention being able to sense power in other people, so I assume you can identify their affinity."

"Yes, I can," I said slowly.

"And what about when you draw active power that someone is in the middle of using? Can you tell if it's plants power or elements power?"

I nodded. "But in those moments it's being actively used according to its affinity. It seems natural enough to be able to tell what sort of mage it's coming from."

"I agree. And now we're back to my initial question. Where does all this leftover power you like to use come from?" He cocked his head, clearly enjoying leading me to what he thought should have already been obvious.

"The leftover power comes from..." I trailed off as my mind ran ahead of my words.

I could sense the affinity in people, and I could sense it in the power itself when they were using it. And that was the same power that was left behind—shreds of it, anyway. It made perfect sense that those bits of leftover power would have an affinity. Why had I never thought of that?

"The power I'm trying to use has an affinity," I said in wonder. "I feel like a fool for not thinking of it before. I suppose it was because I couldn't sense anything in those lingering traces of power." My forehead creased. "But why not? Shouldn't I be able to sense it?"

"I would have thought so." Otto tapped a gnarled finger against his leg. "That's where I can't help you. I can't sense power myself."

"It would make sense that it was more subtle than when it was actively being used," I muttered. "Maybe I just haven't been paying enough attention to it? It was always available so freely, and I never thought of it as anything but one homogeneous whole..."

I looked up suddenly. "But what's the significance? If left-over power has an affinity, does that affect how I can use it?"

"Of course. As you yourself said, the affinity determines what the power can connect with. You may be a power mage, but you're not exempt from that limitation."

"Are you sure?" I asked, battling unreasonable disappointment.

"Ho! Dreaming of creating food out of thin air or something, were you?" He gave me a knowing grin.

"I thought the whole point was that power mages can do things other mages can't." I tried not to sound childishly resentful.

"They can," he said. "They can manipulate power itself in ways no one else can, and they have a flexibility the other affinities lack. Not to mention the potential to perform feats of much greater strength. Don't scoff at the ability to heal people, manipulate the elements, *and* control growing things. That's a very powerful combination."

"Yes, of course," I said hurriedly, already ashamed of myself.

His hard expression softened. "You're young. As difficult as it might be to believe, I do remember being young myself."

"Is that why you're helping me?" I asked, seized by sudden curiosity. "Even though you're from Alia, and I'm allied with Nicabar."

"Well, as to that..." He seemed to lose interest in the conversation. "You really should have stayed in the hidey-hole they found for you."

"What's that supposed to mean?" I asked sharply.

"Merely that while I've often been accused of being interested solely in the past, the rest of my tribe do not share my...failing."

Fear coursed through me, rooting me in place. "You intend to warn them I'm here?"

"I don't need to," he said. "I can assure you that my young

associate will have completed that task some time ago. And by your own admission, you've not yet developed your ability to the point where you can resist a team of strong mages."

My eyes widened. "You're going to tell them what I said, then?"

"Of course." He looked surprised. "They're my tribe. But you needn't look so terrified. Alia merely feels that your unique abilities would be better put to use under our guiding hand."

A sick feeling churned in my stomach, and I glanced over his shoulder at the closed door. "You can't do that! Nicabar and Patrin would never stand for it!"

"Oh, so you did tell them you were coming here, did you?" His knowing expression made my stomach twist even harder.

I glanced again at the door, but he shook his head.

"There's no point hoping to get out that way. She'll have locked it by now."

"And you're all right with this?" I asked, fiery anger burning through me and driving out the sickening fear. "You're just going to let them abduct me?"

"I've spent my whole life learning about power mages, and now I have the chance to work with one within my own tribe," he said. "Why would I oppose them? You'll see. They'll all look to me now. At last my tribe will see the value of my work. When you have lived as many decades as me, you'll better understand why that matters to a person."

"I don't care if I live to be a hundred, I'm not going to start abducting innocent people," I snapped.

His expression didn't change, so I spun on my heel and fled between the rows of plinths. He was far too old to have any hope of catching me, and he obviously knew it because he didn't even try. But behind him, the door clanked and rattled, and I heard the muffled sound of voices.

I was out of time.

Scanning the walls as I ran, I finally found what I was

looking for. Another door. This one was much smaller than the main doors, clearly meant for use by those who ran the exhibit rather than visitors from other tribes. But I didn't hesitate as I grabbed the handle and twisted.

Somewhat to my surprise, it turned without resistance. But no sooner had the door opened a tiny crack than it slammed shut again, snatched from my grip by a strong, steady wind.

I battled against it, seizing the handle and pulling with my whole strength. It wasn't enough. The door remained closed.

Pounding feet and shouting voices approached behind me, but I didn't stop to look over my shoulder. I might not have come into my full ability yet, but that didn't mean I was power-less. Otto was wrong about me.

I snatched at the power that fueled the wind, thrusting it away from me in every direction. I had only meant to fling the power itself, vaguely expecting the wind to die away. Instead the wind followed the power, rushing through the hall and toppling displays on all sides.

Several voices called out in dismay, but again I didn't pause to look behind me. Pulling open the now unresisting door, I dashed through, slamming it closed behind me.

I sprinted a couple more steps before coming to an abrupt stop. In front of me, a large courtyard was ringed by a number of buildings and an enormous, closed gate. It looked familiar and yet also different. I had never been here before, but I had been living somewhere like this ever since I arrived in the city.

The back of the exhibit opened into the Tribe Alia head-quarters.

CHAPTER 17
CADENCE

I looked around wildly, my gaze fixing on the gate. It was closed, the bar across it far too heavy for me to lift alone.

Unless I could use my ability to do it? I hesitated, but only for a moment. Otto might have given me the key to unlocking my full ability, but I didn't have time to attempt something so finicky.

With my pursuers on my heels, I didn't have time to attempt anything at all. They'd be on me within moments.

They knew I was trying to flee, so if they came out here and didn't see me, they would head for the gate first. As soon as that thought entered my mind, I turned and ran in the opposite direction.

Across from the gate, two large, imposing buildings loomed —their many stories full of windows that watched over the square with judging eyes. A small gap separated them—not even enough to be considered a proper alley, but it was wide enough for me.

I sprinted the full length of the buildings, bouncing off one wall and then the other in my haste. When I reached the other end, I found another narrow alley and a high wall, like the one that enclosed Tribe Nicabar's residential buildings. My experience in their holdings told me there would be a door in the wall somewhere, but it was unlikely to be unlocked.

I looked down the alley uncertainly. If I went looking for the door, I could end up trapped, with nowhere to go. Shouts behind me made up my mind.

Taking several steps back down the gap between the buildings, I tried the closest door handle. It turned, so I shoved the door open and peered inside. It was hard to make out much, but I took the darkness as a good sign and whisked myself inside. Closing the door gently, I waited breathlessly as running feet shot past outside without slowing.

Turning, I looked at my surroundings properly. My eyes had adjusted enough to make out shelves lining the walls and rows of hooks, some of them with cloaks and jackets hanging from them. I seemed to have stumbled into some sort of temporary storage room, perhaps for the belongings of day guests.

If the cloaks belonged to people who might leave the building at any moment, I couldn't linger here. I crossed through the long, skinny room to the door on the opposite side. Hesitating, I pressed my ear against it.

Nothing sounded on the other side, so after a moment, I eased it open. A hallway stretched away, lined with closed doors. I eyed them warily. I needed to find a proper storeroom —the kind that was left untouched most days—or an unused guest room or something where I could hide until the search died down. If they thought I'd made it out of the compound already, they might stop looking, and I could sneak out under cover of dark. But if Alia was anything like Nicabar, they probably didn't have many unused rooms at the moment.

If only I had a way to work out what was on the other side of the closed doors. Opening them one by one seemed like an extremely hazardous strategy, to say the least. But the longer I lingered here, the more likely someone would come along.

I began creeping down the hall, walking as quietly as I

could and wincing every time I stepped on a creaking floorboard. Twice I caught the sound of voices behind a closed door and scurried faster for a moment until they faded behind me.

When I'd made it halfway across the enormous building, I came to a corner where a perpendicular corridor led back toward what must be the front door. I paused and peered gingerly around.

More rooms opened off this new corridor, although some of them had open archways instead of actual doors. One of those open rooms, not far from the juncture where I lurked, held a group of people talking in quiet voices.

I pulled my head back around, out of sight, and listened intently. There was no change to the rhythm of the conversation, so I assumed no one had seen me.

I stayed still, trying to think what to do. If I kept going across the corridor, I risked one of them seeing me. I had been able to get a glimpse of several of them, so I had to assume they would have a view of me as well. Should I go back, then?

More time passed as I lingered uncertainly. Perhaps they would soon leave, heading back toward the front of the house and the enormous staircase there. If they didn't go soon, I would have to start trying some of the doors around me. With any luck, I'd find the entrance to the cellars or something.

Footsteps on the polished stone of the main corridor floor made me stiffen. It took all my self-control not to take another peek at what was happening. From the sounds, a single person was moving in my direction.

I tensed, ready to flee. But instinct told me a determined step like that belonged to someone aware of their own importance—the kind of person likely to be heading for a sumptuously furnished sitting room rather than a back corridor.

I was right.

The footsteps stopped, and a harsh voice said something I

couldn't catch. Whatever it was, it provoked a strong reaction, though, because I could hear the responses.

"What? She's escaped?"

"How is that possible?"

The reply came again in a voice too quiet for me to catch.

"Ridiculous," a woman said. "She must be here somewhere."

"This is all your fault," a petulant sounding man with a carrying voice replied. "I'm sure if you hadn't sent Grayson over the border, this wouldn't have happened. He would never have lost her."

Over the border? What did that mean? I edged closer to the corner, my ears straining.

"Me?" The woman gave a hard laugh. "The *enthusiasm* of Grayson that you so admire is the reason he was the one to go. He was the only mage to volunteer for the job." Her voice dripped disdain. "I don't remember you volunteering to face the General."

The General? The hairs on my arms stood on end, my heart somehow managing to beat even faster.

"Naturally not!" The man sounded horrified. "My skills are hardly suited to—"

"Skills?" The woman gave an unpleasant laugh. "No, indeed."

"Must I remind you that we were all in agreement about sending Grayson?" a deep, rumbly voice asked. "Naturally the Calistan raiders are no match for Alia mages, but since the raiders insisted they would only deal with a single individual, Grayson was our best choice. No one disputed it at the time."

There was a pause, and I wondered if he was glaring the others into submission.

"Of course he was our best choice," the woman said, her voice haughty. "It's not just a matter of defending himself. Once the raiders have played their part, and it's time for the vote,

196

he'll be abandoning them fast. Grayson can be trusted to keep them off his tail when he returns to us. We can't have the raiders encroaching too far beyond the border or causing trouble once we hold the throne. That is of more importance than catching one girl."

"Is it?" the first man asked, sounding sulky now. "Must I remind you that if we don't catch her, the throne is by no means a certain thing?"

"Public opinion has already swung back in our favor," a new voice said. "And our trade deal with Tribe Talman has brought even more votes. I'm as eager to get our hands on this so-called power mage as any of you, but I'm not concerned…"

As he gained control of the conversation, successfully switching topics, his voice slowly decreased in volume until I could no longer make out individual words.

It didn't matter. The small part I had heard was shouting so loudly in my mind that I could barely hear anything else. I couldn't stay here and hide now. I had to get word out to the others as soon as possible.

I stumbled back down the corridor, moving too fast for stealth, but unable to slow myself down. I did pause at the door, at least—first listening, and then peering out through a small window in the wall next to it.

No one was visible in the gap between the buildings, so I eased the door open and slipped outside. As soon as it was closed behind me, I ran toward the back wall. The Nicabar door had required a left turn at the end of the building, so I swerved left here, running around the bend and colliding with someone on the other side.

I barely suppressed a scream as I staggered back, recovering my balance just in time to stop myself falling.

"Cadence?!" The familiar voice sounded horrified, but I was so happy to hear it that tears sprang to my eyes.

"What happened?" Zeke asked immediately. "Are you hurt?"

I shook my head. "No, but we need to get out of here. Now!"

He didn't wait for further explanation, seizing my hand and pulling me along the back alley. A shout from the other end, past both buildings, made me look over my shoulder. Someone had seen us.

"Zeke," I gasped, but it didn't matter. We'd reached the small doorway in the wall that mirrored the one we'd once used at the back of the Nicabar holdings.

This door no longer looked much like a door, however. The wood was warped, and green shoots sprang off it in all directions. It had fallen off the hinges, and there was no sign of the lock.

"Zeke!" I said again, shocked this time.

He had done the same to my bedroom door at the Guild once, but this was an external door to the holdings of Tribe Alia. Who knew what the consequences would be?

One look at his set face told me he didn't care, though.

He hurried through the opening, pulling me along behind him. As soon as we reached the increased space of the open street, we broke into a run.

Zeke led me left, and then left again, until we popped out in the large square by the palace. Evening had fallen, and the place was busier than it had been before, with several people waiting at both of the food stalls.

Zeke immediately slowed, a satisfied smile on his face.

"Even if they've followed us, they won't be able to attack here. You're safe."

"I'm sorry." My tears fell properly now. "I thought you were being stupidly cautious and your mother was just being political."

"No, I'm sorry." He pulled me over to sit on the wide lip of the fountain, putting an arm around me. "I shouldn't have dismissed you like that. You had a valid reason for being interested in visiting Tribe Alia, and I never want you to feel like your only choice is to deceive me."

He ran his free hand through his hair, the lines of his face angry, although the anger seemed to be directed inward. "If I'd organized a proper, official visit, they could never have…" His arm tightened around me, the rest of his thought unspoken.

My tears slowed, and I dashed away the ones that remained on my cheeks. Now that the overwhelming relief of getting free had faded, I could think about what had happened more objectively.

"Actually," I said slowly, "I think it turned out for the best. Talking to Otto was helpful—I hope very helpful in the long run. But what happened afterward is more immediately important. And I never would have overheard that conversation if they hadn't tried to grab me."

I angled toward him and gripped his robe with both hands, my voice gaining urgency.

"We have to get to your mother right away. I heard them talking, about someone called Grayson. Apparently he's—"

"One of their most powerful elements mages," Zeke said grimly. "He's a few years older than me, but everyone in my generation knows him. We crossed paths with Tribe Alia several times in my teen years before I left for the Guild, and he was a bully, always quick to fight. I believe they put him in charge of tribe security." He looked contemptuous.

"Well, he's not doing that right now," I said. "They've sent him to the raiders."

"What?" Zeke stared at me, a horrified look growing in his eyes.

"From what I overheard, it sounded like…" I took a deep breath. "It sounded like Tribe Alia are behind more than leaving the defenses on the river. They're behind the raider attack at the border. They led the raiders up the river."

Zeke stood, leaving me to scramble up in his wake. When he looked down at me, there was danger in his gaze.

"It makes sense," I said breathlessly. "The attack was the turning point in public opinion."

"Is that exactly what they said?" he asked in a low voice, his gaze tightly focused on my face. "That they sent Grayson to lead the raiders in an attack on the border? For political advantage?"

I hesitated, trying to remember their precise words. "Not in so many words," I said, haltingly.

A frantic feeling was pushing up my throat. Surely Zeke believed me? If he wouldn't listen, then no one would.

"Their meaning was clear, though," I said quickly. "I'm sure that's what they were talking about. They said he would have to get away from them once they'd played their part. Alia didn't want the raiders causing more trouble once they had the throne."

"Fools!" Zeke spoke so loudly that a passing couple looked at us, startled. He lowered his voice. "I believe you, of course I do. It's everyone else I'm worried about. I assume you don't have any evidence?"

I gave a quick shake of my head, and he continued. "Even if they'd said it as explicitly as that, we'd still have a problem. You're an outsider—and one allied with Alia's political rivals. They'll say you're making it up to discredit them, and we'll have no way to prove the truth of your words. How could we even explain how you ended up in a position to overhear such a conversation?"

I gaped at him. He was right, of course, and I should have seen it immediately.

"So what can we do, then?" I wanted to pace up and down, but I forced myself to stay still, not wanting to attract any more attention from the people passing through the square.

"We'll tell Mother." Zeke sounded grim. "And she'll have to issue a general warning. We don't have a choice. This is too serious to ignore. No one will believe us, and it may be the end of our chance at the throne, but we have to try.”

“Are…are you sure?” I asked hesitantly. “If she knows no one will believe her, does she really need to—”

“Yes, she does,” Zeke said harshly. “Think about it for a minute. You’ve seen the General in action for yourself, as well as some of his followers. Do you think a single nomad mage has a chance against them?”

“No.” It was hard to feel sympathy for the absent Grayson, but as soon as I considered the matter, I knew Zeke was right. “They talked as if the raiders are far inferior to the nomads, but I’m fairly certain Airlie is the only person more powerful than the General. I don’t know where they got the idea that—”

“It’s prejudice, pure and simple,” Zeke said. “I told you that some nomads have a poor opinion of Calista, but it goes further than a general dislike. They despise them and think our ancestors’ success at conquering them means Calistans are weak. It’s caused a problem for some of the refugees. In fact, it’s the reason many of them have hidden their Calistan roots and fully integrated into the various tribes they joined. Those who look down on Calistans aren’t a significant number of people, but there are enough of them to cause trouble. And those same people think the raiders aren’t a problem because they’re Calistan, and therefore they can’t have any significant strength.”

“That’s ridiculous! Surely a tribe as large and powerful as Alia can’t be full of people who think something so illogical and blatantly untrue.”

His mouth twisted. “No, Alia isn’t full of Calistan haters, but there are a couple of influential ones. And just consider for a moment—is the argument that the General isn’t powerful so blatantly untrue?”

“What do you mean?” I asked, outraged. “Of course it is! We’ve seen it for ourselves, and so did all the nomads who came to Tartora as part of your mother’s delegation.”

"Yes, we've seen it," he said. "But just think how it would have looked from afar. Tartora has successfully fended off several attacks now, and not even the Tartorans themselves know it was only because of your unique ability that they managed it. You've unknowingly fed into the idea that the General is weak."

"But what about the nomads who were there and saw for themselves what those attacks were like?"

"That was my mother's delegation and full of our allies. Alia probably believe they're exaggerating the reports of the attacks in order to make the threat seem greater and your ability more important. Besides, they must have set this in motion before the delegation returned, anyway."

"So they sent Grayson," I said slowly, "thinking he could easily control the situation. But actually he doesn't have a chance." I went numb. "Which means the raiders will have either forced him to reveal the path into the city, or they'll have tricked him somehow and followed him."

"Exactly. Tribe Nicabar can't stay silent about this. The risk to the Hidden City and the whole nomad kingdom is too great."

"So you can't stay silent." I met his eyes, my mood despairing. "But no one will believe you. Which means the city will be totally unprepared when the raiders strike."

CHAPTER 18
AIRLIE

We moved as a group at a steady, ground-eating trot. But even at a measured pace, I wasn't sure how long we could all keep it up. We hadn't been trained for this sort of long distance running, and the mountains were deceptively far away.

It didn't help that tension gripped the group, spurring us forward but also keeping us tense and on edge. No one needed to speak for me to know their thoughts were divided between the people we had just abandoned, and the potential dangers ahead. Bodies under this much pressure would eventually give out.

I stopped abruptly, and it took several strides for everyone to notice and stop as well, turning to me with questioning, impatient looks.

"We need to change course and head for the river," I said.

"That's in the wrong direction," Liara said.

"Unless they've changed course?" Paxton asked.

"No, they're still heading northwest. But they're much further north than us. We've only just pulled away from the river, so it won't take much doubling back to reach it. We're a group of elements mages. In the coracles, we can make it to the base of the mountains incredibly quickly. Once we're further north than them, we'll be able to go directly west and cut them off."

A few people exchanged quick, silent looks, but within seconds, everyone was nodding. We started jogging again and soon reached the water.

"I'll fetch the coracles." I reached for the wind and water, using them to scoop up seven of the boats and bring them shooting toward us.

Within another two minutes, we were all skimming over the surface of the river, moving upstream toward the mountains so fast that I feared the coracles might fail.

Evermund and Gia had taken charge of Hayes and Mila, telling me to keep my attention on our quarry. Gia had already proven herself more powerful than I expected, and I was happy to hand the task over and keep my focus undivided.

It didn't take much effort to keep myself moving in the right direction, and I was glad for it since my surveillance efforts became more and more worrisome. As soon as we drew close to the spot where the underground source of the Viridian came pouring out of the mountain, we pulled over to the western bank.

Jumping out of the coracles, we clustered loosely together. Already several people were looking west, ready to start moving again.

"Hold," I said, and everyone responded to my anxious tone, turning to give me worried looks in return.

"What is it?" Paxton asked. "Have you lost them?"

"Not yet." I glanced at Evermund, wondering if he'd felt the same thing. "But they're moving away from us fast—too fast. I'm certain they've picked up speed since I first sensed them. They'll be out of range of my ability soon, and I don't see how we can possibly catch them. They have too much of a head start."

"So we should just give up?" Liara sounded angry.

"I'm not saying that. I'm saying…" I looked nervously at Paxton and Liara. "I guess I'm asking…Are you completely sure the raiders couldn't find the entrance to the tunnel that leads to the Hidden City? Because it's not just that they're moving faster now. I don't know the area well, so I didn't have a clear picture of exactly where they were before. But now that we're here, at the base of the mountains…"

I drew a breath. "They're north of us, I'm sure of it. They're already in the mountains and moving what should be impossibly fast."

I looked at Evermund again, hoping he'd confirm my words —or even better, explain how I'd misinterpreted what I was sensing. He did the former.

"I've lost contact with them now, but I agree," he said. "The final sense I had was north. And my rough estimates would put them far enough west to hit the tunnel mouth—the tunnel where horses and wagons were waiting for us. It would explain their sudden increase in pace."

"Impossible," Paxton said flatly. "No one could just stumble on the tunnel entrance. It's far too well hidden."

"I'm not suggesting they stumbled on anything," Evermund said, his voice steady, but his eyes sympathetic. "They've been moving much too steadily and purposefully for that, I would say. I'm suggesting that somehow they've discovered your secret."

Both nomads opened their mouths to protest, but he kept going. "I have no idea how. All I know is that they're in your mountains right now and moving faster than would be possible if they were in the middle of scaling a mountain face. Their numbers have grown, too. I'm sure I smelled more people just before they moved out of my range."

He looked at me, and I reluctantly nodded. "My guess would be there was one or more other groups of raiders who only came into our range when they converged at the tunnel entrance."

"But if they've discovered the entrance to the tunnel," Liara said, her voice shaking, "they might know the route to the Hidden City as well."

"That is precisely my concern," Evermund said. "And we're too far behind to catch them, which means we can't stop them. But is it possible we could somehow warn the city?"

He looked inquiringly at Mila. "Zeke had a way to send messages across long distances using root systems, I believe."

She shook her head regretfully. "I'm sorry. I don't have the strength for anything like that."

"Do you have some other established mechanism?" I asked Liara and Paxton hopefully.

They both shook their heads, their faces bearing almost identical mixes of panic and fear.

"If there are, I don't know them," Liara said. "I don't know any way to get a message back to our tribes in the city."

"There's only one option." Paxton sounded desperate. "We have to get there ahead of the raiders."

"Is that possible?" I asked.

"No," Liara said sharply. "It's suicide is what it is."

Paxton ignored her. "I think we mentioned there used to be an eastern tunnel route that exited near here, at the top of the Viridian. It hasn't been used for years, but it's a much more direct route to the Hidden City."

"It's also deadly," Liara said. "Which is the reason we don't use it anymore."

"Deadly how?" I asked. "When you mentioned it previously, I assumed it must be blocked from a cave-in or something."

Paxton gave me a contemptuous look. "We do have plants mages, you know. We could have cleared a simple blockage. But no matter how many times we cleared the lichen, it kept growing back. Eventually it wasn't worth the danger—especially with no one using the old trade routes through the fallen kingdom anymore.”

“Lichen?” Gia voiced the question we were all thinking. “What’s so deadly about lichen?”

“There are several types of lichen unique to these mountains,” Liara explained. “You saw one of them on the way down. That one glows and is actually quite beautiful. This one doesn’t glow, meaning you rarely see it before you get close enough to trigger its defenses.”

“Defenses?” I asked with foreboding.

“It senses the vibrations of our feet and releases a cloud of spores into the air. They make a fine dust, a little like pollen. But deadly pollen—the kind that kills you when you inhale it. The eastern route is riddled with the stuff.”

“Why would lichen need to poison everything around it?” Gia asked, horrified.

Liara shrugged. “You’d have to ask the plants mages about that. They studied it intensively back when we still hoped to clear the tunnel.”

“Studied it?” Paxton gave her a significant look. “Don’t you mean created it?”

“What?” She gaped at him with the same expression that must have been on my own face.

“Haven’t you heard that rumor? Everyone official denies it, of course, but my parents believe it. Two generations back, there was a group of plants mages from across several tribes working on developing modified strains of lichen. But when things went wrong, and the deadly strain escaped their control, they abandoned the whole project rather than admit their involvement. The point of developing the glowing lichen is obvious—with that lining the tunnel walls, we wouldn’t have to worry about lights.”

“And the purpose of lichen that releases a poison cloud is equally obvious,” Evermund said, a grim note in his voice. “A handy weapon—if they hadn't lost control. But the important point now is whether we can get past it. Is it possible? Could we send a wind ahead of us through the tunnel to blow it away?"

"We could get some of it that way," Paxton said thoughtfully. "But not all of it. The stuff is insidious, and it doesn't take much to do significant damage."

"How fast does it kill you?" Hayes asked.

We all turned to look at him, but he kept his attention on the two nomads.

"Fast," Liara said. "Which was one of the major problems. But it's not instant, of course. It takes several minutes."

"Well, then." Hayes looked to Evermund. "I vote we take this lichen tunnel. We have to get the warning through to the city, so we can't afford not to. I'll just have to heal everyone as we go."

"Is that possible?" I shook my head at Hayes's stubborn expression. "It won't help anyone if you drop from exhaustion halfway there. From the sound of it, if that happens, we'll all be dead within the half hour."

"I'm strong," he said. "I can do it."

"I can help, too." Mila stepped forward. "I might not be a mage, but I have enough strength to sense lichen ahead of us. I can warn everyone when it's coming up, and you can send the wind through like Evermund suggested. We won't clear all of it out, but it will make the damage Hayes needs to heal more manageable."

Evermund looked from person to person, pausing on Gia. She looked back at him defiantly, and I could read the struggle in his eyes. She was royalty and needed to be protected. But an entire city—including most of the nomads' elderly and infirm, along with many of their children—weighed in the balance. He could have insisted she remain behind, but not only would she fight it, but he'd have to leave her alone since Hayes, Mila, and I were all needed to help us make it past the lichen.

"Does anyone have any objections?" he finally asked after the extended pause.

No one said anything, so he nodded. "All right, then. We take this second tunnel. Paxton, Liara, one of you will need to show us the entrance. And there can be no question of blindfolds this time, of course. You'll just have to trust us."

"The city is at stake," Liara said passionately. "Any risk is worth it. And besides—there's a chance the seven of us might make it, but no one is bringing an army through that tunnel. The lichen replenishes itself incredibly quickly."

"It's this way," Paxton said, indicating his agreement with action.

We all fell into step behind him, a ragged line that stayed silent except for our harsh breathing, each of us no doubt thinking about the danger ahead.

Paxton led us to a section where the mountain suddenly thrust upward out of the grassy hills in a sheer cliff face of stone. We walked beside it, moving away from the river, and I was just growing restless when he disappeared.

I gasped, hurrying forward to look more closely. One minute I was walking along a solid rock wall, the next I could see an opening, hidden by a fold of the rock. You had to see it at just the right angle to even notice it, although it wasn't particularly small once you saw it up close. The nomads could have brought horses and even slim wagons through here back when the tunnel was still passable.

But when I stepped into the cool dark of the mountain, I wasn't standing in a tunnel at all. Instead, we gathered in a large cavern with dank air and the constant drip of some distant water droplets.

I gazed around in bewilderment. I could see neither tunnels nor lichen.

Before anyone could voice a question, however, Paxton strode forward again, and we all rushed to follow. At the back of

the cave, he wove his way through a clump of enormous boul-
ders, stepping around the last of them to reveal the black
opening of a tunnel.

He paused, looking back at us. "Is everyone sure about
this?"

We all nodded, and he gestured for Mila to step up to
join him.

"I have no idea how soon the lichen will start," he said.
"We'd better be on alert immediately."

"But we also need to move quickly," I added, not quite
hiding the anxiety in my voice. Cadence was in the city, an
obvious target for the General and his raiders.

Mila nodded and stepped forward. The rest of us followed
her.

CHAPTER 19

AIRLIE

The five elements mages all created small globes of fire to float above our heads, providing illumination without occupying our hands. I was grateful for the bright light they provided, since the tunnel almost immediately sloped steeply uphill, the stone beneath our feet rough and uneven.

Within minutes I was puffing, feeling the strain of the uphill path. Hayes glanced back at me.

"I'm sorry I won't be able to help with anyone who gets tired. I need to save my strength for our battle with the lichen."

"I'm fine," I said, determined that I would be because I had to be. "We can all make it."

At least we were all young. That thought immediately led to thoughts of the rest of the group who had come down the river, and in particular those who might be lying injured right now. The city had sent healers among the reinforcements, so I could only hope some of them had survived.

"Lichen!" Mila stopped, and we crashed into the back of her, one at a time, only the last two or three managing to stop themselves in time. "We've reached it already."

"I'm not surprised," Paxton said. "It's been free to spread ever since we abandoned this tunnel completely."

I peered around Mila. When I caught sight of the lichen on the wall far ahead of us, I doused all the fire balls.

At least two voices called complaints before suddenly going silent. Without the light we were creating, it was easy to see the steady glow coming from the lichen ahead. I let everyone have a good look before squeezing my hand, sending all five flame balls bursting back to life.

"Sorry." Mila sounded apologetic. "I haven't encountered the different types yet, so I can't tell them apart.

"Don't apologize," I said. "Better to be cautious than not."

She nodded briskly, took a breath, and started walking again. "I think I should be able to identify that glow strain now, so it won't happen again."

I knew Mila's ability was stretching further ahead than my eyes could reach, but I couldn't help scouring the rough rock walls anyway. When another batch of lichen appeared, I jumped. But no deadly cloud released, so Mila had obviously been right not to flag them.

When Mila stopped again, we were all poised for the action, managing to halt in time to avoid any more collisions.

"Up ahead," she said, but her uneasy words were drowned by Liara shouting, "Wind! Quick!"

I grabbed the breeze that had been swirling along at our ankles and thrust it hard down the corridor ahead of us. Other winds traveled with it, sent by the other elements mages. Together, they swelled to fill the entirety of the corridor.

But it wasn't enough. A nearly invisible film of orange in the air made me shrink back, but already a burning sensation was traveling down my throat and into my lungs, carried there by my previous breath.

"Run!" Gia shouted, and we all took off like startled rabbits, bounding up the tunnel as if our lives depended on our speed.

I ran in a blind panic, retaining just enough sense through the burning in my lungs and chest to continue pushing the wind ahead of us. Every breath felt worse than the last, and the pain was spreading to my legs. I wouldn't be able to continue much longer. I pictured my sister's face, thoughts of her giving me an extra spurt of strength.

But even that couldn't last forever. I slowed.

"We've passed it," Mila called, collapsing onto her hands and knees.

I swayed and sank down against the wall of the tunnel. Everything in me screamed for oxygen, forcing deep, shuddering breaths that made my whole body shake with pain.

I watched through shadow-filled eyes as Hayes crawled toward Gia. I was losing my grip on reality, my consciousness driven out by the burning hot pain that expanded to fill the space my thoughts had once occupied.

Hayes put his hand on Gia's arm, and she gave a sobbing cry that might have been relief. She pulled her knees up to her chest and hugged them, resting her face out of sight.

He crawled over to me, extending his arm, but I drew back, stubbornly shaking my head. I had a good reason to refuse, but it took a moment to extract it from where the pain held it hostage.

"Heal yourself first," I gasped out.

He was holding back, probably worried his strength would fail. But it was more likely to fail with him in this state.

"Do it!" I said, forcing more steel into my voice.

He sighed and obeyed, relief filling his face. This time, when he held out his hand to me, I reached for it eagerly. Happy tears of exquisite relief rolled down my cheeks as the pain disappeared instantly, my breathing settling to normal.

"Thank you." I smiled at him as I nodded toward Evermund.

He had made no sound and was still on his feet, but his eyes betrayed his pain. Hayes moved on to him and then each of the members of our small group, healing us all in turn.

As soon as Hayes finished, I hurried over to him.

"How are you?" I asked, unable to keep the worry from my voice. "That was only our first encounter with the stuff, and it was much worse than I was expecting."

Hayes grimaced. "I could do that again for all of us, if I had to. But I don't think I would manage it a third time. Not for everyone. Is it always going to be this bad?"

"We didn't stop soon enough," Liara said. "We'd already set them off. I think it should be better if we have the wind blowing first."

"That was my fault." Mila's face looked shiny, coated with sweat and possibly tears, and utterly miserable. "I failed."

"Don't think like that." I put as much bracing cheer into my voice as I could manage. "That was the first time you've ever sensed this lichen. I'm sure you'll detect it much earlier next time."

Silently, my eyes pleaded with her to catch it earlier. It wasn't only our own lives at risk, but countless others in the city as well.

"I will." Mila already sounded more confident. "I'm sure I can pick it up earlier now that I know what I'm looking for."

We all stood, reforming our ragged line. But no one moved.

Mila, ahead of me, seemed frozen solid, afraid to take another step.

"You can do it," I quietly whispered. "We trust in you."

She managed a tremulous smile over her shoulder, and an equally tremulous step forward. But the first step became another and another.

Soon we were back to jogging again.

When she froze a third time, we all froze only a beat behind her. She peered at the air, and I did as well, looking for the telltale colored mist that would indicate poison had already been released. I could see nothing.

"It's there," she said. "Just out of sight."

I called the wind again, sending it streaming away from us with even more force this time. The others joined me, and a cloud of dust filled the far distances of the corridor. It swept along with the wind, pulled further and further ahead of us.

The wind I was shoving forward found a side tunnel. I seized on it, sending the flow of air and dust around the corner so it carried the deadly powder out of our path entirely. I didn't like the idea of it coating the corridor we still had to walk.

"Run again?" I asked, as soon as all the winds had died down.

"Run," Liara agreed. "And try to breathe as little as possible."

We took off running, shoulders tense and hunched slightly as we prepared ourselves for the same stabbing pain.

This time it didn't hit until I was many strides into the patch of tunnel lined with the poisonous lichen. Twice explosions of colored powder—from pockets of lichen somehow missed by the wind and left untriggered—burst over us, but the air wasn't clogged with the stuff like it had been last time.

Most of us were wheezing and looking eagerly to Hayes by the time Mila called a halt. No one fell to the ground, though, so I considered it significant improvement.

Hayes moved around to each of us, and when he reached me, I reluctantly held out my arm. I didn't like taking more of his strength, but I couldn't keep running with pain stabbing my ribs with every breath.

Once again, relief came instantaneously.

We moved on more quickly this time, although I was keeping a wary eye on Hayes. Twice more, Mila stopped us before a patch of the lichen, and we sent our winds ahead of us, running through the patch in its wake. Neither time did we escape entirely untouched.

The next time after that, Mila in the lead was the only one to get a face-full of it. But after healing her, Hayes was flagging noticeably, stumbling more and more often, the gap between him and Gia in front of him widening.

I could feel the burn in my own legs—this time not a result of the lichen but merely the relentless pace and the steep incline—and I hadn't been expending nearly as much effort using my ability as he had.

Finally, to my secret relief, Evermund called a halt. Hayes sank gratefully to the ground, wheezing, while the rest of us watched him in alarm.

"You said this is a shorter, more direct route," Evermund said to the two nomads. "How much shorter?"

"It's much more direct," Liara said. "That's why so much of it is so much steeper than the western way."

"Are we getting close?" Evermund asked. "Because I don't know how much further Hayes can go."

"I can keep going," Hayes said, but his weak voice belied his words.

"We should be close now," Paxton said. "I've never taken this route myself—I'm too young for that—but my parents have pointed out both the entrance and exit to me before. They even took me down the tunnel a short way, from the direction of the city. We stopped before we reached the first patch of lichen, of course, and I'm fairly certain I recognize that bit of tunnel up there."

I peered at the stone ahead of us but could see no noticeable difference from any other section of tunnel. But then, I hadn't been raised in these mountains.

"We risk it, then," Evermund said decisively. His gaze traveled over each of us. "Airlie and I will accompany you, Paxton. Together the three of us will keep a steady wind going ahead of us and just run for it—as fast as we can for as long as we can. Hopefully we don't encounter any more lichen."

"And the rest of us?" Gia's concerned gaze flicked to Hayes who was still gulping in breaths.

"You, Mila, and Liara stay here and look after Hayes. If the passage ahead is clear of lichen, we'll send a wind back to you as a signal. We'll run ahead to warn the city, but you can rest as long as you need before following us at a slower pace. On the other hand, if you don't get a wind signal coming back, that means we've encountered lichen and you should stay put. Once we make it through to the city, we'll send back help, including more healers."

Gia nodded, as did Liara, both of them looking relieved not to have to do any more running. No one asked what would happen if we encountered enough lichen that we never made it through to the city at all.

I pushed aside the part of me that wanted to sink down to sit beside Hayes on the tunnel floor. We were close. Too close to give up now.

Cadence's face once again filled my mind. She was in the city, ignorant of the coming danger, no doubt worried for me. Were we close enough that she could sense me yet? Would she know I was coming?

"Come on." Evermund's voice was gentle. "Not much further."

I nodded and reached automatically for another wind. My body protested, screaming at me as I pushed it back to a jog, but I ignored it. I had been through worse for Cadence.

Every moment of the run, I expected to breathe in white hot agony again, but it never came. Instead, we staggered around a corner, and the breathtaking vista of the Hidden City appeared before us.

Paxton let out a ragged cheer, but I had no breath left for a similar display. Thankfully Evermund sent the wind rushing back down the tunnel to Gia, leaving me free to do nothing but suck in huge gulps of air.

The sound of wheels from a converging tunnel made me swing around to stare blankly at a wagon. For a horrible moment I thought it was the raiders, but it was only a single wagon, pulled by two horses and driven by a confused looking nomad I didn't recognize.

He glanced back the way we'd come.

"Did you just come out of the old way?" He sounded incredulous.

Paxton stepped forward. "Yes, we did. And we need a ride into the city. There's an attack coming. We have to warn everyone."

"Impossible," the man said, but his eyes widened as he took in our disheveled, exhausted appearance.

"It's true," I said. "The raiders are coming."

Belief slowly grew on his face, and he spoke in new tones of urgency. "Get up, then!"

We all climbed slowly into the bed of his wagon, awkwardly finding places among the barrels and crates that filled it. I sighed, a new kind of pain spreading through my body as my relieved muscles adjusted. It passed, however, leaving a glorious feeling of lightness behind it.

The bridge flew past beneath us, and I let my gaze take in the untouched city in relief. We had obviously made it ahead of the raiders.

When the wheels hit the streets of the city, the man nodded at a bag tucked into one corner. Paxton opened it to find a jumbled collection of small, handheld instruments.

Understanding lit his eyes, and he pulled out an oversized handbell. As the wagon trundled along, he rang it, the clanging startlingly loud against my jangled nerves.

"Attack!" he shouted, ringing the bell again. "Defend your homes! Defend the city! Attack!"

We continued up the street, crowds pouring from the more residential looking buildings. Many of them ran after us, calling questions. Evermund and I answered as best we could, and word spread through the crowd, rippling out.

"Raiders!" I heard people saying. "The raiders are coming!"

A much louder bell rang out from deeper in the city, its clanging reaching into corners untouched by our smaller one.

"Attack!" The call was no longer coming from our wagon, but from every side. "Defend the city!"

People streamed onto the street, hurrying in all directions.

I slowly lowered myself down, staring up at the blue sky above, so strange after the never-ending gray of the tunnel. We had made it. We had warned the city.

And now I wanted to sleep for an age.

"Defend the city!" someone shouted right beside the wagon, and I sat up hurriedly.

I couldn't sleep. The raiders were coming. Our panicked flight through the tunnels had only been the beginning.

CHAPTER 20

CADENCE

I wanted to stay in my room and hide, but I couldn't do that. I already got to lurk out of sight inside the Nicabar buildings while Annora and Zeke faced the ridicule of the tribes. I couldn't hide from my friends and allies as well.

Annora had taken me out the first time, but my presence as an outsider had been more hindrance than help, so I had been left home after that.

Zeke had been right about everything. Annora had felt compelled to attempt warning the tribes, but all she had achieved was turning many of her previous allies against her. In the face of Tribe Alia's horrified denials, the accusation was being viewed as a final desperate, pathetic attempt by a losing candidate.

Annora's confident proud manner didn't crack, but I could see the strain in her eyes. It was taking everything she had to maintain the facade of unconcern. Not only was she facing the ruin of all her tribe's plans, but she carried the burden of knowing danger was coming but no one would listen.

She had organized the strongest of the tribe's mages into shifts, the rotating groups guarding the tunnel exit at all hours. Others had been sent to the lookout tower which Zeke explained wasn't regularly manned but did still house a warning bell large enough to rouse the whole city.

But it wouldn't be enough. We all knew that. The General had been expanding his forces, and if he brought all of them, they would be into the city before a portion of one tribe could stop them. Especially given the unknown means he had of strengthening his mages.

Tribe Patrin, who had been closely allied with Nicabar, were holding themselves neutral on the issue. Annora was furious about it. With their whole tribe in the city, their mobilization would make a big difference. But without evidence, they felt they couldn't judge against Alia—particularly not in the middle of a vote.

And so it was yet another emotion Annora had to contain in public.

I met Annora and Zeke in the courtyard, but one look at their faces told me they had once again failed. Tribe Lothar hadn't been convinced of the coming danger.

Zeke looked tired, so I went straight to him, slipping my arms around his middle and giving him a squeeze. He squeezed me back briefly, a one-armed hug that he quickly ended.

"We meet with Tribe Karel this afternoon?" he asked his mother.

Liara's mother stepped forward, shaking her head. Her mouth was a thin slash across her face, her lips pressed together.

"They sent a message while you were gone."

"They won't even meet with me." Annora said it as a fact, as if she had been expecting as much, but her shoulders dropped fractionally. "They'll no doubt avoid us until after the vote tomorrow."

Mention of the vote made my stomach lurch so violently I thought I might be sick. There was no hope now of Nicabar winning. Not without more time to prove we were right.

A strange clanging in my head made it hard to think, and for a moment I worried I was going to black out. But my vision stayed steady, and the distant, echoing sound grew louder.

"What's that?" I asked, tipping my head toward the gate. "Can you hear something?"

Annora didn't even look at me, her gaze distant, and her whole attitude one of deep weariness. Zeke was watching his mother with concern, but at my words he spun around and frowned.

"Is it...?" His words stopped, his frown deepening. "That's inside the city."

Annora finally stirred at that, looking at us with fear on her face.

"I don't think it's the raiders," I said quickly. "It sounds like a bell...And shouting?"

A much louder clanging made us all jolt and swing toward the palace, eyes wide.

"What's that?" I asked, breathless, my heart racing, although I thought I already knew the answer.

Zeke turned to his mother, a question on his face.

"That's the alarm bell," an older tribesman said from behind Annora. He sounded dazed. "It hasn't been rung in my lifetime."

A handful of people sprinted onto the street from various side streets, scattering in both directions.

"Attack!" they cried as they ran, some stopping to bang on doors or gates. "Attack! Defend the city!"

Annora stepped back out our still open gate onto the street.

"What's happening?" she called to the closest person.

"We're being attacked," he cried, turning in her direction. As soon as he got a good look, he faltered.

For a moment, they stared at each other, and then he bowed from the waist. "You were right, Tribe Nicabar. The raiders are coming. We must defend our city."

Annora stared at him, and for the first time, she looked as if she might actually crumple. But a moment later, she straightened, her face turning stern.

"Continue spreading the word," she said. "I posted sentries near the top of the tunnel. Has the warning come from them?"

He shook his head. "It comes from Tribe Callen—one of the mages who was sent to the border." He noticed me, standing in the street behind Annora. "I didn't see him myself, but I heard your people were there as well." His eyes widened. "They used the eastern route to get word here ahead of the raiders."

"They made it up the old way?" Annora asked. "The closed tunnels?"

I grabbed at Zeke's arm. What did that mean? From their mutual shock, it must be a dangerous thing to do. But the man had said they'd made it. My stomach twisted. Some of them, anyway.

"What's the old way?" I whispered to Zeke.

"That's a dangerous route." His eyes were far too concerned for my liking. "If they risked it, the situation must be dire." He looked down at me. "You were right."

The sick feeling grew. "I wish I hadn't been."

A small pack of riders came galloping down the street from the direction of the palace, riding far too fast for safety given the chaos in the city. They pulled up beside us, the lead rider saluting Annora. He didn't waste time on formalities.

"You were right. The raiders are coming. You're wanted at the palace."

"I have warriors in the tunnels," Annora said. "Can you send someone to warn them? Let them know the city is going into defense mode. The first hint they get of the raiders, they should pull back as fast as possible."

The lead rider turned to the rest of his group, his eyes landing on one of them. The man nodded and pulled his horse out of the clump. Wending his way through the small crowd that had gathered around us, he spurred him back to speed again, shouting for anyone in his way to clear the road.

Within moments he was out of sight.

Someone came out the Nicabar gates leading several horses. Annora mounted one in a fluid motion, wheeling to take up a place beside the Patrin rider who had led the way from the palace. Others of her tribe mounted as well, and she called a few instructions to the man who had brought the horses, her words flowing so fast I struggled to follow them. She seemed to be issuing commands for him to enact existing plans for the tribe to join in the city's defense.

All the horses had riders now except one, and she looked to Zeke. He gazed stubbornly back, clearly immobile. Her eyes flicked to me, and she sighed once, shaking her head. The lead rider flicked his reins, and all the animals began to move, leaving Zeke and me in the middle of the street with the crowd of interested bystanders.

Zeke pulled me back toward the open gates, and I followed eagerly, anxious to be out of the open street.

"Should you have gone with them?" I asked as soon as we were safely in the courtyard.

"I'm not leaving you." He looked at me with such a stubborn expression that I didn't even bother fighting.

"What should we be doing?" I asked instead.

"Staying here and out of sight," he said promptly.

I blinked. "What good will that do the city?"

"There are plenty of mages here to defend the city," he said. "I'm more worried about what happens if the General or any of his people catch sight of you. I'm sure they haven't given up on the idea of capturing you." He hesitated. "That may even be their purpose in coming here."

I stared at him. "You think they're attacking the Hidden City for *me*?"

"I think it's enough of a possibility that I'm not letting you out of my sight, and we're certainly not going off to man the parapets."

Despite everything, a small giggle escaped. "The Hidden City doesn't have any parapets. You don't even have a palace wall."

He rolled his eyes, but I caught the slight smile on his face.

"Are you sure, though?" I asked. "I know you would be a significant help, and I might be able to help as well. I've been thinking a lot about what Otto said about power having an affinity."

The speed of my words increased as a measure of enthusiasm crept in. "I've been thinking back over all the previous times I've used my ability, and I realized I've actually done it before. When our boat hit that blockade, everything was so rushed and panicked that I wasn't thinking clearly. I thought of myself as boosting Airlie's efforts, but that wasn't what I was doing at all. I didn't strengthen her steps on the river surface, I walked on the river myself. It's true I was using her pattern, but not to join her. I was copying it and recreating the effect myself from scratch. In all the chaos, I didn't even think about how that was different. But I think the reason it worked is because I was drawing power exclusively from first Airlie and then the blockade itself, so of course it was all elements power. It had to be since it was tied to the river."

"Have you managed to recreate that?" Zeke asked eagerly. "Have you done anything on your own, without having a pattern to copy? Now would be a great time to be able to protect yourself."

"I'm still working on identifying the affinity of leftover power and separating it out when I collect it," I admitted. "That's been absorbing all my focus. But it'll be different in the case of an attack. I can easily tell the affinity of any raider mage I encounter, which means I'll know how to use any power I take directly from their attacks. I won't just be able to disrupt their efforts, but to actively turn their own power against them."

Speaking it aloud, I felt another rush of enthusiasm. I could make a difference here. I could finally use my ability to its full effect.

But Zeke was shaking his head. "This isn't perfect test conditions. Battle is chaotic and unpredictable. It's hardly the time to be trying something new. While you're working it out, someone else could attack you from a different side. It's better for you to just stay out of sight."

Part of me acknowledged the truth of his words, but the other part fought them. People were going into battle—people would die—and Zeke thought it was possible this was all happening because of me. I couldn't cower safely out of sight when I might be able to help. Especially not if Airlie was in the middle of it all. I had to find out if she had been one of those to make it through.

I could see Zeke wanted to brush away my words, to pull me along in the wake of his forceful confidence. But he must have learned something from last time because he stopped and gave me his full attention.

"I know you want to help," he said. "So do I."

I instantly felt even worse. Of course Zeke would be feeling the same pull to do something—he would be feeling it even more strongly than me. This was his home and his people.

"But we truly aren't needed," he said. "Mother and I have been worried, desperately so, and it might have given you the wrong impression. When it was just our tribe—and with most of our people still camped by the western sea—we didn't know if it would be enough. A surprise attack might have done immense damage before anyone knew what was happening. But this is different. The Hidden City was designed so that it could be defended by the single ruling tribe. But right now, as well as the whole of Tribe Patrin, we have representatives from all forty of the other tribes. The city is as full as it ever is. The General has no idea what he's trying to do. Without surprise on his side, he doesn't stand a chance."

The tightness inside me eased, the roiling in my stomach settling. I still wanted to do what I could, but he was right. It was ridiculous to think the nomads required me to save their capital city.

"I don't think we should stay here, though," he continued. "We don't know how much information they managed to get from Grayson. If they're coming for you, they may know to look here."

"Where else can we go?" I gazed up over the wall to where the top levels of even higher buildings showed. "Should we hide in a storehouse somewhere? There must be hundreds of them in the city."

"It would be better if we were in a building unassociated with Nicabar. But of course I don't have the keys to any of those. And breaking into one might draw attention to the fact there's someone in there."

He paused, his eyes slowly turning to the large storehouse that took up the right of the courtyard. His face lit up with a hint of his normal mischief. "Actually, I might have an idea about that. Come on."

I cast a final glance through the gate, my desire to find Airlie still pulling at me, but I didn't resist. We slipped inside the cavernous space, and Zeke led the way up a set of simple stairs that hugged the wall next to the door. I clung to the wall as I climbed, trying not to look at the place where a rail should be.

We continued up at least two stories in height before step-ping off onto a platform that ran the whole length of the build-ing, like a basic loft. I took two big steps away from the edge before breathing a sigh of relief.

Zeke followed with bounding steps that suggested he'd never felt a fear of heights.

"This way." He beckoned for me to follow him down the shadowy loft, dodging pallets of unknown supplies.

It seemed to take forever to walk to the far end of the building, but we didn't pause until we reached it. As soon as we stopped, he pointed at a small window, and my heart sank.

"Through there?" I regarded it uneasily. "Will you even fit?"

"It might be tight." He threw a laughing look at me. "I've grown since the last time I tried this."

I raised both eyebrows. "Is this the time to be reliving your childish exploits?"

"It is for this particular one. I'll go first, and then I can help you up."

He pushed open the window and grabbed the top of the frame with a reverse grip, easily pulling himself up and through, twisting as he went, so that he ended by sitting on the windowsill with his legs facing back in toward me, and his head and shoulders out of sight through the window. With another smooth movement, he scrambled up until all I could see were the bottom of his legs and his feet which were perched securely on the bottom of the frame. In another moment, he'd disappeared from sight entirely.

I rushed forward to lean out the window and peer upward. His face reappeared, looking over the edge of the roof.

"I fit." He sounded satisfied, but I was too busy looking back down at the ground two stories below.

"Good for you," I said in a choked voice.

"Come on. I'll help you." He reached an arm down to me, and I reluctantly hoisted myself up on the windowsill, scrambling inelegantly until I was balanced precariously with my knees resting on the frame.

Gulping, I froze, but his coaxing voice made me keep moving. I grabbed at his hand, clinging to it tightly as I used it to inch slowly around until I was standing as he had been, my feet on the windowsill and my front pressed against the building.

He must have been lying across the roof because he reached his other arm down.

"I'll pull you the rest of the way."

I reluctantly gave him both hands, scrabbling against the wall with my feet as he hauled me the rest of the way. As soon as I was on the roof, I lay down beside him, breathing fast.

"You used to do that for fun?" I asked.

He laughed. "Actually, this was the fun bit."

Standing, he pointed at a narrow ledge that ran between the storehouse we stood on and the next one. Glancing down, I saw that the wall that surrounded the core Nicabar holdings passed below us, between the two buildings. The storehouse across the gap belonged to a different tribe, but they shared some sort of drainage system.

I eyed it doubtfully. "Please tell me we're not supposed to walk across that. You're not even an elements mage!"

"No, but I have good balance."

A loud cracking sound made us both spin in the direction of the road. But the sound had come from further away. From our new height, I had a clear view across a row of buildings to the bridge that connected the city to the tunnels.

I couldn't see the part of the bridge closest to the city, but my attention was caught on a line of riders racing across at full tilt. They had made it more than halfway and were rapidly approaching the city, one of them lagging slightly due to the extra burden of a second person slung across his mount in front of him.

For a blank moment, I thought it was the raiders, but the group was surely too small.

"Who—?" I asked, just as Zeke spoke.

"Those are the Nicabar sentries."

I gulped. If they were fleeing at that speed, the raiders must be right behind them.

Another crack sounded, and a gap appeared at the far end of the bridge. It wasn't a natural crumbling of the stone, but rather an even gap that disconnected the bridge from the other mountain, as if a section had simply disappeared. The rest of the bridge looked unaffected, the stone steady beneath the pounding hooves of the horses.

I saw the next chunk pulling free from the bridge, widening the gap on the far end. And then another. The separated stones hung for a moment in the air before dropping into the valley below. The final nomads were fleeing back to the city, and the bridge was disintegrating in their wake.

The first of the riders had passed out of sight now, and the others followed one at a time, the bridge falling apart behind them. It was over half gone by now, already useless to anyone approaching from the other side.

A warning shout went up, so loud it reached us on the storeroom roof. At the exit of the tunnel, wagons and a collection of horses appeared. This time, I didn't need to see the familiar hulking figure in the lead to know it really was the raiders.

CHAPTER 21

CADENCE

Swallowing, I looked again at the narrow ledge. We weren't children, looking for mischief. Battle was about to be joined around us, and walking across a ledge was hardly the greatest danger I might encounter.

Zeke must have seen the determination in my eyes because he leaped up without further discussion, walking quickly and surely across to the other building.

"It isn't really far," he called back softly. "But take your time." A trace of worry appeared in his face, as if he was second-guessing his decision.

"I can do it," I said, proud of how calm my voice sounded.

Stepping out, I focused my eyes on my feet. The ledge was wider than they were, so it wasn't as dangerous as it felt, but my sweating palms hadn't heard the message. I shuffled along, not willing to lift my foot all the way off to take a proper step.

I'd made it halfway across when a breeze hit me, and I wobbled. For a horrifying moment, I thought I was losing my balance and grabbed instinctively at the air around me. But the breeze died down, and I stopped shaking, my feet still firmly in place.

Speeding up, I rushed the final few steps, throwing myself

into Zeke's waiting arms. He held me close, murmuring something that might have been a reassurance, if I wasn't too distracted to make out his words.

Power thrummed around me. When had I gathered it? I didn't remember doing so consciously, but it must have been when I grabbed for the air. I hadn't even realized I was wrapping myself in power.

I held it for a moment, about to push it away again, when I paused. I had grabbed at the air, and instead I had gathered power that felt like the air in a way I couldn't entirely verbalize.

In that moment, I had been thinking of crossing the bridge on our first day, and the way Airlie had let me join her in controlling the wind. I had been desperate for the wind to catch me up instead of pushing me down, and apparently I had gathered power around me.

Was it elements power, then? I concentrated on it again. The faint sense of the air was still there. Tentatively, I recalled the sensation of Airlie controlling the wind and pressed the power into the same pattern.

A wind swirled around us, circling around Zeke and me and pressing us closer together. He pulled back, fighting against its force to look down at me.

"Are you doing that?" He sounded startled and confused.

I grinned up at him, forgetting the raiders for a moment. "Yes! Apparently all I needed to do was *stop* thinking about it so hard. I can recognize the affinity of leftover power by instinct better than design. I reached for the air, and my subconscious gathered in power connected to the air. I think I must have been doing something similar when I've worked with you. When I joined with you, following your pattern, I must have been instinctively drawing from plants power. Maybe because I was trying to match it to the power you were using." I grimaced. "Now I just have to learn how to do it on purpose."

"Still, that's excellent."

Another shout distracted him, and we both looked across at the empty space where the destroyed bridge used to stretch. I knew that the nomad plants mages would be able to rebuild the bridge when this was all over, but the sight of the gap separating us from the rest of the world still brought a surge of irrational fear.

"They're coming," Zeke said shortly, and my eyes focused on movement near the tunnel exit.

More than fifty blocks of stone were rising from the valley floor, soaring up to hover in front of the raiders. They leaped onto them, one person per block, and the chunks flew through the air.

Several of them lurched, and two dropped, their occupants screaming. Plants and elements mages among the nomads must be fighting back. Three more of the chunks wavered, flinging off their occupants, and I couldn't help a sick feeling of sympathy.

But before I had time to think further, the General turned to look back from the leading block. He didn't make any other movements, but the people who had disappeared flew back into sight, flung almost violently upward by what must be a powerful wind.

"We need to keep moving," Zeke said grimly. "It's clear at least some of them are going to make it across. The General is too powerful."

I pulled my eyes away from the aerial battle with reluctance. I knew he was right, but it was hard not to watch.

We ran across the new roof which thankfully had only a slight angle. At the far end, Zeke leaned over and pushed open an identical window to the one we had used to escape the Nicabar storeroom. He went first again, slithering easily onto the loft below.

I followed, buoyed by my new ability to control the winds. When my feet touched down, I drew a steadying breath and tried to look around. It was dark in here, though. Apparently this storeroom wasn't in current active use, like the Nicabar one.

"So now we wait?" I asked, my thoughts once again on Airlie.

Was she facing the General right now? She'd done it before and won, but we'd also been able to flee then. Would she be standing alone, or with a host of nomad mages at her side?

I stood up and paced to the nearer wall, moving away from the open drop to the main storehouse floor below. Airlie was out there somewhere, and I needed to...

I stopped. What was I doing? If Airlie was back in the city, she was likely within range. I could find her.

I dropped into a sitting position so nothing would distract me and stretched out my senses. An entire city of people spread around me in every direction, their presence confusing. But I concentrated, pushing through the mental noise to look for the familiar glow of my sister's immense ability. She must be here somewhere. She must.

I skimmed over Annora in the palace, moving outward until I suddenly gave a loud exclamation.

"What? What is it?" Zeke was instantly at my side.

"She's here," I cried.

"Who, Airlie? We knew that. The man in the street said they took the eastern route."

"No, I mean she's *here*. Well, nearly here," I corrected myself. "I was looking for her further out, near the city entrance, but she's here."

"Here at the storeroom?" He stepped over to peer out the open window. "How is that possible?"

"She must be looking for me. Can you feel that breeze?" A slight wind curled around me before flowing out the window. "I think she sent it to look for us."

I was grinning, up on my feet now and bouncing with

delight. Airlie was all right, and she was here. I would see her in minutes.

Zeke, however, stepped immediately back from the opening, slamming the window closed and turning to me with a horrified expression.

I faltered, going still. "What? What is it?"

"If Airlie can find us here with a breeze, then can't the General find us as well?"

My joy drained away instantly.

"Yes," I whispered. I tried to strengthen my voice. "But that's assuming he's looking for me."

Zeke's face told me it wasn't an assumption he was willing to bet my life on.

"What do we do?" I asked. "Should we move somewhere else?"

"Maybe?" Zeke looked torn. "We might still be safer in here. If he didn't manage to get a trace of you in that short time the window was open, he'll struggle to do so now. Whereas if we go outside, any wind he sends could easily find us."

"We should at least wait until Airlie gets here," I said. "Surely the General must only just be arriving in the city. He couldn't be looking for me yet. Airlie will be ahead of him."

Zeke nodded, although he looked reluctant. I bit my lip and looked around the loft again.

Before, the darkness had felt comforting, concealing us and keeping us safe. Now it seemed ominous, every shadow and hidden corner a lurking threat. I shook off the feeling, refusing to give in to childish theatrics.

"What do you think is going on out there?" I asked after several interminable minutes passed with silence inside the storeroom but muffled shouts and bangs outside.

"We're driving out any raiders who made it as far as the city," Zeke said confidently.

I looked at him, trying to assess if he was being positive for my sake or really believed his words. He gave me a knowing look in return.

"My only concern is for you, Cadence. If this is all a distraction so they can send a team after you, then they might have a hope of succeeding. But if their aim is to take the city, they've already failed."

I nodded, reassured. It had seemed so obvious when he first told me, but hiding in the dark with nothing but the sounds of distant battle for company distorted the situation. It was too easy to imagine an endless army of raiders pouring through every street. Every couple of minutes I had to remind myself that the General hadn't buoyed his forces that much. I had even seen their arrival, and there couldn't have been many more than fifty. They were vastly outnumbered.

But the more I built up the reassuring image in my mind, the more uneasy it made me. Zeke was right. This whole attack made far more sense if it had an aim other than taking the Hidden City. They may even have hoped to avoid an open attack at all. But any attempt at a stealth approach had been foiled by our discovery of the Alia plot and then Airlie's warning.

A sensible commander would have withdrawn at that point, but Renley had been certain the General was enraged at Airlie's escape and her defeat of him on that occasion. And if he wasn't thinking clearly, then there was no telling what he might do.

The silence and stillness around us grew even more oppressive. A bang from below made us both jump. Forgetting all about my fear of the drop, I rushed to the side and peered over. Surely, it was Airlie. It had to be Airlie.

Zeke grabbed at my arm, pulling me back, but not before I got a single, swift glance into the partially full warehouse below. In that one second, my eyes locked on to the piercing glare of the General.

He had come for me.

"It's him," I gasped, my words barely audible over a sudden rush of wind inside the building.

Zeke's grip on me slipped, but he dug his fingers in tighter as the wind swept around us both, trying to tear us apart. I reached for him, trying to grab his arm with my other hand, but the wind was too strong.

My feet left the ground, only Zeke's hold on my arm keeping me from being swept over the edge and down to the storeroom floor and the waiting General.

"Zeke!" I screamed his name over the howl of the wind.

His desperate eyes met mine before he cast his gaze first one way and then the other. But we were inside. There were no roots here to spring out of the ground and anchor us or vines to tie us to each other. For all his great strength, he was helpless in this moment.

But I wasn't limited in the same way. Otto's words came rushing back to me. I hadn't had a chance to practice, and the skill was far from fully formed, but I could control the wind, just like the General.

I sucked his power from the air, feeding it back into the wind but directing it away from us instead. But in the panic of the moment, I hadn't thought my actions through. When the wind cut suddenly off, I fell.

I slammed into the floor of the loft hard, Zeke's grip on one arm not enough to save me. Pain filled me, and blind panic as I tried to suck in air and couldn't.

You're just winded, I reminded myself, forcing my logic to take over from the primitive and unreasoning fear. *Just wait a moment, and you'll be able to breathe again.*

A moment passed and another. Zeke let go of my arm, taking up a defensive stance above me. I tried to suck in another breath, and this time succeeded. Relief flooded me as intensively as the precious oxygen.

Pushing myself into a sitting position, I scrambled up to

stand beside Zeke. Somewhere beneath my terror and pain, exhilaration filled me. I had done it. In the heat of the moment, I had managed to control the wind, just like an elements mage. Just like Airlie.

No sooner had I thought Airlie's name than an enormous force slammed into my legs. For one confused moment, I thought a pallet had come to life and was attacking us, and then I realized another wind was driving it. But this one had sprung up behind us without warning, partially lifting one of the pallets and sending it sliding into us.

I staggered as the pallet slammed me again. This time my legs gave way completely, and it pushed me straight off the edge of the loft.

I fell, flailing my arms and trying to suck in power to cushion my fall. The air around me hardened, catching and slowing me, and for a second, I thought I had somehow succeeded. But the cushioning air swept me toward a stationary figure near the splintered door. It hadn't come from me at all.

CHAPTER 22

CADENCE

I fought it, thrashing and kicking, but there was nothing to kick against but air. A crash behind me made my heart seize. I gave up fighting and tried to twist around instead.

It wasn't Zeke, it wasn't Zeke, it wasn't Zeke, I told myself, but I didn't believe the words. A tangled, confusing mass of plants power had sprouted from a spot in the storeroom floor, just out of my sight. And I could no longer sense the glowing inferno that burned at the center of Zeke anywhere in the building.

I finally managed to crane around far enough to see a pallet smashed across the ground, half of it buried in the crater it had created in the floor. And just visible beneath a length of material that had spilled from the packaging was an arm, sprawled unmoving on the edge of the crater.

"No!" I screamed, fighting again, although I already knew it was fruitless.

In my rage, I was grabbing all the power around me indiscriminately, and I couldn't get it to do anything. Even the air holding me didn't let go. I couldn't imagine how much power the General must be expending to pour more and more into his effort to keep me bound and moving toward him.

"What have you done?" I screamed as soon as I was dragged directly in front of him.

"What have I done?" He spoke coolly, but his eyes burned with barely restrained rage. "You made me do this. You and your sister. If you had just come with us in the first place, no one had to be hurt. We are your true people. You don't belong with the nomads any more than you belong with the Tartorans. Like it or not, you're coming home to Calista, power mage."

Everything whirled around me when he said the word *hurt*. That was Zeke back there, lying as still as— My mind shied away, unable to even think the word.

I screamed my wordless rage and spat at the General. The wad hit him right in the eye, and he reared back. Just as his weight shifted, someone tackled him from behind, their shoulder colliding with the middle of his back and sending him flying forward.

The air around me thinned, and for the second time, I dropped. This time I landed on my hip, a shock of pain racing through me. But at least I could breathe.

When I tried to stand, though, my leg gave way, and I crashed back down. Giving up on the idea of standing, I scuttled backward, like a spider, trying to get away from the General and his attacker.

The other person was smaller than I expected, her long brown hair flying everywhere as she fought to keep the General pinned to the ground. Her smaller stature made the job difficult, and after a frenzied moment, he surged to his feet, throwing her off.

"Airlie!" I cried as she landed on her rear beside me.

More people poured in through the door the General had destroyed, Evermund in the lead. He halted before the General, giving him a threatening look that would have made me turn and run. The General glared back, but he was breathing heavily, and he must have expended an enormous amount of power earlier to keep up with what I had been sucking away from him. His eyes flicked to the crowd who were still cramming in to swell the numbers behind Evermund.

With a snarl, the General turned and fled, Evermund and the others chasing after him. I let them go, turning to my sister.

"Cadence!" Airlie threw both arms around me. "Are you all right?"

"I've hurt my hip, but that doesn't matter. Zeke…"

I began to crawl back toward the crater in the ground, ignoring the pain in my hip as I maneuvered around the strewn contents of the pallet, and the smashed lengths of wood that had formed it.

"Is Hayes with you?" I gasped out.

"No," she said. "But—" She looked toward the door where some of the people who had come to our rescue still lingered. "We need a healer!" she called. "Now!"

Voices repeated the cry, the sound moving out through the doorway. I ignored it all, dragging myself painfully forward. Healers could heal almost any injury. As long as he was still alive…He had to be alive.

I caught sight of his arm again, and my pace increased.

"Zeke!" I called. "Can you hear me? Zeke?"

A rough groan emerged from the crater. It was the most beautiful sound I had ever heard.

"Zeke." I was crying with relief as I dragged myself up far enough to peer down at him.

He lay in a surprisingly deep hole, much of the pallet contents pinning him in place. It had been a large pallet, but I had no idea how it had smashed so deeply into the ground. Plants power still coated everything, and now that I was closer, I could sense the faint flicker at the center of Zeke, hidden by the mass of power around him.

"Just hold on!" I said. "A healer is coming."

I peered over my shoulder, hoping the words were true. A

number of people were hurrying toward us. Surely one of them would be…I reached out with my power and felt the presence of a healer.

"Are you the injured?" A middle-aged woman asked briskly, reaching her hand for me.

I shied away from her. "No, no, it's Zeke." I pointed into the hole, and she gave a smothered exclamation.

Sliding down the edge of the crater, she managed to make contact with his outstretched arm. She muttered several incomprehensible things to herself, my anxiety peaking at the concern in her tone.

A man approached, and she beckoned him to Zeke's other side. I held my breath as he made contact with Zeke's shoulder, his concerned murmurs joining the woman's.

Several other people moved around them, working together to carefully lift the broken pieces of the pallet out of the hole without disturbing the work of the healers. Within minutes, they had cleared everything off him.

I stared down at the three people left in the crater, although my eyes could see no action at all. Inside Zeke, my ability told me a different story, however, as the power of the healers fought to repair his body.

Slowly his own blaze grew stronger, until it no longer flickered. I sat back, tears pouring down my face.

"Will he be all right?" Airlie whispered.

"I think so." I threw my arms around her and buried my face in her shoulder, while she patted my back and made soothing sounds.

"Do you still need a healer?" a younger voice asked from behind us.

"Yes," Airlie said firmly before I could say anything. "My sister is injured."

The man put his hand on the top of my head, and cool relief from the pain spread down through me. I thanked him in a rush, more interested in the movement at the bottom of the crater.

Airlie and I both scrambled to our feet to offer our help as the three people climbed out, their limbs weak from exhaustion. As soon as Zeke was properly on his feet, I wrapped my arms around him.

"Is he fully healed?" I asked the woman.

"I'm fine," Zeke said, in a voice that seemed impossibly calm for the situation.

I still looked to the healer, however. She nodded, swaying slightly. Airlie hurried over to offer her support while fresh tears streaked down my cheeks. Zeke must have been near the edge and badly injured if it had taken so much out of two healers to fix him.

"Thank you," I managed to whisper.

She shook her head. "I'm grateful to have a chance to discharge my debt."

"Your debt?" I looked up at Zeke, but he just shook his head slightly.

"Tribe Nicabar attempted to warn us, and we accused them of petty lies," she said. "The whole of the nomad kingdom owes them a debt of gratitude."

"Oh." I was still in too much shock to properly absorb her words.

The woman turned to Airlie. "And I believe you were part of the team that came up through the eastern tunnels. My thanks go to you as well."

Airlie nodded graciously, looking regal despite the dust and dirt that clung to her clothes and skin, and the lines of exhaustion on her face.

A new crowd pushed into the building, their faces vaguely familiar. I couldn't recall their names, but I knew they belonged to Tribe Nicabar. After a brief inquiry into our health, they surrounded us, sweeping the three of us the short distance to the Nicabar gates.

"I suppose we're going to have to offer payment to whichever tribe owns that storeroom," I said. "It's been half destroyed."

"If that healer is any indication, they won't accept the offer," Airlie replied.

I pressed into Zeke's side. He still hadn't removed his arm from around my shoulders, and I wasn't sure if I could bear for him to ever do so. It still seemed too unbelievable that he was here and whole.

But in the middle of my wonder and gratitude, my curiosity reared its head.

"I know it was a good-sized pallet," I said. "But why did it make such an enormous crater? I thought there was solid stone under the floors of all these buildings."

"There was," said Zeke. "But I can't make the air catch me mid-fall. All I could do was pulverize the stone beneath the impact spot. I turned it into dust as far down as I could before I hit. I still hit the floorboards, and the pallet still landed on top of me, but the soft landing underneath saved my life."

"That was quick thinking," Airlie said admiringly.

"Unlike me who panicked and made a mess of everything," I said.

Zeke frowned down at me, his arm tightening around my shoulders. "What are you talking about?"

"I panicked and pulled all the power around me. If I'd only drained it from the General, instead of contaminating it with the leftover power in the air, I could have turned it back against him."

"I'm not entirely sure what you're talking about," Airlie said, sounding unreasonably cheerful, "but you still drained his power, which is a lot more than nothing. In fact, it's probably the only reason he ran. He's incredibly powerful, and he's beaten Evermund before, but he must have known he was dangerously tired."

"Why are you so happy?" I muttered, not quite willing to accept her generous reading of my foolish mistake.

"Because we made it in time!" she exclaimed. "And you're both healed, and the nomads have driven out the raiders. I'm not sure what there is to be unhappy about!"

"So it's over?" Zeke asked, as we stepped into the familiar courtyard.

A small group of people turned to look at us, Evermund in their center, and both twins at his side. Airlie raced forward to join them, while Zeke and I followed at a more sedate pace. Renley appeared from behind Nikolas, relief on his face.

"There you are! I tried to find you when the fighting began, but there was no sign of you anywhere."

"We were hiding," I said ruefully. "But unfortunately not from the one person we were trying to avoid." I looked to Evermund. "Where is the General?"

"I'm afraid he got away." Evermund exchanged a look with Gia.

"Got away?" Zeke frowned. "How did he evade half the city?"

"It's my fault," Evermund said gravely. "I was already exhausted, and I wasn't able to combat his speed. A few of us followed him across the chasm, but he ran off down one of the tunnels."

"It's not your fault," Airlie said quickly. "I don't know how you chased him at all. I was so tired I lost my head completely and physically tackled him." She shook her head as if unable to believe she'd done something so ridiculous.

"It worked, though," I said. "But why didn't anyone else go into the tunnel after him? You weren't the only one chasing him. Surely the nomads—"

"He didn't just go down any tunnel." Gia glanced at Airlie.

"He appeared just as Mila, Liara, Hayes, and I were emerging from one. Nik, Master Augusta, and Captain Huxley were there, having come in search of me, and the General was clearly too weak to take on so many of us. I suppose he assumed that if we were coming out of the tunnel, it must mean it was a way out."

"Well, he's right about that," Airlie said, looking stunned. "But he'll never reach the exit. Not alone. And no one will have been expecting him to run in that direction, so it's no wonder he got away."

"I don't understand." I looked around the circle. "It's been a long few days. Could someone please explain?"

"That route has been closed for many years due to a particular deadly type of lichen that grows there," Airlie explained. "We barely made it through alive, and that was only because we had a plants mage and a powerful healing mage with us. Alone, an elements mage doesn't stand a chance."

"You're telling me the General is dead?" I asked, unable to process the thought.

"He must be," Evermund said.

"Then that means, we've won." I tried to force my numb brain to properly absorb so many shocks in a row. "So now—"

"Now we sleep," Annora said from the gate. "And then we vote."

CHAPTER 23
CADENCE

It wasn't as simple as that, of course. At least as far as the sleeping was concerned. I wasn't the only one reluctant to part from the people I loved, even to sleep, and everyone wanted to know what everyone else had been doing during those crucial hours.

When I heard that Annora had helped Tribe Patrin coordinate the city's defense from the palace, I expressed surprise that she was back with us so quickly. Zeke had to explain that as a candidate for the vote, she was excluded from the palace from sunset.

"So Tribe Nicabar doesn't get a vote?" I asked.

"We don't get to be there at all," he said.

"And what of public opinion?" I asked. "If that healer is anything to go by, the attack must have changed things."

"I hope so," Zeke agreed. "We should have won back our previous allies, at the very least. But those who are loyal to Alia may take more convincing before they believe Alia had a hand in this unprecedented breach of our city."

"Is there no evidence?" I asked, looking to Annora.

"Time is against us there," she said. "If we had longer, I wouldn't doubt the outcome. The raiders chose to use stealth, following Grayson at a great enough distance to escape his detection."

"Which they could easily do," I said, "given the strength of the General's ability. He found me in a whole city of storehouses. He could easily have tracked Grayson from afar."

"Precisely," she said. "Especially since Tribe Alia had discounted the rumors of his strength, so Grayson wasn't guarding against a tracking ability like that. Grayson made it almost to the city, only stopping because the Nicabar sentries arrested him once he reached their position. At that point, he was still ignorant of his part in leading the raiders to us. Our people brought him back to the city over one of their horses, and he's even now with Tribe Patrin being questioned by their healers. I have no doubt all will be revealed, and the truth of our accusations will be ascertained. When that happens, Tribe Patrin will spread the word as quickly as possible, but..."

"Time is against you," Evermund repeated. "I'm sure the most stubborn will wish to examine the evidence for themselves."

"In normal circumstances, I would praise their desire to do so," Annora said. "But I know for some it will just be an excuse to avoid having to acknowledge the truth—that their favored tribe has shown themselves unworthy of the crown. It's a bitter admission."

"But surely handing that tribe the crown would be worse," I protested.

She shrugged. "Anyone who wishes to rule must recognize that people are more often driven by emotion than by logic. Until you can accept that, you'll neither be able to understand nor predict the actions of your people."

I didn't say anything, unsure why she felt the need to tutor me on ruling. Even if she won the vote, and I ended up joining the nomads, Zeke would never be eligible for the throne. Tribe

Nicabar wouldn't be able to nominate for a second monarchy in a row.

Evermund was still standing with us, but his attention had been captured by something over my shoulder, a strange expression on his face. I turned to see two people huddled together in the corner of the room.

I excused myself and hurried in Airlie and Renley's direction. Unlike Evermund, I wasn't going to hang back and watch from afar.

"You two don't look like we just won the battle," I said in a quiet voice when I reached them. "What's wrong?"

"When the raiders attacked us by the border, there was someone with them who shouldn't have been there," Airlie told me, looking sideways at Renley, worry etched into her face.

"What do you mean?" I looked between them.

"Marissa is practically a second mother to me," Renley said. "There is no way she would ever work for the General."

"By choice, at least," Airlie said, and Renley's face transformed instantly from defensive to angry.

"It's the only explanation," he agreed. "But if it's true, then most of the settlement is in great danger. If the General is forcing anyone with a power affinity to help him, then they may have already suffered more internal damage than a healer could easily heal."

"The General can't do that!" I gasped.

"In the past he's preferred to stick to persuasion," Renley said slowly. "But if he was enraged enough at all his losses to attack this city, then I would believe he could have done this, too."

I stirred uneasily. Airlie and I were the reason for the General's rage. I hated the idea of him taking it out on other people.

"We'll just have to rescue them," Airlie said briskly. "I have to believe it's not too late for them to be healed. Cadence and I will both help, won't we, Cadence?"

I nodded. "If the General's truly dead, we won't find much resistance. Especially not given how many of his people he brought here."

Airlie didn't look as pleased as I expected at this idea. "If he's coercing the settlement, he'll have left mages behind to keep them under control." She hesitated. "I haven't seen any sign of Lawson among the casualties or the prisoners."

"Even if Lawson's there, ruling in the General's name, we still have to try to rescue them," Renley said quickly. "My father is still there, along with everyone I grew up with."

Airlie and I rushed to agree, assuring him that we weren't going to run and cower because of Lawson.

"Between the lot of you and Evermund, someone would be excused for thinking we lost," a bright voice said from behind me.

I swung around to Gia, but it was Renley who answered.

"Would you prefer to dance instead? I'm willing if you are."

His eyes were glinting at her, and she laughed in reply, but her brother stepped up beside her, and there was no laughter on his face.

"Very humorous," he said sourly, giving Renley an intimidating look.

Renley didn't falter, however, his expression still laughing in Gia's direction. She threw a look up at her brother before sighing.

"One day you'll learn how to enjoy yourself, Nik. I just hope I'm still around in that dim and distant future." She threw a smile to Renley. "You'll have to save me a dance for next time."

"I'll hold you to that," Renley replied. "But for now, I'm taking myself off to bed where I can mourn the lost opportunity in peace."

Gia giggled, and Nik snorted. When I looked at Renley in some confusion, he winked at me.

A small giggle of my own escaped. After the time we'd spent

stuck in the city together, waiting for the others to return from the border, Renley had lost his awe of Nikolas's position, and it made me like him more.

When he moved off, I looked over at Zeke. He was swaying even while sitting down, utterly spent after his severe injury and extensive healing. I crossed over to join him and learned that the last of the Nicabar tribe members had returned to headquarters, many with stories of having helped capture raiders. Unfortunately some nomads had been killed, but their number was few, and none of them belonged to Zeke's tribe.

"In that case, there's no reason for you to remain awake," I told him, and he reluctantly agreed.

I sent him off with a final hug and headed for my own bed, Airlie trailing behind. At least we would be able to share a room. I didn't feel like being alone after the General's attack. I kept thinking of those who had been killed, their deaths heavy on my conscience, although I knew I had never done anything to provoke the General, other than existing.

"Do you really believe he's dead?" I asked Airlie as we slipped into the two beds. "Is it terrible that I find I can't believe it? Until I see his body with my own eyes, I think I'll still be looking over my shoulder for him."

"I know what you mean," she agreed. "I feel a little the same way. But then...I walked that tunnel. I don't see how he could possibly survive." She hesitated. "A team with plenty of healing mages could make it, though. If Annora wins the crown, I'll ask her to send a team to retrieve his body."

I had to be content with that, sliding between the sheets, my mind too full to make rest seem at all realistic. I kept remembering the sensation of being shoved into open air and reliving the sound of Zeke's body hitting the ground.

"Tell me what happened to you," I said to Airlie. "I've heard bits of it in the last few hours, but tell me the whole story."

She did, and I told her everything that had happened to me

while she was gone. She was still outraged at Annora's revelation to the tribes about my affinity, and my own acceptance of the situation only seemed to inflame her feelings further.

Eventually my eyes began to droop, and I mumbled a goodnight. My last thoughts were that I wasn't ready to say goodbye to my sister again. We had already had too many goodbyes.

I woke late, the light edging around the curtains making me instantly aware I had overslept. Even so, Airlie was still asleep, so I got up and dressed quietly, slipping out to the breakfast room in the hopes of finding Zeke.

He was there, still filling his plate, and he gave me a smile that set my heart racing.

"How are you feeling?" I asked anxiously, and he laughed at me.

"I feel fine, as you must know. Two healers pronounced me entirely healed, remember?"

I gave him a mock glare. "You didn't see yourself lying there, looking dead. After that trauma, I'm allowed to ask as many times as I like."

"My apologies," he said meekly, although his eyes laughed at me.

"What time is the vote?" I asked as we sat down next to each other in the middle of the long table.

"The first vote has already happened," he said calmly.

"What?" I exclaimed, nearly dropping my spoon.

"Don't worry," he said. "It's a protracted process. You haven't missed anything important. The exact numbers aren't released to the nominated tribes, but Tribe Darshan received the fewest votes. They are therefore dropped from the list and the next round of voting occurs. The lowest tribe in the second vote will be excluded, and then the final vote will choose between the remaining two tribes. They give a lengthy gap between each vote so the tribe representatives can consult with their tribe. Of course, in reality, everyone knows who they'll vote for in every possible eventuality, but it's custom to allow the time."

"That sounds confusing," I said, feeling dazed and wondering why I hadn't asked about the voting process previously.

"It's the fairest system," he said, "and the only way smaller tribes are able to attract initial votes. If there was only a single vote between all nominations, representatives would be reluctant to vote for a tribe who had no chance of winning, thus wasting their vote and giving up their chance to have a true say in the choice of monarch. Plus, as each tribe is dropped from the list, they join the ranks of those voting, so a full 39 tribes vote between the final two candidates."

"I suppose that makes sense. But why is it so important to include smaller tribes?"

"Because if we didn't have a way to include them, we might have settled into a system of alternating back and forth between a tiny handful of powerful tribes. It already happens too much, as it is. Patrin has just finished its rule, and before them was Alia. Before Alia's last reign, it was Patrin again. Way back then, Nicabar was a smaller tribe no one would have considered a true candidate. But we nominated against Alia, and then a second time against Patrin, and now we're considered one of the true contenders this time. The other tribes have seen the growth in support we've achieved over those decades, and it helps to sway opinion toward us."

"Not Alia's opinion," I muttered, and he chuckled.

"No, not that. They consider us upstarts, challenging a true royal clan."

I gazed out the window, considering his words until I was distracted by the quality of the sunshine.

"Should this really be lunch?" I asked.

He grinned. "It might have been except I think the entire tribe slept almost as late as us. I suspect many of us were glad to do so. Waiting through a voting day when you're not participating in the process is...difficult."

I nodded, seeing exactly what he meant as I considered the hours we would still need to wait.

A man I didn't recognize stuck his head in the door, his eyes skipping over the few other people in the room to fasten on Zeke.

"They've just announced the second round results. No surprises. Tribe Esterla came last and have now been dropped from contention."

Zeke nodded, and the man disappeared, leaving a rustle of murmurs in his wake.

"There were only four nominated tribes left after Talman pulled out earlier," I said. "So that must mean there's only one round of voting left. This will be over soon after all."

"Not as soon as I'd like," Zeke said. "They'll give the longest break now, since this is the most important vote."

"In that case," I said slowly, "I think I should speak to your mother before the result is announced. I want her to know that my decision isn't influenced by whether she wins or loses."

Zeke went still. "Your decision?" he asked carefully.

"I want to be here with you, Zeke," I said. His face brightened, so I rushed on. "But I'm not ready to leave my sister. She left for the border as soon as we got here, and being separated again...we've hardly had any time together still. I'm just not ready to live in separate cities."

"And how does she feel?" he asked, his tone unexpectedly harsh.

"She feels the same way," I said quietly, reminding myself that it was understandable he would be hurt by my words. "Why do you ask?"

"I..." He paused and ran a hand through his hair, sighing. "If you must know, I think she's keeping something from you. I don't like seeing you putting such blind faith in her when..."

"Keeping something from me?" I stared at him. "What makes you think that?"

"Instinct?" He sounded bitter now. "Long experience with family keeping secrets, perhaps. I apologize. I don't want to drive a wedge between you and your sister. I know how important she is to you. I just don't want to see you hurt."

"And perhaps you don't like having a rival for most important person in my life?" I looked at him steadily, and he winced.

"I suppose, if I'm being completely honest, there might be some of that in there somewhere," he admitted.

I leaned over and slipped both arms around his middle. "Airlie is my anchor to my past, Zeke. She'll never not be important to me. But you're my anchor to my future. You're the one I want to spend my life with."

He frowned. "Then why—"

"You didn't let me finish earlier. I want to ask your mother if she'll allow you to come back to Tartora with me. Just for a year or two. And in exchange, I'll agree to come back here with you after that." I watched him nervously. "Would you be willing to do that? If your mother wins the vote, you'll become a prince, and I'm sure you'd prefer to be here. But maybe you could take on a diplomatic role to the Tartoran court? I'm sure there will be lots of liaison needed if we're going to find a way to fight the wild power together."

Zeke said nothing, and my anxiety grew.

"Say something," I whispered. "Do you hate the idea? Or do you just think she'll say no?"

He stood abruptly. "I think you need to talk to her."

I stood as well. "I want to talk to her, of course. But I need to know what you think of the idea. I can't suggest it if you're not interested or willing to come back to Tartora for a while."

"I think that you should talk to her," he repeated.

"Zeke!" I cried, exasperated. But he just left the room at a fast stride, making me jog to keep up. "Seriously, what's going on?"

We reached the door of his mother's favorite sitting room, and Zeke paused. "Before I left for Tartora, my mother made me take a vow. I've been working on her to release me from that vow for a while now, but she's refused. And so, I'll repeat, you need to talk to her."

"Who needs to talk to who?" Airlie asked, wandering in our direction, her face still drowsy, and her pace slow.

"I..." I looked up at Zeke, desperately confused and unsure how he would feel about her presence, especially given his earlier outburst. But to my surprise he nodded, as if pleased with her sudden appearance.

"You should be here for this, too, Airlie." He opened the door without knocking, pushing us both gently into the room ahead of him.

Annora looked mildly surprised at our unexpected descent on her private space, but she nodded graciously and wished us all a good afternoon.

"This isn't a time for pleasantries, Mother," Zeke said. "It's time—and past—for plain talking."

She gave him a sharp look, and he returned it in equal measure.

"You said I could leave after the vote, Annora," I said. "So I've come to tell you I wish to do that. Do you still intend to honor your assurances?"

Airlie said nothing, but she drifted closer to me, and I could feel the pleasure radiating off her.

"Of course I do." Annora regarded us both equally. "But I would caution you not to lose sight of what really matters."

I glanced instinctively at Zeke before turning back to her. "And what's that?"

"Calista, of course," she said calmly.

"Calista?" I hadn't been expecting that, but perhaps I should have been. "You mean the threat from the wild power?"

"No," she said, "I mean a kingdom that has for too long sat empty, its people cast out and its fields fallow. It is time to reclaim the fallen kingdom, and that is far bigger than either of our preferences."

"Reclaim the fallen kingdom?" I asked dazedly. She had mentioned freeing Calista before, but I had thought her focus was on the threat of the wild power. This seemed much greater in scope.

"I don't know what you think I'm capable of," I said after a moment, but I'm—"

"A power mage," she said. "That is what's important. And you love my son. Really, nothing could be more perfect. It's arranged itself far more neatly than I could have hoped for."

"What does that mean?" Airlie asked, all signs of sleepiness long gone. "Do you imagine yourself ruling across a double kingdom?"

"Me?" Annora's eyebrows arched up toward her hairline. "I have no Calistan blood and no claim to the throne in Calinara. I aspire to rule my own people, but that is all. Any ambitions I have are for my son and my son alone."

"Wait. You want *Zeke* to take the Calistan throne?" I asked, my throat suddenly dry.

"Of course," she said simply. "He is not only the direct heir on his father's side, but the only remaining person with Calistan royal blood. The throne in Calinara is his birthright."

A whooshing filled my ears as I turned slowly to Zeke. Every past conversation about his status and potential royal title rolled through my head with new meaning. All his comments about pressure, and the complexities I'd observed in his relationship with his mother.

"You're the true king of Calista?" I asked. "How could you not tell me?"

"I told you out in the hall," he said. "My mother's condition for allowing me to go to Tartora was that I swear an oath—the most sacred oath we have as nomads—not to tell anyone the truth about my heritage. She said it was for my own safety, and I didn't think anything of it since this has always been our greatest secret. I didn't predict meeting you and wanting to tell you everything. I was honest when I said I wanted nothing like that between us. I've been arguing with my mother for months to release me." He glared at her.

"Is there anything more?" I asked. "Any more startling revelations?"

"Just one," Annora said. "And you really shouldn't blame Zeke for any of this. He's been furious with me for putting him in a position of either hiding something from you or breaking his vow."

"Just one?" Airlie asked in disbelief. "And what's that, may I ask?"

"Before I was born, Nicabar was a small tribe, and not especially influential," she said. "We've grown in both size and power for one simple reason. Before Calista fell, our tribe leader at the time had struck up a close friendship with the Calistan Master of Plants." She shook her head. "Such a small thing to change so much. After the wild power was released, Calistan refugees fled in all directions. The attackers had first targeted the power mages, and both they and their families were completely wiped out—with one notable exception." She nodded toward Airlie and me.

"But their focus on the power mages gave time for other Calistans to escape. When the attackers next turned their attention on the mages of the other three affinities—as those most likely to put up a successful fight—many were killed. But the Master of Plants led the remaining plants, elements, and healing mages from the Calistan Guild to Tribe Nicabar, smuggling the king's youngest son with them."

"All of them came to you?" I asked.

She nodded. "And from the safety of our tribe, they were able to observe what happened next. The ordinary people with a power affinity never emerged from Calista at all, but all the other ordinary citizens fled far and wide to be met with suspicion and hostility. The mages realized their strength would make them even less welcome in the kingdoms of their enemies, so they kept their secret. And for nearly a hundred years, Nicabar has sheltered and protected them. In return, we have gained power thanks to that influx of new members—all with strong abilities."

"So half of Tribe Nicabar aren't even nomads?" I asked, shocked.

"Of course they are." Her voice cracked like a whip. "They have sworn themselves to our tribe, as did their parents, and their grandparents before them. They are both nomads and Calistans, as is Zeke."

"And if somehow Zeke does manage to take back Calista?" Airlie asked. "Will they return to their families' old home?"

"That will be up to each individual to choose," Annora said. "Some will choose one way and some another, I'm sure. It's the same decision that many Tartorans and nomads will have to make—many have Calistan ancestors at this point. But Zeke cannot reclaim Calista alone. If that was possible, we wouldn't have waited three generations to act. We've been waiting for you, Cadence."

"Me?"

"Well, not you specifically. We were waiting for a power mage of sufficient strength. There have always been rumors that one, at least, escaped. And Tribe Nicabar has long searched for the person behind those rumors without success.

"The old Calistan king was a suspicious man, and while the wild power wasn't a protection he set in place, the mistaken idea didn't come from nowhere. He did have protections, and he created them to require both someone of royal blood and a power mage to unlock. Zeke is the true king of Calista, but we've been waiting for you, Cadence, so he can take back his birthright."

"You want to send Cadence and Zeke into Calista to remove the wild power?" Airlie sounded outraged. "Never mind that we don't have a way for them to do that!"

"There will be a way," Annora said calmly. "The protections are the key."

"How?" Airlie crossed her arms.

"I don't know," Annora admitted. "But those who fled Calista were clear. If we could only find a power mage to accompany the heir, we would find the answer to Calista's salvation hidden in Calinara. Zeke and Cadence must travel there and find those answers. It's the only way to save all three kingdoms from the wild power."

"You want to send your son and my sister into the heart of danger on something as amorphous as that?"

Airlie's outraged voice seemed to be the only thing anchoring me to the moment, my head spinning so fast, I worried my legs might give out. Annora intended a throne not only for herself, but for her son—and me beside him. She wanted me to be queen of Calista. The idea was laughable.

"Isn't one throne enough for you?" I asked. "Why do you need two?"

"*I* will not have two," she said. "But what could be better for a fledgling Calista, still in the process of rebuilding itself, than having the closest of allegiances with the nomad throne?"

"What will the rest of the nomads think of that?" Airlie asked.

"It will be a small repayment for rescuing us from the largest threat our kingdom has ever faced," Annora said. "And there are other mutual benefits to be had besides—not the least of which is guaranteed peace."

"And all this has been planned for generations?" I asked, a little awed.

"Not everything." Annora's voice grew heavy. "Not all things can be planned for. If my husband had not had that accident..." She and Zeke exchanged a sorrowful look, and I realized what I should have seen immediately.

"So you were meant to be queen of Calista," I said, "at your husband's side. But he died before he had a chance to retake his throne, so you set your sights on a different throne instead."

She laughed. "I can't dispute any of the facts, as you lay them out. But the heart of the matter was quite different, I assure you. I had no thought of thrones back then. I had no reason to think anything would be different from how it had been for our parents. We had no power mage to help us reclaim Calista. Instead, my husband was voted head of our tribe, and I had never been so proud. I served at his side, and I was happy with our life. Especially when Zeke came along."

She smiled at her son before continuing. "And then my husband died. I thought my world was ending. My world as it was *had* ended. And I thought I would never be happy again. But I realized in that moment I had a choice. I could step aside, give allegiance to a new head, and narrow my world to my son, or I could put myself forward as a replacement for my husband —a leader in my own right."

"Do you ever regret your choice?" Zeke asked.

"Sometimes I wonder if it might have been better for you," she said. "But I couldn't deny my talents and my nature—not even for you. At your father's side, I learned that I excelled at leadership and the dance and thrust of politics. I had helped our tribe, and I could continue to do so. I was born to be a leader, and I could see the fullness of the vision in that moment of choice. Under my leadership, Nicabar could make it all the way to the throne." She paused. "Do you wish I'd made a different choice? I might have been a better mother. But you wouldn't be here now, with a chance to win your throne, if I had. And you would never have gone to Tartora."

"That's no choice at all," said Zeke. "How could I wish for a life other than my own? A life without Cadence. It's unthinkable."

Annora sighed softly. "Indeed. And perhaps I wouldn't have been a better mother at all. Perhaps I would have chafed at the loss of my natural purpose and position, growing less and less satisfied until I became the worst shadow of myself. We can never know what that other path would have looked like. All we can do is make the most of the chances we have worked so hard in order to find before us. In a few hours, we'll know if I have won a throne. But it's up to Cadence if you ever have the chance to win yours."

"I—" I faltered.

I didn't pretend to understand the choices Annora had faced back then, or the many she had made since. But when it narrowed down to that one question, what really mattered was my own choice.

Zeke had hidden this enormous thing from me, but I had forgiven Airlie for the promises she made to our father, and I could forgive Zeke for keeping an oath he made to his mother. I could admire him for it, even, in a detached sort of way. He had held his integrity in the face of great emotion—it was a good characteristic for a king.

A king. Could I really fight for a throne for Zeke? And if we succeeded, could I sit beside him?

My mind shied away from that question. It seemed far in the future, anyway—in the distant, hazy reality where we had defeated the wild power. A reality that might well never come.

But as soon as I focused my thoughts on the wild power, I knew it was no choice at all. It never had been. If I was the one remaining key to defeating the wild power, the last hope for all three kingdoms, then I couldn't say no, regardless of the risks involved.

And though there were risks, Annora wasn't sending us on a suicide mission. She truly believed we could succeed. This was a woman who had taken a tribe from obscurity to the edge of a throne. If she believed it, then the chance of success was significant enough that I had to take the risk.

"I don't care about thrones," I said aloud. "But I do care about defeating the wild power. For that alone, I would brave every danger in the fallen kingdom. And Airlie and I were already planning to go as far as the settlement anyway."

"Are you sure?" Zeke asked, holding my eyes. "If it was merely a choice between you and a crown, I would—"

I shook my head, holding up a hand to silence him. "I know. But for everyone's sake, we have to try this. The General might be gone, but the wild power is still an enormous threat, and one that's growing worse. He's destabilized Calista, and I believe it's too late for that process to be reversed."

"Secrets," Airlie muttered. "Always more secrets." She looked intently at Annora. "Are you sure there aren't any more?"

Annora met her gaze. "None of my keeping."

It sounded like a challenge, and Airlie gave way before it, her eyes dropping down.

Zeke looked at me significantly, but I shook my head. Airlie was thinking of the secret she was keeping from Evermund, not one she was keeping from me.

"I'll come with you, of course," she said abruptly. "You might need an elements mage."

I threw my arms around her. "Thank you, Airlie. It wouldn't seem right to go back into Calista without you."

For a moment, she stiffened beneath my arms, but at my words, she softened, hugging me back. Before she could speak, however, the door to the sitting room opened.

"The vote is completed," the newcomer said. "We are summoned to the meeting hall."

CHAPTER 24
AIRLIE

No one objected, so the entire Tartoran delegation followed along with the nomads as we marched up the street to the palace. I might have been surprised at the building's indefensible layout if I hadn't just watched how effectively the nomads dealt with intruders. All the damage from the battle was already gone, the city looking as it had on the day I first saw it. I had even seen a glimpse of the intact bridge on our way here.

We crossed to a hall that sounded like the one Cadence had described to me, its circular shape and tiered levels allowing every tribe their own place. We entered on the heels of the last of the Alia tribe members, and at sight of them an angry murmur swept our group.

But Annora held up a hand, and silence fell again as we filled the remaining empty place around the circle.

The entire room had their attention split between us and Tribe Alia who were positioned almost directly across from us. My mind was still buzzing with Annora's declaration and request for help, but the sight of the other tribe filled me with loathing. Just seeing them brought back the phantom sensation of burning lungs and aching legs.

The sound of a bell made me jump, swinging to look at the door. But only a lone man came through, and no one else reacted, so my heartbeat slowly resumed its normal rhythm. Clearly this wasn't the same as the alarm bell.

The man, who wore a plain, midnight blue robe, walked to the middle of the room before speaking.

"Welcome, tribes of the kingdom." His voice easily reached every level. "Tribe Patrin hosts you for the last time under this monarchy. We stand together to choose a new monarch."

Everyone around me cried out in unison, "We stand together."

"The voting is now complete," the man said. "All have witnessed it save the nominated tribes. We will stand together behind the new monarch."

As the crowd chanted, "We will stand together," my tension mounted. How long would this go on? When would we find out the winner? I admired Annora's calm appearance. Underneath, she must be both incredibly tense and utterly impatient.

"We will stand together behind Tribe Nicabar and Queen Annora," the man suddenly roared, and the crowds of people around the room broke into loud cheers.

Annora smiled, nodding in all directions to acknowledge the passionate outpouring.

"We will stand together," the man in the center said disapprovingly, reminding the crowd of their line which they diligently repeated. As soon as they had done so, all the members of Nicabar broke into their own celebration, hugging each other and exclaiming. Many of them were openly crying.

Annora smiled at them all once before gliding along our tier to the nearest set of steps and walking down to join the man in the center of the room.

"Tribe Nicabar thanks Tribe Patrin for your service," she said. "Be released from your load and free to roam once more.

We will take it and carry it for you. We will be faithful to the tribes."

"May you enjoy a long and fruitful reign." The man bowed to her. "Tribe Patrin pays tribute to our new sovereign."

From somewhere, he produced a velvet cushion holding an elaborate golden crown, studded with rubies. Lifting it high, he placed in on Annora's bowed head.

"Serve us well, Queen Annora," he said.

She lifted her head to beam at the crowd, and he strode up the steps to join the rest of his tribe in their place in the circle.

Immediately the head of Tribe Alia left his place. For a tense moment, I feared he meant to challenge Annora, and she certainly greeted him with none of the warmth she'd shown the man from Tribe Patrin.

But to my surprise, the leader from Alia bowed to her, and said, "Tribe Alia pays tribute to our new sovereign."

He held out a length of material which he shook out to show a cloak of royal purple, trimmed with white, and with an enormous train. He placed it around her shoulders.

"Alia is known for its fine clothing," Zeke whispered in my ear. "They always bring a royal cloak as tribute. And as the losing tribe, they have to go first."

After that, the floodgates were opened. Tribe Esterla came next, and then Tribe Darshan, in the opposite order to their being voted out. Then came Talman, and Callen, and Karel, and Orelie, and Calahan, and Lothar, and on and on, until all forty tribes had sent their leader to bow and offer a valuable item as tribute. Anything she couldn't wear was placed at Annora's feet, and it spread out from her like a blanket across the ground.

When the last tribe had returned to their places, Annora looked as if she meant to speak. But before she could do so, there was further movement from the tiers.

It came from our section, and I had to lean around someone before I managed to see two figures detaching themselves from the group. Gia and Nik walked slowly down the stairs, carrying the chest Gia had fished from the river between them.

When they reached Annora, they both gave shallow bows and placed it as close to her feet as they could get.

"Tartora extends greetings and well wishes to the new sovereign of the nomads. Queen Annora, please accept this gift from King Marius as a sign of his respect and his desire for an alliance of mutual trust and cooperation."

Annora inclined her head. "Please give King Marius our thanks for his gift. We, too, look forward to a future of friendship between our peoples."

Gia and Nikolas nodded and returned to their places. Annora waited until they were completely gone before gazing across each tribe in turn, taking her time before straightening to speak again.

"I thank each of you for the trust you have placed in Tribe Nicabar." Her confident voice easily reached every ear. "We will do all in our power to live up to that trust. Just yesterday our kingdom faced the unprecedented—an attack on our city itself. The raiders have now had their numbers decimated, many of them held as our prisoners. But their attack—so effectively turned back by our combined efforts—is not the only unprecedented threat we face."

She once again swept the circle with her piercing gaze. "We must stand together against the wild power that creeps ever closer with its corrupting force. I pledge myself to fight it with every weapon Tribe Nicabar can bring to bear, and with everything the tribes of the kingdom can contribute." She paused.

"Some questioned my bringing Tartorans into our midst, but this wild power threatens every living person and creature across both lands. We must fight together, or we will all fall. And I will never let the tribes fall!" She thrust a closed fist into the sky with her final word, and the crowd erupted into a second round of cheers, even louder than the first.

Even I was swept up in the moment, cheering with the others, although I hadn't entirely overcome my distrust of Annora. Her mission was noble, but she had demonstrated she was willing to put it before everything—even her own son, and certainly Cadence.

Maybe you're just jealous, an unwelcome voice in the back of my mind said. *She didn't allow herself to be tied down by others' expectations and needs. She knew what she was capable of, and she rose to meet it.*

I shook the thoughts away. I had decades of life ahead of me to discover my place and purpose. I couldn't allow insidious thoughts to distract me from the urgent needs of the moment. I had spent enough time in my home kingdom to know the danger Cadence and Zeke would face.

Still, I watched Annora, though. Had my deception been unnecessary? Did she already know of the paser trees? I couldn't help but think they must somehow be the key to defeating the wild power. Perhaps the protection hidden by the old king was somehow linked with the remaining seeds. Maybe they were waiting for us in Calinara.

My father had seemed to live inside a dream of the future— one where he was already in Calinara. Perhaps that was what had made him boast about possessing them.

I would have to tell the other two about the paser trees at some point. The thought made me uneasy. How would they react to finding out I had hidden it from them? Cadence had proven herself forgiving time and time again, but Zeke watched me with a wariness in his eyes, almost as if he suspected me. If I gave him this ammunition, would he use it to pry Cadence away from me?

"Is everything all right, Airlie?" Evermund asked, jolting me from my thoughts. He was watching me with concern.

With a start, I looked around and discovered everyone was streaming from the hall. We would soon be the only ones left.

"Yes, yes, I..." I stopped. "No, actually," I said, making a swift decision.

Cadence had Zeke now, and I needed an ally, too. My own actions meant I could never look to Evermund for my world and my future, like Cadence looked to Zeke, but there was no one I trusted more.

"Annora is sending Cadence and Zeke into Calista, and I'm going with them. But I'm afraid the three of us won't be enough."

"What?" Gia cried, stepping into view.

I groaned. Clearly I had reacted too swiftly. We weren't alone after all.

"Cadence can't do that," Nikolas said stiffly. "Our father won't allow it. We can't afford to throw away our only power mage."

Realizing there was nothing for it now, I quickly outlined everything Annora had told us. Unlike Zeke, I had taken no vow of secrecy.

I didn't need one, I reminded myself bitterly. I was keeping my secrets just fine on my own.

"I agree with Cadence," Evermund said. "If there's a chance, we must take it. But I also agree with Nik. Cadence must be protected. I will willingly accompany you, but we must return to Tartora first and leave from there. There's something I need to do there before I'm free to leave." His face gave no indication of great perturbation, although I could guess at the meaning of his words, and my heart sank for him.

"We'll come to Calista, too, of course," Gia said immediately.

"Absolutely not!" Evermund and I both said in unison, our identical tones making us grin at each other.

"Your parents would never allow it," I added.

"We'll see about that." Gia's face took on a determined look.

"You're coming back with me to Tartora," Evermund said, his voice as hard as granite.

"Of course," Gia agreed. "There's something I need to do there as well."

I stared at her, bemused, the emotion growing when I saw the blood drain from Evermund's face.

"Gia," he said in a low, warning tone.

"Don't bother, Evermund," she snapped. "If Nik and my parents haven't made me change my mind over all these years, what hope do you think you have?"

Her argument must have worked because Evermund said no more about it, although he was clearly unhappy.

"Father will never approve this mission, regardless of what either of you do," Nikolas said bitterly.

"I think you'll find you're wrong about that," Evermund said. "But we will see. With Annora on the throne, an initial alliance agreement shouldn't take long. And we'll be traveling downriver this time. The help of the current will make the trip far less onerous. We should be able to be home within the week."

Somehow this whole situation had spiraled out of my control. I had wanted Evermund to advise me, not to throw everything away to put himself in danger. Why was he doing it? Surely not out of a sense of responsibility for me as his apprentice? If that was it, I had to find a way to stop him.

My stomach wound itself tightly, making my legs feel weak. Somehow, when we were back in Tartora, I needed to find the courage to tell him the truth—without causing the whole lot of them to turn against me. If they did that, their poor opinion might flow through to Cadence and the entire mission.

I took hold of my panicking thoughts. I still had over a week to work it out. I would find a way. I had to.

"It will be all right, Airlie," Evermund said softly, recognizing my distress as he always did, although he didn't know the cause. "I won't abandon you."

For a brief moment, I lost myself in the strength of his gaze, allowing the spark at its depth to jump across and warm me from the inside out. It wasn't a luxury I would have much longer.

Outside those doors, he had an alliance to make, we had a settlement to liberate, Cadence had a kingdom to save, and I had trust to shatter. But right now, just for this moment, I had Evermund. And I never wanted the moment to end.

NOTE FROM THE AUTHOR

Find out what happens in the fallen kingdom in the fourth and final book, Forests of Grandeur and Malice.

Or for more fantasy, romance, adventure, and intrigue, try my completed Spoken Mage series—where a world of written magic is upended by the first spoken mage—starting with Voice of Power.

To be informed of future releases, as well as A Mage's Influence bonus shorts, please sign up to my mailing list at www.melaniecellier.com.

And if you enjoyed Thorns of Hope and Betrayal, please spread the word and help other readers find it! You could start by leaving a review on Amazon or Goodreads or Facebook or any other social media site. Your review would be very much appreciated and would make a big difference!

NOMAD LANDS
Hidden City
NOMAD LANDS
KINGDOM OF CALISTA
CELADON RIVER
VIRIDIAN RIVER
CALINARA
LAKE ATERRA
CADENCE'S HOUSE
HUNTING LODGE
CELADON RIVER
KINGDOM OF TARTORA
TARONA
VIRIDIAN RIVER
N
W
E
S

Acknowledgments

This is my thirtieth book, a milestone that would have been hard for me to believe back when I first started my writing journey.

I'm so grateful for the opportunity to write books and share them with the world. And my gratitude for my amazing team only grows with each of those books. But after thirty titles, the acknowledgements can get a little repetitive. So I'm going to merely say, to all of you, I appreciate you more than words could ever express.

And to all my readers, thanks for continuing this journey with me. I hope I can entertain you for many more books to come.

About the Author

Melanie Cellier grew up on a staple diet of books, books and more books. And although she got older, she never stopped loving children's and young adult novels.

She always wanted to write one herself, but it took three careers and three different continents before she actually managed it.

She now feels incredibly fortunate to spend her time writing from her home in Adelaide, Australia where she keeps an eye out for koalas in her backyard. Her staple diet hasn't changed much, although she's added choc mint Rooibos tea and Chicken Crimpies to the list.

She writes young adult fantasy including books in her *Spoken Mage* world, her *Mage's Influence* world, and her various *Four Kingdoms* and *Kingdoms of Legacy* series that are made up of linked stand-alone stories that retell classic fairy tales.